INCARNADINE

The True Memoirs of COUNT DRACULA

VOLUME ONE

Edited and with an introduction

By R. H. Greene

iUniverse, Inc.

New York   Bloomington

Incarnadine: The True Memoirs of Count Dracula
Volume One

This is a work of fiction. All of the characters, names, incidents, organizations, and dialogue
in this novel are either the products of the author's imagination or are used fictitiously.

iUniverse books may be ordered through booksellers or by contacting:

iUniverse
1663 Liberty Drive
Bloomington, IN 47403
www.iuniverse.com
1-800-Authors (1-800-288-4677)

Because of the dynamic nature of the Internet, any Web addresses or links contained in this book
may have changed since publication and may no longer be valid. The views expressed in this work
are solely those of the author and do not necessarily reflect the views of the publisher, and the
publisher hereby disclaims any responsibility for them.

ISBN: 978-1-4401-5943-5 (sc)
ISBN: 978-1-4401-5945-9 (dj)
ISBN: 978-1-4401-5944-2 (ebk)

Printed in the United States of America

iUniverse rev. date: 8/31/2009

For "Baby B."

"Or shall the Adversary thus obtain
His end, and frustrate thine? Shall he fulfill
His malice, and thy goodness bring to nought,
Or proud return, though to his heavier doom,
Yet with revenge accomplish'd, and to Hell
Draw after him the whole race of mankind,
By him corrupted?" – John Milton, *Paradise Lost*

"Reach a certain moment in your life and
you discover that your days are spent as
much with the dead as they are with the
living." – Paul Auster

Foreword

by R. H. Greene

Y ou hold in your hands a piece of revisionist literature, based on one of the most famous novels ever written.

Bram Stoker's classic tale *Dracula* features a title character so iconic that it can be safely said his name recognition falls somewhere between Moses and Jesus Christ. A watershed of Gothic literature as well as a fractured kaleidoscope of the repressed sexual hysterias so associated today with the Victorian era, *Dracula* has been purchased more times and adapted into other media more often than any tale other than the Bible.

The True Memoirs of Count Dracula is an early example of what some have called the literary genre of "counter-myth," in which a well-known story is reimagined—and in some cases refuted—by a trick of literary voice and viewpoint (in English, modern classics of the form would include John Gardner's *Grendel*, William Styron's *Confessions of Nat Turner*, and Gregory Maguire's *Wicked*, which is shaping up as a rather enduring reimagining of the works of L. Frank Baum). In *The True Memoirs of Count Dracula,* we have a wildly different take on many of Stoker's characters and events (with many additions) told in autobiographical form by the evil antagonist himself, under the *nom de plume* Konstantin Kuzmanov. What makes the work particularly intriguing (irrespective of the question of its literary merits) is its odd provenance and the related fact of its century of suppression.

Although forensic testing indicates a manuscript well over 100 years old, *The True Memoirs of Count Dracula* was discovered in the foundation of an old Soviet-era farmhouse in northern Bulgaria less than half a decade ago. This is not quite as bizarre as it sounds.

Because Bulgaria is a country that is still organized in part according to quasi-feudal principles of agricultural self-sufficiency dating back centuries, the likelihood of a well-hidden object lying undisturbed on one of its many subsistence farms is higher than it might be elsewhere.

The farmhouse in question was owned by a parsimonious eighty-year-old man who passed away in it, giving rise to wild rumors among his neighbors that he had hidden his fortune (sacks of gold, naturally) in the foundation of his home—a structure built in 1950, but on the then-100-year-old stone foundation of a teetering mud-brick relic from the Ottoman era. Rumors of horded riches abound in modern Balkan villages, because under communism citizens were forbidden to save money or to own objects of excessive material value, such as jewelry, lest the individual's complete dependence on the state be corrupted by the bourgeois influence of personal wealth. Treasure had to be hidden if it was to be kept. As a result, more than one Slavic attic has been found to contain forgotten lodes of currency, coins, and gems—small jackpots, typically, but large enough to keep alive an unsavory tradition of looting unguarded properties within the struggling economies of the former Eastern Bloc.

The century-old foundation was judged solid enough in 1950 that it had been built over and left undisturbed until the neighbors began prospecting for "miser's gold" within it. They found no money, but they did manage to excavate a minor literary payload in the form of the multi-volume handwritten manuscript whose first half, translated into English, you are about to read.

So who buried *The True Memoirs of Count Dracula* in a Bulgarian cornerstone more than a century ago, and why? The why we will get to shortly; the who is so fascinating it begs to be dealt with first.

The oldest available title for this property contains a provocative disclosure: The Bulgarian resting place of this text was, for a brief period in the late 1890s and early 1900s, the vacation domicile of an affluent British widow named Wilhelmina Murray Harker—the same Mina Harker who was fictionalized against her will by Bram Stoker, and who sued unsuccessfully to suppress his book. (Thankfully for world literature, she lost her case—in part because in one of his last acts before his early death from gout, her husband Jonathan, by then a powerful figure in the shadowy world of London finance, gave Stoker his whole-hearted and public blessing. This could not have helped Mrs. Harker's chances at court in those patriarchal times).

Wilhelmina Harker was a peripatetic and troubled soul in her later years, and her affinity for things Slavic (which may have been one of the real-life details that drew Stoker to use her as a model) has been well established. She has been described by those favorable toward her eccentricities as the "Schliemann of the Balkans," an analogy likening her to the accomplished but controversial German archaeologist of the Victorian era who discovered the alleged ancient city of Troy and the equally alleged tomb of the Homeric warrior king Agamemnon—with little more than a pick axe in his hand and a worn copy of Homer's *The Iliad* in his pocket.

Wilhelmina Harker's forays into Slavic lands were less celebrated than Schliemann's exploits, but they did bring back a store of treasures. It was during just such a journey that she briefly took possession of the site where *The True Memoirs of Count Dracula* was secreted, using the farm plot as a sort of southern headquarters for her Slavic campaigns of 1899 and 1903 into the far reaches of northern Bulgaria, Romania and the Carpathian Mountains. As the dates of her excursions roughly correspond with the age of the manuscript itself, the circumstantial evidence would suggest that *The*

True Memoirs of Count Dracula was squirreled away in its hiding place by Mrs. Harker's own hand.

In her search for what she rather grandly referred to as "the soul of the Slavs," Wilhelmina Harker would have been instantly attracted to the *Memoir* author's remarkable facility with the dead tongue that is at the root of most Eastern European languages: Old Church Slavonic, a root dialect dating back to Saint Cyril, who is himself referenced disapprovingly within the work. But if Old Church Slavonic was part of the manuscript's allure, it's likely that Mrs. Harker believed the book to have had at least some claim on authenticity (being herself depicted in its second half, she could hardly have failed to notice the fictional embellishments contained there).

If so, Mrs. Harker deceived herself over the manuscript's provenance, because the writer's sentence structures give him away as a passionate amateur linguist of the mid-to-late 1800s who has somehow developed a miraculous facility in an obscure tongue. His sentences flow in a decidedly Victorian fashion (no mean trick in the elaborate and formal Slavonic dialect), and so we have the bizarre juxtaposition of a dead medieval tongue being used to craft entire paragraphs that would be structurally acceptable in the writings of Joseph Pennell or A. Conan Doyle.

To span both worlds, the author would have to have been as old as Dracula himself, which may be the point of this Quixotic exercise in pseudo-authenticity: The writer may have believed that to convince a Victorian readership of the manuscript's legitimacy, he would need to adopt a Victorian cadence (one of the assumptions that would mark this the work of an "out of the loop" amateur, since the Victorian era was a high-water mark of obscurities translated into English, and an epoch not just open but eager to assimilate extraordinary linguistic challenges).

Conversely, the author might simply have been incapable of transcending his roots in the Victorian period, despite the obvious incongruities this introduced—another sure sign of the amateur. Or finally, the writer may have learned Old Church Slavonic as his mother tongue and then lived long enough to have his dialect influenced by Estuary English. In other words, the writer might be Dracula. Delicious as that possibility may seem, the reader should note that if the above exegesis has any analytical merit, the odds of the *Memoirs* being written by their ostensible subject are running two to one against.

Nonetheless, the Old Church Slavonic original is a blessing to the contemporary English-language reader in one sense, because this book was translated for the first time ever not in the nineteenth or twentieth but in the twenty-first century. And this has allowed us to use a slightly more contemporary vocabulary than might have been expected in a text well over a century old. Where an anachronistic term captured the concept best, we have not hesitated to incorporate it.

Hence we have Dracula talking of the "psyche" well before the popularization of Sigmund Freud, anticipating contemporary astronomy by complaining of being pulled "into the unwavering orbit" of a superior object, speaking like B. F. Skinner of Donka's "learned response," likening a Roma woman's interaction with a defrocked priest to "a householder paying off a grocer" (the Victorians would have used "shopkeeper," or "greengrocer" if they were feeling *au courant*), and later referring to this same Roma woman as "a nervous type." These are just a few of many possible examples where we have chosen to modernize the *Memoirs* in translation, in the belief the work should speak to the reader without a bogus interlocutor based on one of the great Victorian translators (say, Richard Laurence) or some other long-dead scholar who never got his or her chance with this particular text.

Our purpose in making this choice is to try to ensure some measure of lasting clarity at a moment when the language itself is in an accelerated ferment of flux and change, as anyone who has ever encountered an emoticon already knows. But there were limits to how far we would go in our quest for the contemporary. For example, one term brooded over was "sunstroke," which went in and out of the translated manuscript several times. It is clearly the concept being described, but the word itself sounded too much like something a California surfer might say to put it into the mouth of an unholy terror of the Middle Ages. The narrator also seemed to us to be struggling to define what was a new concept for him, one he would therefore be unlikely to apply a term of common usage to. So we instead settled on the invented "sun sickness"—in Old Church Slavonic, "это не слово."

At the same time, we've striven to allow a hint of the slightly ornate and elongated rhythms of Victorian expression, believing that if an echo of the original voice is the best a translator can offer, the original author is still entitled to that echo. This is a translation, though, and its flaws should therefore be laid at the feet of this writer, who supervised the current text's creation, rather than at Konstantin Kuzmanov's feet.

Preliminary mutterings from within the groves of academia indicate that our most controversial choice may end up being the decision to publish *The True Memoirs of Count Dracula* in two volumes. We plead your indulgence. First and foremost, there are legalities involved. For though the real-world Victorian figures Bram Stoker adapted to his purposes are long dead, their bloodlines still course throughout contemporary Britain, where the slander laws are among the most severe and punitive in the world, thanks in large part to the durability of the Royal Family both as an institution and an object of fascination for Britain's carnivorous tabloid press. The second half of the *Memoirs* takes a far different view than Stoker's, not only of the Harkers but of other figures based on real women and men, and though the case law favors our right to publish, there are today several hundred descendants and/or relations of the Murrays, the Westenras, the Sewards, the Holmwoods, and even the Van Helsings spread throughout Britain, Scotland, Canada, Northern Ireland, and the Falkland Islands, all of whom could try to assert a claim of some imagined patronymic injury based on the revisionism that characterizes the *Memoirs'* second half.

Our publisher therefore hesitates to bring the complete work to market before completing a painstaking exploration of the complex legalities at issue in its latter pages—an exercise in due diligence that will probably take several years to accomplish, if it ever can be. While we considered following the Victorian practice of publishing real names using dashes (L__ W_____ for Lucy Westenra, Dr. V__ H_____ for literature's most famous vampire hunter), we concluded that the archaism would be a betrayal of our attempt to make the *Memoirs* as readable as possible for a contemporary audience. We remain reluctant to embrace such stylistic evasions without first pursuing all other options.

After much deliberation, we therefore decided that the first half of the full manuscript could stand alone as a novel in its own right, and that this may indeed have been part of the author's original intent. It was a judgment call based on several factors:

- The natural schism that occurs in the *Memoirs* (which vault approximately 300 years at almost precisely the halfway point before launching into an extremely argumentative but in many ways close reinterpretation of Stoker's event structure)

- The novelty of the *Memoirs'* first half—a kind of revisionist origin myth with no precedent in Stoker's work (indeed, it seems more to favor the Brothers Grimm)

- Forensic distinctions (of parchment, ink, and even mild variations of penmanship) that separate the contents of this volume from the proposed contents of *Memoirs II* and suggest different periods of authorship

- The nature of the *Memoirs'* conversation with *Dracula* itself, which in the second volume becomes a sustained quarrel over Stoker's plotting, narrative approach, characterizations, and even his cosmological view of the human condition

Also, before letting a complete if scrappy unknown go toe-to-toe against one of literature's best-loved works, we wanted to allow Konstantin Kuzmanov to present himself to the reader without the inevitable parsing and comparisons that promise to greet the second volume. But the refs say it was a close decision, and if a statutory path can be cleared for the second half of the manuscript, the possibility of a combined edition could be revisited on the basis of reader reaction later on.

The last important mystery we need to clear up is how this manuscript came into Wilhelmina Harker's hands and why she buried it in the cornerstone of a farmhouse in northern Bulgaria. But perhaps that's not such a mystery after all.

We know for a historical fact that Mrs. Harker's relationship to her much-honored husband was a troubled one, and it is believed that when the final break came, she may have blamed as a root cause the weird notoriety brought to their name via Bram Stoker's novel. Desperate to unravel what had gone so horribly wrong in her personal life, she ended her days roaming the recently liberated former Ottoman territories as a monomaniacal collector of all things related to the lore and superstitions of Eastern Europe, and she is known to have paid top dollar for rare works and primary artifacts.

This makes it entirely possible that *The True Memoirs of Count Dracula* was generated for an audience of one, as a literary con against a grieving and wealthy British widow with too much time and money on her hands. Mrs. Harker's facility with Old Church Slavonic was known to be intermittent but functional, and she would have been particularly susceptible to the work's autobiographical structure, since the Stoker novel she blamed for wrecking her household was written in the epistolary form to give it a similar ersatz authenticity. What we can say with certainty is that Wilhelmina Harker clearly responded with singular emotion to the forgery, as her moving coda to the second volume—in which she plays along with the construct to a worrisome degree that indicates incipient psychosis—is unquestionably authentic. But it's also entirely possible, and indeed probable, that she uncovered the deception of the *Memoirs* later and, mortified and in a last moment of lucidity, decided to bury the evidence in the literary equivalent of an unmarked tomb.

If so, it was an unquiet grave. For this manuscript has risen again, moldering perhaps, and surely blood-soaked, from its fitful sleep. There can be no more fitting outcome for a yarn steeped in the lore and traditions of the Dracula myth. And so, with apologies to Bram Stoker, *The True Memoirs of Count Dracula, Volume One.*

- R. H. Greene
Rousse, Bulgaria

PROLOGUE:
In a Time of Silence

There is in my mind even now a single and horrible image that never leaves my thoughts: the empty cross, that symbol of the Immortal Adversary's primacy over the fetid tumescence of sinew and flesh. It does me no comfort to consider that this wretched ornament of servitude is thought lovely by millions of my onetime species, for it is their devotion to such icons of their indenture that besets me and that I have striven to escape from, and even to reverse.

Hold a crucifix before me, with the Adversary's effigy pinned to it the way an entomologist might pin a beetle-bug before dissection, and my joy is unbounded. The Foe is imprisoned. Harmless. Constrained to partake by some small measure in the unrestrained suffering He has meted out to others in their billions down the blood-soaked ages.

The vacated cross is another matter: God's malevolent parlor magic made manifest, with all His grim trickeries revealed, enlarged and set like traps before the weak and thoughtless hordes who would rather writhe for a lifetime in His appalling grasp than taste the crisp and terrifying atmosphere of a single un-poppetted breath. Transfigured by some squalid vision of religious ecstasy, with hymnals to the benevolence of his Cruel Master deafening him, and puerile candy-colored phantasms of some fictive and invisible reward blinding his sight, the man who brandishes so profane an object is not the religious warrior of his own imaginings but a slave who kisses his chains. I shrink from this man, but not from his alleged and self-awarded sanctity, for he has none. I shrink instead from the vacancy on that uninhabited cross, an emblem of my own failure in a centuries-old war yet to be concluded. He has escaped me. What raw red mischief is He working somewhere? And who is to die this time for His unquantifiable sins?

I have traveled the world from end to edge and am older than forests. Men, of the sort I was once but am no longer, have spent centuries trying to finish me in ways both direct and imaginative, and I have faced unnumbered perils by spear and sword and gun and bow. The blades that bit deep into my body, bullets that cleaved my skin and organs and tissues then passed harmless by, images seared into my eyes of man's viciousness toward innocent others—few of these things have left more than a glancing mark upon my mind and heart.

Of a thousand-thousand horrors ingested, it is the vacated cross that preeminently haunts my dreams.

My struggle against that unholy artifact now reaches for its decisive moment, and while many of my actions have not gone unspoken of, the Adversary's minions have too frequently been my interlocutors. I am named Demon, Usurper, the Unconsecrated and Dread Prince. Peasant mystery stories accrue to me, heightening my depravities, clovening my hoof. And so the fetid odor of a grave I have eluded and taught others to evade scents my every gesture, a befouled and manufactured atmosphere that transmogrifies my one unquestioned accomplishment into something like its opposite, and sends those I might reach for across the mortal abyss scurrying from my hand—rushing for the shameful magic of ritual, crucifix, and prayer.

I alone have perpetrated the one offense the Adversary abides least of all. I alone have conspired successfully to end God's monopoly on time.

In the indeterminate twilight of our pitiless campaign, the Wiley Foe may yet triumph against me, and my foundering offensive end in rout and ignominy. Against that outcome, I leave behind this testament, that fair-minded creatures of another time may see past my own imperfections as an insurrectionist and judge me by my motives and true deeds.

Whether this is to be the final diary of a greater emancipation than the world has yet known of, or the object lesson of a defeat to rival bright Lucifer's, can only be revealed in the fullness of a time yet to come. But that time draws near. And so I set down this story of a reluctant and fretful Spartacus and his inconceivable sufferings, that others unborn may take what is usable or consoling for their own skirmishes against the Great Antagonist out of the raw stuff of my pitiable and unachieved life.

I set this down freely, of my own will and by my own hand, and avow that everything contained herein is true and factual, however incredible the exterior details may appear.

- Konstantin Kuzmanov, nee "Dracula"
London, Tuesday 4th October, 1887

PART ONE:
A Memory of Dust and Smoke

Chapter One

O f my amoral start in life, there are many things I could say. I, who have been called monstrous and a voluptuary on the basis of my latter-day repute, was far more blemished and far more of an affront to the Divine Order of things as they actually are in those, my earliest days of worldliness and carnality. But it was not worldliness or carnality that separated me from the vast and invisible connections between all things, for to live within the body given us is no sin. I lived inside that skin, drew breaths that tasted of grass, air, and mud, and was in every sensual aspect fully human, as you are. But I was thoughtless also, callow and selfish, a man of brisk violence and squalid pleasure, without shade or gradation or concern for any other than myself. Such is the life of a soldier.

In those days, the Ottoman Yoke was only partly fastened, and so the war launched at Constantinople on a fateful Tuesday in 1453 continued to rage everywhere, unslaked and unabated. As a condottiere, I served whoever paid me best or whoever allowed me to set my own wage in pillage from the spoils of war—my preferred form of salary. I sacked for the Turk and the Bulgar, looted for the Rumanian and the Goth, and made friends and slew enemies on either side of the battlefield, on one frenzied occasion even managing to take up opposing colors within a single day.

In my cynicism, I had few close acquaintances, all of my associations being opportunistic and therefore changeable. But there was one man from my own village who had been close to me in childhood, and whom I valued as a friend. This was Malaga, a bluff and laughing giant of fearsome mien in battle and passionate religious devotion away from it.

Had we not formed our relationship in childhood before time worked its changes on our personalities, I doubt either of us would have felt the fealty we did. Where my loyalties were a product of the marketplace, Malaga's were immutably dedicated to a single flag and the One True Cross. But despite this schism in our thinking, our love was like brother for brother, unchanging and true. As we were sometimes on the same side in the hostilities, we would generally seek each other's company where we could. We also had a standing agreement that, if possible, neither of us would die by the other man's hand.

Malaga was appalled and fascinated by the Turks and wanted to know my personal impressions of them from my time in their service. Was the God they worshipped the same as the Christian one? I told him that, in my understanding, it was. If that was so, how could they justify consuming the flesh of Christian babies? I told him that, to my knowledge, this was rumor and conjecture created to rally public sentiment, with no basis in fact. Aside from aversions to mead and pig meat, they had no dietary irregularities. "Well," said Malaga, "if not to keep themselves supplied with Christian children, why do they make war on us, so far from their home?"

As one who has known war at close quarters, I should here interject some statement as to my idea of its theory and practice, for no subject in all of human discourse has been treated to so much distortion and false romanticism. This is understandable, since it is a very unnatural thing to ask a man to put himself into a context where his death or mutilation is almost a certainty; so his eyes must be wrapped in waving banners and his ears deafened by applause and trumpets lest his knees buckle at the first clear indication of just how completely he has put his foot wrong. More than a few knees buckle anyway, despite the circuses put on in their honor, and the men attached to them are given the defamatory label of coward for their trouble, instead of a sobriquet more reflective of their instinctive wisdom.

What passes for bravery on the battlefield is often actually a lack of imagination, for the bravest soldier is one who cannot imagine himself dead. He can imagine his loved ones praying over his corpse, and the lamentation of women who have passed too quickly through his hands. If ethereal, he can imagine himself as a poem; if patriotic, he can imagine some dim monument with a flag fluttering over it where he will live on as a figure of stone. But in this context his lifeless form becomes a sort of stage prop allowing him, while still alive, to savor the regret and remorse that will afflict others in the unlikely event that his personal drama terminates in the heroic tragedy he has been instructed to both avert his eyes from and to anticipate.

All this is a way for the soldier to imagine a story that continues to include him after he has left the stage. What he cannot imagine— and I say this as one even more familiar with death than with war—is the dead's total unresponsiveness, their unyielding disinterest. To die is not just to cease to be, but to un-become.

So why make war, an activity whose most immediate by-product is an un-becoming of a massive type? It would be too facile to simply cite the obvious motivations of greed and a scarcity of resources, though these certainly have their part in the deliberations that occur in the unbreathable air where nations make decisions of polity. The real allure of warfare, at least to the warrior in the field, is that it grants him an unholy dispensation, a residency in another country where everything proscribed by the crimping standards of goodness becomes not just permissible but desirable.

The soldier metes out murder as casually as you or I might shop for vegetables. If he helps take a city, everything it contains, including its inhabitants, becomes his to do with as he will, and so rape and casual sadism are added to his fearsome repertoire. He may steal as long as it's from his foe, or set whole villages to the torch merely to warm his hands. That scaly atavism in every human heart, so thwarted by the cautious and deliberate tempo of ordinariness, is taken out of its box and poked with a stick until it roars and lunges and he himself becomes that monster in its most vivid and enlivened form. The warrior gets all this and the circuses besides, telling him in endless repetition that his actions are righteous and good, and that his many sins and slaughters are heroisms.

I could not have delivered such a sermon to Malaga, of course, but as one who has been maligned down the long years as a fiend and an ogre, I find it appropriate to place it here. For you, gentle Reader, will bear witness to my centuries of wantonness, and though my story is indeed steeped in horrors, I promise you they will not amount to the despoiling work of one middling squadron on an indolent day in the field.

To Malaga's question of Turkish motivation, I merely said, "Treasure and a greater access to the sea," and then we said our goodnights and went to sleep.

Chapter Two

It was hard not to notice the change in Malaga the next time we raised our swords on the same side of the field, for he was thinner, more sadistic in his battlefield actions, and far less jovial at camp. The source of the change was easy to trace. Not only had we been steeped for years in daily brutalities, but also the general tendency of the war was unavoidable: the Turks were going to win.

This left Malaga with a conundrum. On the one hand, he was a Christian and a patriot, and could not deviate from these commitments without stripping the patina of nobility from his previous actions and revealing them as the cruelties they were. Understandably, this was something he was unprepared to do.

On the other hand, the noble Turks had an unpleasant tendency to execute every Christian they captured, in the nasty but prudent belief this would prohibit the prisoners from taking up further arms against them. And while Malaga was unshakable in the belief that he would one day see God and lift his voice with the Choir Eternal, he was in no hurry to commit their songs to memory. It did not help his pessimistic mood that I had told him as a courtesy this might be our last collaboration in slaughter, as I would most likely spend the rest of the war on the Ottoman side, where the looting and pillaging was becoming distinctly more reliable as a source of livelihood.

You must here consider the mindset of the medieval peasant, which may be alien to you. It is as unsubtle and tactile as the hundred daily chores it takes to tease a crop out of even the smallest plot of land—the product of a closed process where things are placed in the ground, are attended to regularly, flourish, and are cut down. So preoccupied is the peasant by the actual he has no space in him for the reflective, and so even philosophical abstractions are rendered in his outlook as completely tangible—fungible goods to be marketed in the event of a pressing necessity.

It was therefore not especially extraordinary when Malaga queried me about my religious standing under the Turks (I swore an insincere oath to their Prophet whenever I fought on that side) and then suggested that we temporarily swap our religions.

This was an actual custom of the time, and it illustrates perfectly the literal-mindedness of peasant thinking. When I fought with the Turks, I was a Muslim and thereby sheltered from their religious slaughters when the battle was decided for their side. I was also a member of their army and thereby due my portion of glory and treasure in the event of a victory. In the peasant mind, I had two forms of protection against the Ottoman scimitar, and was only in need of one. This was an ideal situation for a mutually beneficial bit of barter.

Malaga recommended a temporary transaction, whereby he would become a covert Islamist for the duration of the war and I would be the clandestine carrier of his rather more burnished and habituated Christianity. This would also extend some small protections to me as well, for in the increasingly unlikely event of my capture by Malaga's side, I would face a ragged and depleted but still well-armed foe that had proved no less inventive than the Turks in his religious butcheries.

I asked Malaga to describe his theology for me so I could see what kind of bargain he was offering.

"Well," he said, "there's this big fellow and a little one, and they are one thing, because to worship more than one thing the way our grandfathers did is wrong. The little fellow is a magician—he can make wine without grapes, I remember that, and wouldn't we all like to know the secret there, ho?

"In the end, things get good and bloody, and the little fellow won't raise a hand over it, being small and therefore meek. So the big fellow builds a great oven, and they stuff all their enemies in it and build a good fire. Ho! Oh yes, and there's a white bird comes into it somewhere—he's also one thing. I wish I could say more of him but being a bird he never held my interest."

After so learned a discourse, there was no other choice. I told Malaga I would gladly make the trade and that such an intelligible creed would be a bargain at twice the price. Then, in what I recognize now as both a provincial travesty of Christian ritual and a strange foreshadowing of my future path, we got out our knives and a dirty wooden bowl and sealed the bargain with the accepted ceremony:

We drank each other's blood.

In this way I took Malaga's faith and draped it over my shoulders as lightly as a widow puts on her evening shawl. And the arrangement felt weightless, as all spiritual transactions should.

Chapter Three

I f the scales tip far enough in one direction, the fun goes out of a war. Soon the towns are depleted, offering little in the way of proceeds that aren't scraggly, diseased, and thin. Instead of defending themselves, villages shower you with gratitude for taking them, and then ask you for provisions. The armies pitted against you start to run out of men, and one fine morning you find yourself wielding your axe without enthusiasm against little boys and grandfathers. And where's the sport in that?

It was toward the end of one of these depressing days late in the struggle that we on the Ottoman side took what surely had to be the last substantial force that would ever be arrayed against us: some thousands of ill-kempt warriors who, though starving and without a visible command structure, gave every appearance of being battle-hardened men.

The Pasha in command of our legions had long since grown bored with butchery. He barely looked up as he gave the command for us to form up for the obligatory post-victory slaughter of the Christian forces. But some unscripted business rekindled his interest, for from the captured enemy hordes, a brassy rumble issued forth, shouting, "Ho! You can't kill me! I'm an Islamist-er!"

It was unquestionably Malaga.

The Pasha's eyes brightened, for here at a minimum would be some low comedy to leaven the high tedium of his grisly post. "What's that you say?" he called. "Step forward."

He made a sign to the guard, and Malaga was permitted to come to him. "Excuse me, your Muslim-ness. But I've had a bit of barter with one of your men, and swapped his religion against mine as a protection against just this outcome. If you kill me, you'll be killing one of your own."

Despite the look of disbelief on the Pasha's face, and the treacherous shoals we'd begun navigating, I felt obligated to jump in.

"It's true, Effendi. He made the swap with me."

The Pasha's eyes gleamed with mirth then, although he maintained his inflexible attitude of command. "Ah!" he said to Malaga. "So it's this devout and pious defender of the faith you've made common cause with, is it?" He looked me over, his appraisal as dispassionate as a farmer appraising a horse at auction. "And here I took this man for a lowly mercenary—a condottiere. Well, Prisoner, let's gauge what sort of enterprise you've invested in, shall we?"

His eyes weren't smiling anymore, and I could feel sweat building on my scalp and over my lip. The Pasha turned to me.

"What is the holiest city of our faith?" he asked.

"I'm sorry, Effendi, I—"

"Answer please!"

Though there was no oath or magistrate, I was all of a sudden on trial as surely as any prisoner in the dock. The Pasha was certain I had joined Malaga in making mock of the Muslim faith, and he was going to prove the point and let me face the presumably dire consequences. And while I trusted my good right arm in most situations, the Pasha of course had an entire army at his back.

Despite years of military campaigns, I'd never really prayed before, which made me something of a battlefield anomaly to be sure. But I prayed then, as fervently as any nun in her cloister. My flustering entreaties flew to God like a flock of drunken doves, pleading for His mercy and assistance. There are friars and bishops who wear holes in their knees with their daily devotions and never hear anything but silence. Call it beginner's luck, but amazingly, in an instant, I had His answer!

For suddenly my agitated brain was aflame with specialized knowledge of things never before revealed to me. The gentle wisdom of the Prophet. The fierce demands of his law. Places, dates, and concepts of Islam. Arcane passages of Koranic scripture. A wealth of information I could not have come by through any other means than divine revelation. It was all suddenly available to me, the way another person might remember his mother's face or his own name.

Tranquil with the self-confidence that flows from such a miraculous occurrence, I was ready for the Pasha when he asked again, "What is the holiest city of our faith?"

Upright and untroubled, I gave him the answer that had come unbidden into my receptive mind. "Constantinople," I said.

The Pasha nodded approvingly. Then, with a benevolent smile, he reached down and removed a fat calfskin purse from his kaftan. He threw the well-filled pocketbook to Malaga, who grinned as the coins in it jingled against his hand.

"My friend," the Pasha said to Malaga. "May I introduce you to the one god the condottiere is on intimate terms with."

Malaga was so delighted to hold a purse full of gold he did not realize the turn things were taking.

"I thought that you should hold this undeniably potent deity a moment," the Pasha continued, "seeing as you were swindled in your original dealings."

He turned to me. "Condottiere, retrieve my purse from this man."

I went to Malaga who, still grinning, handed me the purse.

"Well done," said the Pasha. "And now Condottiere, kindly draw your sword and remove this feeble-minded gentleman's empty head from his thick neck."

Malaga turned to him, beginning to stammer. "But I . . . I got his faith! You . . . you can't kill me. I'm Is-Is-Is-Islamist-er! I got his faith, I got—"

"He has no faith," the Pasha said with forced deliberateness, as if talking either to a moronic child or a very bright pack animal. "The answer to that ridiculously simple question is Mecca." He turned to me again. "His head, please. Immediately."

"Effendi, please I—"

The Pasha drew his sword. "His head, or I'll have yours."

The code of the mercenary is a simple one. There is no faith but in the self. No allegiance to anything but the self. No cause worth dying for but the self. The mercenary inhabits a nation of one. And that's what he defends when he goes into battle, and he defends it at all costs.

I drew my sword.

Malaga looked at me, and his eyes were a curse. He started to pray. "Praise be to—" But then my hand struck, and his head was smashed and rolling, and whether his prayer was to Allah, or to God, to Jesus or the Devil, is more than I can say.

The Pasha was merry at the upshot of his jest. "Well, there's a surprise," he said. "The giant wasn't empty-headed after all. Shall we get on with the massacre?"

Chapter Four

The profound mental collapse that followed this event was unique in my experience of warfare. I'd killed a hundred men and seen ten thousand die. There was nothing in me of squeamishness. No vision of spilt innards or splintered skull could possibly appall me.

But still, when I struck Malaga down, something inside myself was also sheared clean and severed. And it was I who rolled in the dust.

For the soldier can only function while his enemy is a thing. He puts that thing in a box, in the same way a pig keeper puts his pigs in a stall during the winter. The pig keeper may like his pigs; he may talk to them like they're his babies and raise them with the tenderness of a new mother. Still, his hand doesn't tremble when he slits their throats.

So it is with a soldier. And Malaga's curse on me, the one he communicated with his final baleful glance, was that for the first time I was forced to address the fact that I was killing not a what but a who—a human being instead of a thing. For the first time in a decade of butcheries small and large, I became in my own eyes a murderer.

It was not just Malaga's unquiet ghost that haunted me after that. Shades came at me in fistfuls. The men I'd gashed, the children I'd hacked, the women I'd ravished and lacerated. They seemed to delight in my anguish, and sometimes in my feverish fancy they would join hands and dance around me as I labored through the unsleeping night, an unholy brood of fiends come to gloat over my dismay.

The other warriors were quickly exasperated by my tendency to shriek without ceasing from the first sign of darkness until morning light, and I cannot blame them for it, for an army's access to rest is as much a weapon of battle as any serrated armament. It was decided I was mad, and I was relieved of duty and told to go home.

"You do realize it was all in good fun," said the Pasha, who was not without conscience about my fate. "No matter what you said, he was going to die anyway."

I did not reply, but merely fought down tears as I did most of the time in those days. Then the Pasha did something he meant as a kindness but which unmanned whatever strength was left in me. He handed me something heavy and closed my fingers around it. "For the journey," he said, and then rode away.

When I looked down at what my hand held, it was the object I most feared it would be.

That same overflowing calfskin purse.

In my experience of it, the foremost attribute of madness is its complete lack of specificity. What's missing from the brain is the ability to focus attention on a single thing at a time and to give it precedence over other things. You meander down a road and find yourself bleeding against a stone because the road was no more important than the stone and so you drifted from one to the other. You start to eat a meal and become fascinated by the table, or the spoon, or even the shape of the food rather than the fact that it's meant to nourish you, and the result is you go hungry—not that this matters any more than any other thing.

The only point that can be made on behalf of madness is that the common people have a healthy respect for it. They draw near to the babbling lunatic and find cryptic wisdoms in his gibbering utterances. They cross themselves and genuflect as he goes by. Rotted food is left for him in wooden dishes, and eventually the smell or the flies draw the imbecile's inconstant attention, and so he survives for another day. Most important, the folk avoid physical contact with the madman out of a superstitious belief that his disorder may be an infectious disease. This is the only explanation I can give for the fact that when my thoughts cleared after several weeks of nomadic squalor, I was still clutching the Pasha's overflowing calfskin purse in my filth-encrusted hand.

The first object to take precedence in my thinking since I left the Ottoman camp was a cooking fire. Above it was a sausage on a stick. Connected to the stick was a hand, and attached to that by arm, shoulder, trunk, and all the usual accoutrements was the tonsured head of a round-faced man, smiling at me above a brown swathe that was his rough sackcloth robe.

"Come back to us, have ye?" he said. "Praise God."

"Who are you?" I tried to say, and then realized my mouth was swollen from several recently broken teeth.

"I'm a poor monk," he said, intuiting my question, "driven out of his holy sanctuary and scattered to the winds like his brothers by the surging fortunes of the Infidel."

Having had some small hand in those infidel successes, I hung my head, abashed.

"Here," he said consolingly, without embarrassing me by asking for the source of my obvious grief. "Have a sausage."

Chapter Five

His name was Brother Ivan, and he was the most self-assured man I'd ever known. If my mind was a riot of guilts, shames, and blood-soaked recollections, his was as orderly as the angle at which the beam hits the crossbar on a crucifix.

Haunted as I was by my gruesome past, I confessed as soon as my swollen mouth would let me that I had served with the Turks. "It doesn't matter," Brother Ivan said, amazing me with the equanimity of his response. "You were just fulfilling your function in God's Holy Plan."

In Brother Ivan's cosmology, God's Holy Plan accounted for everything and was perfect, so nothing anyone ever did could be objected to. This didn't mean that he rejected the notion of sin; in fact, he was ruled by it, as were most of his calling. But in meting out punishment or judgment against the sinner, he would not have assumed an attitude of righteous wrath. To do so would be to grant the sinner the god-like power of choice over his own actions (one could only get angry if the sinner had *elected* to do wrong, after all) and therefore to confer legitimacy on the idea that life is a series of formless contrivances. While Brother Ivan admitted that it often seemed that way, he was firm in stating it was not.

The sinner could not have done other than to sin. God had ordained all human actions since before time, because no human actions could occur independently of Him and He was both all-powerful and all-knowing. As a monk, this proposition was altogether plain to Ivan, as was the fact that his primary role in the godly order was to understand the great scheme better than most others did and to try to explain it to them. For this reason, he made my edification a sort of special cause, and I found myself living in the ill-provisioned camp of this holy vagabond.

Seeing what a lost soul I was, and uncertain about the future of his religious order in the coming era of Islamic ascendancy, Brother Ivan asked me if I would like to take religious instruction with him. "It's a stimulating time for the Faith," he said, trying to sound optimistic. "We're going to have to cut away some of the fat and go back underground, like the Apostles and proto-Christians. Soon we'll be at holes and corners again—code words, *noms de guerre*, secret signs." He here drew a stick-figure fish on the ground. "I've already selected my summer name. What do you think of 'The Brown Fox'?"

In the time-honored tradition of the missionary, the goodly man was shrewd enough to attach an offer of regular meals to his pitch—a fisher of men who understood the efficacy of bait. Among the many benefits of the arrangement was that Brother Ivan began my curriculum by teaching me the rudiments of the Cyrillic alphabet, and he provided me with a worn Psalter from among his possessions, thereby initiating the process by which ultimately I learned to read.

My days were soon filled with the sound of Brother Ivan's voice telling wondrous tales of hardship and miracles, sudden blinding revelations, godly wrath, and divine filial pieties. The Old Testament's Warrior God appealed strongly to what was left of the soldier in me. Having done my own share of smiting, I appreciated His hot temper and refusal to negotiate over even the most trifling of slights. How I would have liked to become a consuming column of flame or a great and crushing wall of water to drown my enemies during some of the desperate battles that were part of my previous life!

Under Brother Ivan's influence, the visions that haunted me began to take a different shape. Soon it wasn't a ring of festering corpses that danced around my bed, but white-robed seraphim and

Bible prophets. In place of the gouts that spouted from Malaga's gushing neck, the wounds of the gentle Christ filled my thinking, and the Great Lord himself even appeared to me once while I dozed of an afternoon, and asked me to take His stigmatic hand.

"It felt more like a dream than a vision," I said diffidently to Brother Ivan upon waking, unsure how to deal with such an axiomatic religious hallucination. I also told him of my experience of false revelation during my interrogation by the Pasha, and my resultant suspicion about my own appropriateness as a vessel of God's message.

"No," Brother Ivan said. "Don't you see? It's Malaga's death that set you on the Holy Road. You're not ready yet for the great gift that's been offered to you. But don't worry. You will be, I know it. It's all in the Plan."

Killing Malaga to send a message to me seemed a dubious proposition. But I was so grateful to Brother Ivan for helping me escape the nightmare of my former deliriums I resolved not to argue the point.

One day, Brother Ivan decided I was improved enough for him to take up the matter of the calfskin purse with me. He had noted me clutching it feverishly during our first encounter, but discreetly avoided discussing it for fear I had come by the gold through some foul deed that was the source of my distemper. Impoverished for life by the vows of his order, Brother Ivan had strong opinions on the evils of money, even when it was come by honestly. His certainty that the Turk's purse was the artifact of roadside murder or some other foul brigandage made his conviction against it all the more fervent. And my habit of sleeping with the overstuffed reticule wedged under my pillow did not reassure him.

"It's a wonder you can hear God's voice at all with Mammon's auric claws clanking away against your head all night," he said to me peevishly as we were roasting our dinner over the fire. "God is asking you to rise above your past. That pile of gold is what's weighing you down, my lad. Make no mistake." He then provided me with many passages of holy precedent on the subject of human greed, including the tale of the unfaithful Israelites and their Golden Calf (yet another leaf from the Book of Smites), Judas and his thirty pieces of silver, and the Gospel parable laying odds about a rich man's entry into heaven against a camel's passage through the eye of a needle in favor of the camel.

In truth, I had never felt anything but anguish over the means by which I came to possess the Turk's gold. I slept over that infidel pocketbook the way an apostate might sleep over a bed of coals—that is to say, fitfully and without comfort. For me, the Ottoman moneybag was both my punishment and the inflexible adjudicator of my guilt. As such, I was not at all adverse to Brother Ivan's idea that cutting lose from this weighted object was the only way for the religious transformation he sought in me to take wing.

I asked him what I should do.

He scratched his head. "Ordinarily, there'd be an easy answer for that," he said. "Give it to the Church." Our problem was that, in the moment, there did not appear to be a Church to give the money to.

With the Ottoman ascendancy all but completed, chaos and unrest rippled throughout the religious orders. After having declaimed for years from narthex to chancel that an Ottoman victory would have the most grotesque consequences for Mother Church, it was inevitable the clergy had come to believe in its own rhetoric and now expected an orgy of impalement, dismemberment, and slower tortures to be launched against it. At the same time, the Christian capitulation was still uncompleted. A few of the larger Orthodox churches had settled with the Ottomans, and the Turks were making a great show of leniency toward them in the hope of expediting similar arrangements elsewhere. But official church doctrine was that negotiation with the Ottoman authorities was an act of schism and deviltry. And so, from the most exalted bishopric to the lowliest novitiate, a state of fluctuation and uncertainty reigned.

Brother Ivan patted my leg reassuringly. "It's a puzzler," he said. "But you just leave it to the Brown Fox. I'll think of something. Here. Have another sausage."

Chapter Six

Brother Ivan's scheme, when it came to him, was an audacious one. The cloister he'd abandoned was part of the oldest enduring structure of significance in the entire region—a vast, fortress-like religious compound carved into the stone face of a sheer cliff inside a mountain hollow. The site's history was indicative of the savage era we were still living through. Four hundred years earlier, a crown prince was lured to the ravine by his usurping brother. The usurper, who was next in the succession, had the crown prince killed, dismembered, and his body parts hurled over the steep precipice, obliterating all evidence of his crime on the hungry rocks. The Tsar grew suspicious, and the murdering brother became the focus of some rather imaginative tortures, whereupon he gave the Tsar a detailed account of the more favored son's murder and of the whereabouts of what remained of the crown prince.

The grieving Tsar decreed that a vast moral edifice should be erected on the spot of his son's death, taking as its text educational stories from scripture dealing in similar acts of betrayal, punishment, and death. The greatest artisans in the land were brought together for the task, an undertaking that would last so long that several generations of stonecutters came to it as apprentices and left as master carvers. Bit by bit, the immense face of a remote escarpment was reimagined as a decorative headstone on a massive scale. When the task was completed, the entire rock face was adorned with bas-relief sculptures—some over fifty feet high—depicting Bible horror stories of deception, vengeance, and God's unceasing wrath. The result was said to be one of the most spectacular and disturbing monuments to human suffering ever created. It became known in honor of the prince, whose macerated bones it still contained, as *Monastьɪrj na Krovi*, the Monastery On the Blood.

I'd never seen this continent of wonders, but Brother Ivan proposed to change all that. For although he'd fled his cell at the Monastery On the Blood in anticipation of an Ottoman incursion, his loyalty to his former home was absolute, and his fury over the manner of his leave-taking had not abated but rather intensified over time. Equally strong was his commitment to free me from the evil influence of my Turkish purse. It was unsurprising, then, when all these things fused together in his mind and produced a single mad scheme.

"You know the Turks, I know the monastery," Brother Ivan said, clearly relishing his self-assigned role as that laughing rebel, the Brown Fox. "We'll hide the purse so well, they'll never find it, or even know it's there, and the gold will be a curse in the dark we hurl at them every day. Between us, we should be able to move in and out like an avenging wind."

I pointed out that it seemed rather odd to give alms to a nonfunctioning—and indeed, overrun—church.

"The tide of rebellion must rise somewhere, my lad. Believe me, they'll sing songs about this one day. What better act of resistance can there be than to leave an offering to the God the Infidel denies right under the Infidel's unholy nose?"

And so, after acquiring a pair of undernourished horses, a sack of mealy beans, and a day's supply of pig sausage from some elderly religious folk in the town, we set out for Monastery On the Blood. And Brother Ivan's heart was so light he sang psalms for me for much of the way.

This seems an advantageous moment to introduce you to a leading character in the formative portion of my personal drama: the forest itself, a wild and primeval place of a type, dear Reader, it is impossible for you to imagine without my assistance. I make this overconfident claim not to insult my audience but because of the moment in time where I sit as I set these thoughts to paper, and all the developments occurring in the world in the centuries since Brother Ivan and I set out on our journey. Wonders though they are, the gas lamp and the electric lantern have changed the relationship of human beings to the robust, generative, and harrowing domain they were once an integral part of. Here in the latter portion of the 19th century, men sit in rooms as inorganic as stained glass and read to their children from fairy tales about wolves hiding behind blankets or North American lumberjacks who fell entire jungles with one swing of an axe. In their modernized minds, there is no corner where light can't find them, and precedent terrors are always put to sleep comfortably on shelves and between covers before the unblooded man of today kisses his progeny and turns out the artificial light.

In the medieval era, the forest was not a place but a living entity, an unresolved monster for which there were no reliable maps. Into this refuge of unholy mysteries and pagan ghosts, human beings frequently ventured with the smallest of objectives in mind and then simply vanished, gone without trace and with no particle of their corporeal selves ever showing itself again. This was as true of excursions that set out by day as it was of those more stout-hearted journeys initiated after nightfall. Danger was not a conception encountered in the forest. It was an animate and breathing inhabitant of the wood.

Centuries of stewardship and husbandry have conditioned people to think of forests as vast and naturally occurring gardens— dominions under a benign human protectorate. But the relationship between the ancient and undying forest and the barely established town of my time was more like that of two warring kingdoms often engaged in a death struggle. And the handful of wise humans who fitfully speckle any era alongside the prevailing follies would not have argued that the town was the likelier hegemon among the two.

We will parse these matters further, for both town and forest will extend their claims on our attentions presently. For now, it's enough to say that as the branches overhead thickened in density and concentration until they were more like a ceiling than a trellis, and the thirsty vulpine calls of creature to creature and like to like overwhelmed our ears, Brother Ivan's jolly mood diminished and his songs slowly died in the air, until his boisterous personality became so creased and folded that it was at best a third or a sixth of its normal size.

He looked around him at the deepening wood, hushing like a fidgety boy at a funeral. "Here's something the Turks will never conquer," he said quietly.

Chapter Seven

We were fortunate in that the Monastery On the Blood's remote location and the general immobility of the treasures it contained made it a lesser priority for the invading hordes, for even the triumphant Ottoman was incapable of carting away a cliff. We saw little evidence of a garrison in the area, though once or twice we left the road and hid ourselves until small cadres of unobservant Turkish soldiers went by.

The holy fortress itself seemed unremarkable from the angle of our approach, so much so that it took Brother Ivan climbing down from his horse before I realized we had arrived. "We're here?" I said, looking at an unremarkable clump of stone in front of me, which was no more than twelve feet high.

Brother Ivan looked irritated. "What did you expect, that we'd walk in through the front door like two pilgrims on a religious holiday? We're an avenging wind, remember? We get in through the unplastered cracks."

We tied off our horses, and within moments we were two dimly glowing shades traveling through an ingeniously apportioned netherworld of fissures and splits. The unassuming pile of stones was in fact a portal that let us approach the bluffs at some distance and from the flank, and what this unguarded access-way revealed was that the cliff was not one face but many faces pressed together as tightly as skulls in an ossuary. Within this jostling horde were naturally occurring inlets and basins, dead riverbeds bereft of waterways, that seemed at first glance to be untouched and in their primal state. Closer examination revealed hundreds of minute alterations—a rounded stair-step here, a false façade there—steering our path precisely so that it was always illuminated by indirect light.

In those murderous times, preservation of the innate cover was an obvious motivation for such intricate subtleties, and as Brother Ivan and I moved together through wavering pools of shadow and brightness, occasionally hearing distant murmurings in the Turkish tongue, I was grateful to the architects of the Monastery On the Blood for our well-wrought camouflage. But the artisans had also done something remarkable for men of that blunt and thrashing era: they had accepted what was immutable about the promontory and, relinquishing their desire to conquer it, yielded like bridegrooms to the edifice's inner quirks and foibles because they found more beauty in what was naturally occurring than anything that could have come from their hands.

Soon we could see the end of the passageway. Brother Ivan stopped. "You're younger, thinner, and more apt to understand what they're on about," he whispered. "Have a look."

I stepped forward, sticking my head out for a better view, and had an absurd impression of a birthing baby's head crowning. I peered carefully out into the light.

The vista was anticlimactic in any number of ways. The celebrated sculptures the Monastery On the Blood took its name from did not reveal themselves to my eye, nor did some seething horde of Turkish swordsmen panting for battle. Instead, I saw only the columns and arches of the monkish residences, cut into the cliff wall with such undeviating geometric regularity it was as though honeybees had acquired the skill to dig in stone.

As to Turks, there were perhaps six visible from my position, all armed with swords and spears, but soft-looking men for that, and behaving with a casualness that indicated no strong sense of alertness or even a competent command. Despite Brother Ivan's passion for his home, this monastery clearly did not elevate the Ottoman pulse the way it did the monkish one—it was as close to undefended as it could be and still be claimed as property of the Empire. The only visually stirring element of the scene was something that *wasn't* there: an implication of grandeur in the line of the cloister's cells as they rose toward a massive presence that could somehow be felt just outside the field of vision, which was exactly the way Brother Ivan sometimes described God.

I reported back to the Brown Fox. "It's thinly guarded. Had I retained my weapons when I left their service, I could subdue them all."

"A pity you didn't, then," said Brother Ivan. "But patience can be a weapon too." He somehow managed to remove a pair of previously cooked sausages from his sackcloth robe. "We'll wait for their backs to turn, and then we'll go in. Shall we lunch?"

Chapter Eight

We were several hours waiting for the Turks' backs to turn, but turn they did. So small was the perhaps ten-soldier retinue that it was incapable of watching over the entirety of the compound's vaulted vastness. And so undisciplined were these second-tier soldiers that they clustered together to talk and joke, rather than spreading themselves to maximize their watch, and shifted their post's position as a body to shelter from the heat of the sun. This meant the Turks' placement within the monastery grounds was easily anticipated and that when they left the area we were hiding in, they likely would not return for what remained of the day. For all its eccentricities, Brother Ivan's plan to lay our tribute in the home of his order no longer seemed unachievable or far-fetched. If we couldn't sneak in and out of the monastery on these terms, we were hopeless rebels indeed.

And so, after allowing the sun to push the Turks as far from us as possible, we snuck out into the daylight and quickly scurried across to the monks' cloister. For Brother Ivan's eccentric plan had but one thought of an appropriate hiding place for my accursed treasure-bag: we were to bury it beneath the floor of his own monkish cell.

When we stepped inside, I was sure the tiny, cave-like room had been looted, for it contained nothing but a bare cross on its wall and a splintered wooden plank that to my surprise turned out to be Brother Ivan's bed. The walls were so close together that it was impossible to extend both arms fully and hold them out at the shoulder, and there was no window, just an open entryway that served as a door.

Brother Ivan smiled as if he was a king who had just returned to his palace from exhausting affairs of state. "It's good to be home," he said, indicating there was nothing unusual about the cell's nakedness.

The floor was of dirt and clay, and came up easily in our hands. We dug quickly and sank a small hole about six feet deep into the ground, leaving our Ottoman spoils well hidden in the earth. We had just finished tamping the soil down again and were almost through raking the floor with our feet to obscure the marks of our industry when Turkish voices could be heard echoing off the cliffs nearby.

Fastidious Brother Ivan ignored the sound and kept on clearing the floor. "Leave it!" I whispered hotly.

Judging that the voices were near to our original access point, I asked if we could exit by a different route than the one our entry had taken. Brother Ivan nodded. "Follow me."

Our new path was a more dangerous one. It took us along a rock face out in the open and included a sharp twist around a sheer ledge where it was impossible to see what we were stepping into—a deadly moment indeed if the Turkish guard was on the other side of the turn. But Ivan said the risk was worth taking because we'd be out of the monastery far more quickly. He also thought it unlikely the drowsy Turks were near, as we were moving toward the most unrestful and forbidding area of the entire compound, and their general commitment seemingly was to leisure.

With some difficulty, Ivan stepped around the cornered ledge and bade me follow. Turning from the narrow pass, we stepped out into a vast open area where I caught my first glimpse of the storied rock carvings of the Monastery On the Blood.

I promptly swooned into Brother Ivan's startled arms.

Yes, swooned like a maiden on a balcony who catches her first glimpse of Milos Gloriouso, the swaggering soldier come to ravish her. For such was the power of the massive, rough-hewn sculptures that they carried me off in a spiritual euphoria, burning themselves into my eyes like a brand so that I could still see them, even as I dozed, insensible and dreaming.

There lay Egypt, its bloodied babies slaughtered, Pharaoh and his centurions bashed and asphyxiated by God's torrential anger. Here innocent John the Baptist twitched in agony, his fingers curled like fishhooks, while long-limbed Salome kissed his dribbling head and danced. Lot's wife stood stricken, Gomorrah fragmented and flared. Judas the betrayer dangled from the Tree of Life, his distended neck captured in the very act of cracking under the heavy ballast of his abandonment by God.

In a place of unmistakable prominence (as fitted the fratricidal circumstances of the monastery's commissioning), the feral and barbarous form of Cain bludgeoned his brother Abel with a blunt stone axe. The ferocity of the image was overwhelming—the clenched swing of the truncheon, the spewed fragments of blood and skull. But the real power in the representation came from Abel's serene and startled face, upturned toward heaven in a posture of supplication. Launching his soul into the ether, Abel was even now well past the petty concerns of the immediate, which his fiendish brother stood mired in. God-filled and unafraid, Abel had already moved on.

Of themselves, these fearsome figures could well have overwhelmed me. But I have described just half the exhibition. Adamantine and unremitting as they were, these stony forms seeped anemia compared with the sanguinary spectacle splayed over the wall of rock that formed the other half of the diptych.

For here the artisans had taken as their theme the blood of Christ—that reeking river of martyrdom and gruel. All the thousand saints who met their end by violence were presented in the act of their dying. Fires were slaked; arrows chewed flesh and quaffed gore. Stones shattered necks and chins; eyeballs protruded at the severing intrusion of the headsman's axe.

And centered on the plane, towering over all in a figure fifty feet high, the tortured Savior writhed against the Roman spike as blood burst from Him and stabbed downward, a jagged river of liquid lightning, inundating the martyrs and engulfing cities and towns full of prostrate multitudes, until God's blood seemed to clot the world.

I dreamed these things after the smallest glimpse of them, and in this dreaming they claimed me. For it was in that moment, with the Turkish guard surrounding us and our escape but half-achieved, that Brother Ivan's patient tilling of my soul's soil yielded its crop. I had struggled in the net long enough. God had me.

And then suddenly my eyes are open, and I see concern in Brother Ivan's face. I see his fear but am unafraid, and it's as if the top of my head has come off in his hands to let in the hot white light. And I am laughing, I am laughing, I am crying, a child again and shouting, calling out His great name. Brother Ivan's eyes widen as my raised voice echoes against the bleeding cliffs, and then there are shouts above us and running footsteps, and the spears come for us, but my light is so bright they cannot find me, and the two sentries throw wide. I take up the spears and hold them against my body and run at the soldiers, so foolhardy they gawp at me just long enough, and then their blood is everywhere, baptizing the ground, baptizing me and Brother Ivan, baptizing all the thirsting chiseled gore inside the rough rocks.

Then Brother Ivan's arms are around me, pushing me, and we are running in half-light in a tight corridor of stone. And then another spear comes and he is stumbling, stumbling as we emerge in the place where our animals are, and he is crying but not for joy like me, and I am throwing him over his horse, and we are galloping, galloping away into the tree-sifted light. There is so much blood that I can't tell who's bleeding anymore—Brother Ivan, the horses, the whole world, or just me?

Chapter Nine

I was probably never happier than I became during the early stages of my religious conversion. We forget what a strain the everyday business of being can be—the groping in the dark, the constant shifting of position, the loneliness. Suddenly I had fixed my place in the universe as pristinely as a sextant fixes a star, and in the great flux of comings and goings it was the universe and I who held our positions while everything wheeled around us.

Brother Ivan didn't die from his wounds, but he suffered. In fact, my untimely rebirth in the Spirit presented him with an extremely difficult theological problem, and that was a form of suffering, too. He brooded over it, and he was not a man prone to brooding.

"There's no way around it," he said at last, as I patiently drained the fluid from the place in his side where the spear had struck at him. "God wanted me to suffer this injury, or he would not have revealed Himself to you at such an awkward moment. For all my discomforts, the Plan is unyielding on this point: things happen for a reason. So what is the reason God wanted me to suffer?"

"Perhaps in emulation of the Savior," I said serenely. "For surely it has occurred to you that He, too, received an enemy's spear in the side."

"That's—ahhhh!—very consoling," Brother Ivan said, flinching against my ablutions. "Rather than worry over this injury, perhaps I should just count my blessings and be grateful the Lord didn't see fit to also put a few Ottoman nails through my palms into the bargain." Then he laughed, insofar as his injuries would allow it.

To Brother Ivan's surprise, I rounded on him for the first time ever in our association. "For shame, brother!" I said hotly. "It would be an honor to take on the Lord's pains! You should pray for such a boon, and a crown of lordly thorns besides!" Less than a week in the faith, and I was already turning into something of a Jesuit.

"Well tendered," Brother Ivan replied, but his tone was uncertain. "But see here, brother, half the day is gone. Shouldn't you be at your prayers?"

In truth, the idea of personal suffering as a path to redemption was exerting a stronger and stronger hold on my imagination. For me, the Monastery On the Blood had been a waking vision, and what it communicated in figure after figure was that the body is the soul's prison, to be struggled against and discarded with contempt as soon as the spirit can get free.

When I closed my eyes now, I saw the stony countenances of Cain and Abel—the one mired in petty rages and jealousies of the moment, the other launched toward the eternal, his earthly load as light as a seed. In my imagining, the two opposing façades had converged, with Cain the face I showed the world and Abel the immortal soul that grappled with him underneath.

As with the figures in the rock, the struggle was a fight to the death. I scorned my outer Cain and wanted him torn and punished so that the interior Abel might become visible and freed.

Brother Ivan noticed the change immediately the next time I came to tend to him. "Brother, what's happened to your sandals?" he said.

"I've discarded them, for they confined me."

"Was that wise?" For keep in mind we camped at the edge of the forest, where brambles and rubble made a constant assault on the feet.

He sat up then, noticing as he looked more closely that there was blood running down my ankle and that saplings of thorns had been wound around my legs, and were visible below the hem of my garments.

"Good heavens!" he said. "What are you doing?"

"The Lord calls on us to suffer for his sake. So I am suffering."

"But surely that's a misinterpretation of the text! The call is to accept suffering, not to seek it."

"We disagree there, brother," I said, all tranquility, and then knelt beside him, feeling the sweet anguish of the thorns grinding deep into my knees. "Perhaps that's why one of us groans on his pillow, while the other attends to him."

Through such exchanges, I quickly became intolerable to my former friend. But as my religious motivations were unquestionably sincere and Brother Ivan himself had made it his task to bring about such a transformation, he was unable to approach the matter directly. Still, as he recovered his strength, it became clear in the worried looks and glances he gave that we would soon part company. Meanwhile, my obsession with self-mortification continued to grow. Bathing, for example, was soon dismissed as a vanity. On the day Brother Ivan was at last able to mount his horse and take his leave, there was little distinguishing my outer appearance from that of the filth-encrusted madman he had saved from insanity.

But of course, I was different. For whereas before I was unable to concentrate on a single thought among many cascading impressions, my mind was now focused inflexibly on one thing only. And my subjugation to that idea was so complete that I imagined a fixation had at last made me entirely free.

"I suppose there are many paths to salvation," Brother Ivan said with uncertainty as he took his leave of me. "And though our roads are parted, I am confident they both lead toward God's radiant glory."

By this point, I was less sure of the efficacy of Brother Ivan's ultimate destination than he was, and so said nothing.

"You're sure you don't want some of my provisions?" he said, in a last vestige of his former paternal worry for me.

"The Lord provides for the beasts of the field, and as I have become like them, I know he will provide for me."

"Well tendered," Brother Ivan said again, always a bit unsure how to respond to one of my declamations. And then turning his horse to the road, he began singing a psalm in a robust voice, and so set out on the pathway of the next passage in his personal journey.

Chapter Ten

In at least one respect, my predictions about my prospects proved correct. For as I threw myself on the mercy of the unfeeling world and sought my way among the fields and in the town, I found quickly that the world was more than willing to provide for me.

It turned out self-abuse was a great validation of holiness in the eyes of the peasantry. It's no secret that the peasant's lot is one of routine suffering. A rent gets raised, a crop fails, the peasant encounters an unexpected pestilence of cow or sheep and soon he's a shattered man, begging alms in the street. If his youth is dazzling enough to win the maiden of his fancy, he will sit beside her and watch their loveliness grow prematurely jowly and slack under the duress of daily toil and strife, even as clock and calendar tell them they are still young. And as husband and wife they will cry together, again and again, for fully half their children will die in infancy.

All this woe makes peasants receptive to the deranged spectacle of the man who courts suffering. "Aye," they think. "There's one who lives in the world as it is, not like all them bishops with their chalices and lordly graces." For these reasons, many of both town and farm felt kinship with my self-mortification, seeing in me an outward demonstration of their own interior beings.

This explains the penitenté's emotional appeal to the peasantry, but I found also that my behavior appealed to the logicians among the mob. For if Heaven truly was as promulgated and there really was nothing of comparable worth on the earth, why *not* reject everything in the visible world as corrupt? Few would want to follow that example, but it had its allure if only as the logical extension of an argument. And if any of these creatures of reason heard the still, small voice of religious doubt whisper in their ear (as reasoners often do), they would see me coming toward them in my fetid rags and say, "Well, *he* certainly believes the great reward comes elsewhere." And then feel reassured.

And of course, as ever, there were also those who simply found it comforting to come upon a man whose manifest afflictions seemed so much greater than their own.

As a result, I soon found myself with the stirrings of a small following within the town—a surprise not only to me but to more illustrious religious personages, as will be seen. I would walk down the streets shedding filth and leaving bloodied footprints on the stones, and instead of giving me the thrashing that might have been reasonably expected, the crowd would part before me with cries of "Make way for the Fool of Christ," a term of honor, not of derogation.

When I held out my bowl for the meager alms I needed to sustain me, hands were thrust back at me so thick and fast I had to wave them off, and still I was forced by my success as a pauper to make regular trips to the town's shuttered nave, where I would leave my excess bread and porridge at the door so other unfortunates might feed there. This in turn was taken as an enlarging proof of my saintliness, for it was a rash insult to the Turks to leave alms at a church they had closed, and it was also obvious I could have used the food and other items to increase my own comfort, had I been so inclined.

Soon certain of the town would trail me in a sort of religious rapture when I walked among them, and women began bringing their babes to me for my sanction, and even hiking up their skirts to ask benediction on their child-carrying bellies. Babies weren't the only items these folks asked me to bless. I fondled goiters, tickled tumors, caressed corns, and stroked broken teeth, becoming acquainted with the thousand forms and varieties of physical suffering the poor are prone to. Animals, too, I laid my hands upon, and it was inevitable given the sheer volume and variety of afflictions thrust at me that some whom I touched recovered, and thus spread still more word of my saintly powers.

Although my knowledge of scripture was as nothing compared to that of Brother Ivan's, I began experimenting with sermonizing. I drew a crowd whenever I spoke, and people would nod gravely at whatever spontaneously arrived-at doctrine I chose to preach. In general, my text was on blood and suffering—subjects that continue to fascinate me.

It was in the aftermath of one of these homilies that a melancholy young woman was brought before me by her parents to receive my blessing. Her hair had been shorn as with wool shears, and in some places the ends appeared singed by flame. Her eyes seemed to look away rather than toward things, and she exuded both a fatalistic belief that there was no hope of escape and an overwhelming desire to flee. I had seen enough men captured by war to recognize another sort of prisoner when one came before me.

"She's the terror of the fields," her dowdy mother said, shaking her head. "A real itch for the boys, this one has."

"Had," the human slagheap that was her father said emphatically. And that one word was like the rap of a cudgel on the girl's white skin. She flinched at the sound of it.

"Please, your saintliness," the mother said. "You who have given up so many of the soft snares of this life, help our Anya to put her foot on the hard road that is the One True Way."

I turned to the girl, who still refused to look at me. "Well, Anya," I said. "Is there anything you'd like to say in your defense?"

Anya raised her sad blue eyes then, looking into mine with an expression of absolute supplication. And she utterly conquered me.

In the effort to explain the indescribable emotion that is love, the poets have essentially thrown up their hands and settled for a smattering of stock epithets. Love is an arrow that hits the besotted lover's heart. It is a bolt of lightning that electrifies his soul.

You will note the only thing the two analogies have in common is that, made literal, they are each likely to cause a fatality.

But neither of these romantic slogans is adequate to describe the earthshaking catastrophe of my response when Anya first looked at me. "Struck by a runaway oxcart laden with barley" might be a way to express it, though admittedly that wouldn't scan well in the mouth of a balladeer. "Obliterated by a cascade of barn-sized boulders," perhaps.

It isn't just that I was not as I was, but that I was not. I reacted to this girl's face, which looked as though an artist had drawn it using nothing but circles so that men might cry "Oh! Oh! Oh!" And then for long seconds I simply ceased to be, except as the aftermath of that reaction.

In the moment, there were three things that kept my love from declaring itself to Anya with every loose strand of my unraveled being. The first is a cliché—I had lost my power of speech. This should not have been the bar to communication it would be normally, for so substantial (and I might even say physiological) was my response to Anya's beauty that even without words it should have had no more trouble announcing itself than a burning house has announcing it's on fire.

But despite the feverish riot in my blood, my unyielding policy of personal degradation had rendered anything other than my outer blots and blemishes virtually invisible. I would shortly have access to the first mirror I had seen in many months. I would find in looking at it that what looked back was less like a man than a human shrubbery.

Even my eyes, said to be the portals of the soul (and indeed Anya's proved to be such for me), were no gateway to my haunted spirit but more an index of some long and wasting illness, a hodgepodge clutter of rheumatic yellows, filmy whites, and corpuscle burgundies. While I have no doubt my eyes—and indeed my whole being—flashed at Anya like an English lighthouse sending out a coded distress signal, the fog of suffering I had enshrouded myself in was far too thick for there to be anything interpretable for her to see.

For these two reasons, Anya was able to look upon the chaos in my soul and see only the deranged prophet her parents were foisting on her, not the meek and bleating lamb ready to sacrifice itself so willingly on the altar of her beauty. "Holy Father," Anya said, in a dusky voice made of rosewater and sugar that blossomed like a puff pastry in the kiln of the ear. "Please tell me how to be good. What is it I should do?"

I should have said so many things. I should have said, "Dear girl, I stand here abashed and beg your forgiveness for being asked to judge you. This evil notion of unworthiness is something that's been put upon you by this thuggish man and his toadish wife. You've done nothing to deserve their cruelties; your soul is as light as theirs are charcoal black. And Anya, your eyes didn't wander to the boys, I know it. It was certainly the boys who were drawn like insects to your fire. For if the boys had eyes, Anya, they surely had eyes for you."

Instead of this soliloquy, I was trying to get my tongue to form something simpler. "I love you," perhaps, or "Please marry me." Then the third reason my feelings for Anya had to remain unexpressed that day clamped itself down on my shoulder and shook me roughly.

For it was precisely at this moment of high and intimate feeling that the Turks decided to arrest me. And the hands that clutched at me then were nothing like an overcooked lover's simile.

Anya's parents fled as they realized what was happening, but Anya stood unafraid and looked on as the pair of soldiers clubbed me with their fists and dragged me off. The last thing I saw as they marched me away was Anya's stubbled head and angel face, with her melancholy eyes watching after me.

"'Fool of Christ,' huh?" one of the Turks said.

And the other said, "Well, we'll just see."

Chapter Eleven

You may expect, gentle Reader, that this is the moment when my patchwork quilt of a life at last unraveled and dire consequences came to me. Bound and blindfolded, thrown into a tumbrel cart, and hauled like refuse to a location I couldn't see, I was sure that death or some other terrible reckoning was at hand. Perhaps the Turks had connected the Fool of Christ with the slaughter of the two sentries at the Monastery On the Blood, or maybe they had simply tired of my pious affronts to their authority. I had no way of knowing, though I was sure to find out presently.

The jouncing ride, interspersed with Turkish jabs and kicks, could not have been more painful. As the paradoxical Fool of Christ, I should have welcomed this torment. But something shifted in me when I looked upon the girl. Perhaps in her aspect, I at last saw something in the world that Heaven could not improve upon, and so life again seemed imaginable as a thing to be lived in, and not just endured. I cannot put the change this chance encounter worked on me fully into words, but from this moment, a process began, after which I would no longer take refuge in a perverse drive toward suffering.

The tumbrel cart stopped, and the Turks grabbed me by the elbows and threw me to the ground, getting in a few last kicks as our time together was drawing to its close. Then they marched me up a long stone staircase until a voice cried, "Halt!" and they removed my blindfold.

I was in the midst of the most ornate church building I had ever seen. Golden columns caught the sun and radiated honeyed light in all directions. Men in priestly garments walked with measured step on marble stairs, their hands lightly brushing against gilded balustrades. Murals of saints and prophets, so delicately painted the figures on them seemed to wink and breathe, looked impassively at and through me, their eyes fixed on mine but focused elsewhere—perhaps on God.

I stood inside the Church of Churches. The Holy Synod, seat of the Orthodox Faith.

A florid little man scurried up to us. He wore foppish blue clothes with a golden pendant on his breast that marked him as a public official—a Boyar, charged by his new Turkish masters with assisting their local administration. The bright blue mortarboard that crowned the Boyar's costume made him seem both pedantic and ludicrous, for it was grandly made but a bit too big for his sweating head.

The Boyar looked me over, his eyes narrowing. "He seems to have been struck about the face," he said to the Ottoman guards.

The guards didn't blink. The first one said, "It's a rough job we have, sir, and no mistake."

The little man hesitated, weighing the guard's response, as he weighed everything, to see if it was an attack on his authority. Then the Boyar threw his head back, trying to look superior. "His Excellency is waiting for us. Give me a moment to go inside, and then bring this man along."

The Patriarch's office wasn't luxurious, but it was certainly comfortable. The furniture was all meticulously carved and lacquered, its dim hues adding weight to the room's already considerable spiritual gravitas. A sculpted crucifix writhed on the wall, and modest painted icons showed the lives of two great Christianizers: Saint Methodius and Saint Nahum of Ohrid, both of whom the Patriarch claimed as progenitors to his own activist line.

The Patriarch himself looked as though he might have fallen out of one of the icons if his extravagant personality could have flattened itself long enough to be contained there. He was a great bearded giant with flashing eyes and a gilded bishop's hat, and he surely would have tamed a pagan wilderness or two if there were any remaining in all of Europe that were worthy of his garrulous attention.

He stood to greet me—a great honor under any circumstance, but even more so given my deranged appearance. "I am Acacius," he said, "Patriarch of this region."

The Boyar twitched nervously in a chair to one side, shifting and diffident, refusing to look me in the eye. He barely took up one third of the Patriarch's shadow.

The Patriarch sighed and, indicating the little man beside him as if it were an unpleasant formality, said, "This is the Boyar. He hears in Turkish now. So he doesn't speak when he's in this room. He just listens." Then the Patriarch sat, and his thick fingers drummed a moment on the top of his desk, a heavy rain spilling out of this torrential man. "So. You are the Fool of God everyone speaks of."

"Fool of Christ," the fidgeting Boyar corrected.

"As I say," the Patriarch said sharply, "the Boyar does not speak." The Patriarch's nose wrinkled as if something unpleasant had wafted his way. "Fool of God," he said, "you are a filthy, wretched thing." He snapped his fingers. An Abbott appeared as if by a conjuring trick, carrying a small handheld mirror that was thrust in front of me. I recoiled at the battered sight of my own face, and the Patriarch smiled.

"You see? And you think God wants this? You know what God says when he sees this kind of thing? He says 'Blecchhhhhhhhhh.'"

"I would not presume to know what God wants, Effendi—"

The Turkish honorific landed in the room like a slap on the cheek.

"I mean Excellency," I added hurriedly. "I do not presume to know God's mind."

"That's good, Fool of God. You know why? Because our Christian faith is organized as a Patriarchate. In a Patriarchate, only one man knows what God wants. Can you guess who that man is? In a Patriarchate? Come, say the word with me. Puh—Puh—Puh—"

"Patriarch?" I said.

"Correct! The Patriarch! Bravo! You are not the fool they take you for, Fool of God."

He leaned forward. "So now we understand each other, and we can talk about the important thing. The thing that caused this silent Boyar here to send out his Turkish troublemakers so they could give you those nice bruises and bring you here to me." He cleared his throat, seeking for the right words. "We are," he said at last, "in a very delicate time religiously . . ."

The Boyar nodded—yes, yes, very delicate, very delicate indeed.

". . . and it is not helpful . . ."

Now the Boyar shook his head—no, no, not helpful, no not at all.

". . . for you to be inflaming . . ."

The Boyar's head shook so emphatically that it was as if a flapping Ottoman battle flag had somehow mated with an epileptic seizure.

The Patriarch pounded his desk. "Will you STOP doing that?" The little Boyar shrank by another eighth before the Patriarch continued. "As I said, it is not useful for you to be raising religious feeling among the people just now. That church, where you lay bread for the poor? It will be a Turkish mosque soon, I'm afraid."

"Excellency!" I said.

He shrugged. "What can we do? They won, it's an excellent location. The point is, the Orthodox faith is strong and will continue— even the Turks know that. They can take people's homes from them or their goods or their animals, but if they try to take away their souls the fighting will never stop. So the only time we have a problem now is when the new administrators or their minions become nervous." He looked at the Boyar with undisguised contempt. "Then people like this Boyar here start looking for someone to make an example of."

Nothing changed in the Patriarch's tone, but somehow his next words came out as a threat. "And Fool of God, your actions in the town are making the Boyar very nervous. So he would like to make an example out of *you*. Boyar, I give you permission to agree with me."

The Boyar nodded vigorously, and I knew I was done for.

In my mind's eye, I saw the sheer crags and bluffs of *Monastырj na Krovi* then. The rock-faced martyrs seemed to open their arms at my approach, and the stony rivers of blood washed over me.

"I'm not afraid to die, Excellency."

The Patriarch laughed. "Yes, well, that's all fine and good. But I've known some martyrs—if asked, the Turks might even say that I've made some martyrs. And let me tell you a little something about martyrdom, shall I?"

I nodded.

"It's overrated—all that screaming and blood. And if the Turks are smart, they don't even let anyone know they did it to you. That way nobody makes anything out of it. No church with your name on it, no sainthood. Just pfffttt. And then maybe ten years from now, some peasant says, 'Remember that Fool of Christ? I wonder what happened to him. He was such a crazy guy.'"

"You mean Fool of God," the Boyar said, correcting. The Patriarch sighed.

"God would still know, Excellency," I said. "If I died, God would know."

"That's true. But God would also know if you found a less dramatic but more lasting way to serve him. Over the next few years, we're going to be allowed to build a few smaller and less impressive churches to make up for the one the Muslims are taking away. If you're willing to trim the beard, take a bath, and give up on your aspirations to become the Slavic John the Baptist, I'd like to invite a man of your proven appeal to take holy orders and then give one of the parishes to you.

"Excellency!"

"A small one," the Boyar added hurriedly. "And very far away."

"I'm overwhelmed," I said. "I don't know what to say."

"Then say yes," the Patriarch said, and his bright eyes flashed seductively. "It's a very easy word. Just one syllable."

For a moment, Anya's sorrowing face quivered inside my thoughts. There was a question in her eyes, as there had been when the Turks dragged me away and her face had seemed to embody all the patient suffering of the world.

But our encounter had happened so quickly, and been over so fast. Anya was already receding from my memory, her features becoming indistinct, like a dream.

"Of course I will, Excellency," I said at last.

With a little smile of triumph, the Patriarch held out his ring. I went over to him and kissed it. "Good!" he shouted, rapping the flat of his hand on his desk. "There, you see how easy life can be?"

I didn't respond, because for some reason that eluded me I suddenly felt quite sad.

The Patriarch noticed my somber mood, and he leaned back in his chair. His eyes narrowed as he looked at me. "You know, I've done you a kindness here, Fool of God, and probably saved your life. So why do I feel like you're judging me?"

"There's only one judge, Excellency," I said, hiding myself from his probing eyes by a routine piety. "And I would not presume to take His place."

"Very true," the Patriarch said. "And that judge looks beyond this meager moment and thinks in centuries. This little man beside me, this Boyar, with his funny hat and his Turkish chain? He'll be gone in an eye-blink, and his funny hat will be gone, too. I'll be gone then also, Fool of God. But my funny hat? It will always be here. Important for us all to remember that, don't you think?"

Chapter Twelve

How strange it is to set one's life on paper, to watch it flow away from you in broken lines. The man on the page twists and turns, now this way, now that. You want to call to him: "Not that door, Fool! Avoid that corridor! Do you hear how your step reverberates against its frosted floor? Do you recognize the clatter that you're making? It's the hobbled tap and crooked foot of a man who walks alone."

But the immutable past ignores your cries, and the lines break and flow on.

In subsequent times, when I became anathema to "goodly folk," it was said I was a shape-shifter, and this unholy talent was used as proof of my deviltry. On the journey you and I have taken so far, I've shown you only the supposed saintlier fragments in the mosaic of my life. Tell me, Reader, has there ever been a creature that was more of a changeling than the man I was? Soldier, madman, disciple, prophet, and now novice in the Holy Synod—a metamorphic, adjusting his stance like a desperate wrestler whose arms can't quite reach entirely around his foe.

If transformation is the mark of evil, I was never more evil than you find me during this confused and restless period of my life. An empty man, I filled myself at any fountain, never caring if the water was pure or brackish.

After that day in the Patriarch's office, I didn't leave the Holy Synod and its outbuildings for longer than one afternoon in thirty for over two years. Under the Church's patient tutelage, I lived like a vine in an English greenhouse, growing toward whatever light they showed me.

Fasting, prayer, and scriptural study occupied all of my time, and the intensity of this spiritual curriculum, coupled with the ecclesiastical grandiosity of my surroundings, altered me. At the end of my novitiate, I left the Synod a more balanced and thoughtful man.

Just before we were assigned to our parishes, we were taken as a group on a pilgrimage to a sacred site: *Monastьrj na Krovi*, the Monastery On the Blood. Brother Ivan had been right in predicting a glorious return of his sect, though wrong in assuming an Ottoman overthrow would precede it. The monks had returned to their cloisters about six months after he and I staged our two-man raid on the Turks, and they had resumed the rhythms of their former lives as if they had not been interrupted. The monastery grounds were clean, well tended, and completely devoid of Ottoman guards on the day we novices arrived.

My first thought was to find Brother Ivan, the old friend who had been such an important mentor to me, and whom I had so grievously offended with my airs of pious superiority at our parting. As soon as we entered the monastery, I received permission to part from the group and walked quickly to Brother Ivan's monkish cell. To my surprise, it had been combined with the two nearest to it and transformed into a small chapel with a stone altar, an everlasting candle, and space for about twenty to kneel.

The Abbot who was master of the monastery was just finishing a quiet moment of solitary prayer as I came in. He looked up when I entered, sensing my surprise and wonder.

"Yes," he said. "What is it?"

"I'm sorry, Father. I must be confused. I thought this was Brother Ivan's room."

"It was. In a way, it still is. He's among those whose memory this chapel is dedicated to."

"Memory, Father?"

"He never returned to us, nor did nine of his brethren. All are presumed dead at the hands of the murdering Turk."

I could feel my lip tremble then, and hot tears starting behind the lenses of my eyes. The Abbot came over to where I stood and put a hand on my shoulder. "You'll see him again, son. Surely you know this?"

I nodded. It was the expected thing to do.

As I was turning to leave, I thought of the other member of our expedition: the Ottoman purse. I looked back. The massive foundation stone of the altar rested on the very spot where we'd buried our sunken treasure.

"Father," I said. "How far down does the base of that altar go?"

"It's very deep. About seven feet. Why?"

"Was anything discovered when you excavated the floor there?"

"Just clay and stone."

"Just clay and stone," I repeated. "Thank you, Father."

So. The Turks got the gold, too. It had been a fool's errand after all.

The murderous stony cliffs were as dramatic and beautiful as I remembered them, but I didn't swoon when I saw them this time. Instead, they were what we'd like old friends to be: unchanged. And willing to wait for us. Indefinitely.

PART TWO:
Profanities

Chapter Thirteen

The life of a country priest is an eventful one. As the members of his flock sail through the great tidal ebb and flow of their days, the priest is called upon to both sanctify and bear witness at each river crossing. A child is born into the hands of a midwife and then reborn in the priest's hands at the baptismal font. Adolescent children begin to blush and waken, and as they open to the world like roses in springtime, the priest affirms their blossoming in the sacrament of Confirmation.

He blesses throats to ward off sickness, lays ashes upon foreheads to remind his parishioners of the stern grip of hurrying time. If a young man and woman seek to join their bodies in that most sacrosanct and pleasurable of human actions, they may first come to him, and then, in celebration and by the priest's consecrating hand, declare their private union before the eyes of the whole world.

These are simple things, and common, but their mundane nature should not disguise their fundamental lyricism. As fields rise and are cut down, and the priest blesses both the planting and the harvest, as he draws babies out of wombs and then that same day throws the first fistful of earth on a grandmother's casket, this priest, this simple country priest, basks daily at the very mouth of the River of Life.

Hardest among his many tasks is the time he spends among the diseased and dying. For though I had been a warrior and seen many men spilled out on the earth in fragments, all soldiers die in part by their own consent, having staked their lives on the violent undertaking that claims them. They are not ravaged by degrees and inches, the way most men are, but look into the abyss directly and then leap or are thrown into the dark it contains, either to be held there or wakened to another kind of light, depending on where you, dear Reader, place your own sensibilities.

A warrior's quick death in the splendor of youth may be an affront, but it is less painful to witness than the more common shape the thieving knave Mortality takes, as both an affront and a humiliation. The average body doesn't rot on some bloody battlefield where crows peck at it but rather withers on a straw-mattressed bed, with the man still inside it. Flesh degrades, discolors, and wilts; eyes go blind; the brain twitches in fevered delirium. And yet the sufferer clings to his rebellious skin and will not leave it, despite the humble priest's entreaties that peace and slumber wait for this living corpse on the other side of an insubstantial line.

If ever I had qualms about my chosen calling, it was in these stench-filled rooms of purpling morbidity, where I was as often cursed as welcomed and where my voice hardly carried over the sound of agonized keening.

And still, for all the gathering darkness of these thoughts, in that time I led an eventful life and thought myself a happy man.

Though promised a congregation of my own by the Patriarch, it was thought wise that I first serve a sort of clerical apprenticeship under another pastor. It was in this capacity that I bore daily witness to all these little signs and wonders, while the Church groomed me for more illustrious service elsewhere. After some months of this benign servitude, the Patriarch called me once more into his presence.

The Holy Synod was as impressive as before, but during my absence it had at last been touched by the fluctuating times. The golden columns were stripped of gilt, revealing blanched and common stone, and the great marble staircase was replaced with makeshift steps of cheap and rough-carpentered wood.

The Patriarch was his robust self and honored me again by standing to receive me. This time when I met with him, the flinching Boyar was nowhere to be seen.

"Ah, him!" the Patriarch said merrily. "It seems he didn't learn to curtsey small enough. Or perhaps the Pashas and potentates found his fiddling fidgets as irksome as I did. I saluted the last time I saw him, but he didn't acknowledge me, being preoccupied by the rope connecting his neck to an Ottoman gibbet. But he looked well for all of that. Somebody finally had the good taste to remove that ridiculous hat."

The Patriarch clasped my shoulders, a proud father on his son's wedding day. "So! Fool of God, look at you. Wasn't I right? Isn't this a better way to serve the Lord?"

"I owe you everything, Excellency."

"Well, you owe me a lot, but don't overdo it. Let's give God his portion. And you yourself. I've had excellent reports of you at every juncture."

We sat. The Patriarch's fingers immediately began drumming again—the restless rainfall that always spilled out when this elemental man assumed a posture of rest. "It's time to fulfill my promise and give you that parish you're owed," he said. "But you'll have to work for it a little. You aren't afraid of a little work?"

"Let there more work be laid upon the men," I said, quoting from Exodus to prove to him my studies had not been wasted, "that they may labor therein."

"Hmm. Yes. You're going to have to stop quoting spiritual aphorisms to me. It makes me nervous, and when you do it you seem less intelligent than you are. So, to our problem. The Turks have let the Church continue, but they've recently confiscated anything we had that could help it grow. You've seen our foyer, I assume. Denuded as Adam on the seventh day."

"I wasn't sure how to react. I thought—a renovation, perhaps."

"Yes, we've decided to humble ourselves, like you did when you wore nettles for shoes. Actually, the Turks presented it to us with a lot of legalisms, as a kind of tax. Backdated, of course, to a time before they had even arrived here. They've bankrupted us, just a little." He rubbed his thick hands against each other, and I almost expected lightning to issue from them. "So why do I tell you my troubles? Because as much as I'd like to give you a church of your own, I can't afford to build one. And so it's I who need your assistance. Because fortunately, my former Fool of God, you have a great deal of experience with the fine art of begging."

"I'm at your service, Excellency."

He nodded brusquely. "Indeed you are."

"Please tell me what it is you want me to do."

Chapter Fourteen

There were already men who had adjusted well to the new way of things, flourishing under the Ottoman yoke as they never had in less restrictive times. Many of these had converted to Islam, which was the surest path to winning Ottoman favor, just as converting from pagan to Christian had been an excellent means of advancement and self-preservation in the time of Saint Cyril. But some few men, through a rare combination of mercantile opportunism and personal charm, had thrived in Turkish trade and still retained their links to the Orthodox faith—a very rare combination.

Such a man was Cosmas the Merchant, into whose shining presence the Patriarch now sent me. Cosmas was a bit of a mystery to the local folk. He had arrived with the Turks from some place no one could name, and had immediately negotiated between the local farmers and the Turkish army to become the primary supplier of bulgur wheat, a rare form of that ubiquitous crop in our region, but the one most to the Ottoman's liking.

Thriving immediately by this contrivance, Cosmas paid in gold for the finest house and grounds available, then had the house torn down and replaced by a finer one. Though never seen in public worship, he was believed religious because he'd built a small church on his grounds where local clerics were permitted to say a daily mass. But for all of that, his manner was thought increasingly Ottoman, and there were rumblings about his supposed embrace of some of their more decadent customs.

The Patriarch wasn't bothered by any of these rumors. "He's a rich man, and indulgent. They usually are. His salvation is God's problem. Ours is to persuade Cosmas to atone for at least as many of his sins as it takes for us to buy you a new chapel."

According to the Patriarch, Cosmas had become familiar with my former reputation as the Fool of Christ and was intrigued enough by what he'd heard to want to meet me. This was taken as a good auger of a coming success, and so at Cosmas's request I was sent out alone and by horse to see the great man.

His house was indeed a fine one by the local standards, with a painted white façade and a domed tower that gave a subtle suggestion of a minaret at the top—no doubt a design that made the Ottomans feel at home when they visited. Though elegantly appointed, the place had the whiff of the bawdy house about it once the visitor stepped inside. All the house servants were comely young women of regional origin, and Cosmas had dressed them in a pastiche of local and Turkish styles created with an eye toward sensuality that skirted the border of what was then considered allowable, and in many places crossed over it.

Lush eastern rugs carpeted the floors, some with religious themes in their weaving, others depicting forthright images of carnality. To take my mind off these worldly sights, I focused my attentions on a collection of vases done in the style of Greek antiquity, depicting pagan rituals and ceremony. Upon closer examination, I realized each vase was double-sided, with the facing side showing the mundane conventions of pagan religious practice (incense burning, prostration, and the like) and the reverse portraying sexual actions so robust and imaginative that even the exhibitionist Cosmas was chaste enough to turn these revelers to the wall, where they could frolic in relative privacy.

"Those are religious acts they perform, Father," a jolly voice called out. "The benevolent god Bacchus makes such rigorous athleticism a daily requirement of all acolytes who worship him."

I turned quickly, and to my utter astonishment saw Brother Ivan grinning at me, reinvented as the successful bulgur wheat merchant Cosmas. He had gained at least thirty pounds and was dressed like a caricature of a Turkish sultan, from the bruised jewel in his sky-blue turban to the curled tips of his shoes. He looked as though he'd just arrived by flying carpet, and he must have sensed my amazement because he was half serious when he said, "You're not going to swoon in my arms again, are you, Father?" Then he held out his flamboyantly outfitted arms, and we embraced.

"I'm sorry to play such a joke on you," Ivan said. "I should have come to visit you at your church, but I had no idea what became of you after our rather odd parting. Then the Patriarch invited me to the Synod—to beseech me for a donation, of course, without seeming to do so—and told me of this Fool of Christ he wanted to build a church for. I knew it had to be you. I'm pleased to see that, in different ways, each of us has used our time apart to thrive."

"But Ivan," I said, "how on earth—"

"On earth indeed. And all because of that damnable Turkish purse."

He then recounted for me a fractured mirror image of our time together, in which he completely devastated every impression I ever had of his goodness and sanctity. He was indeed separated from his home in the monastery by the Turkish invasion, but was far from finding this a burden. After years of enforced asceticism and self-denial, he was overwhelmed by all the sights and smells and tastes the unbounded world contained, and he quickly resolved never again to abandon this realm of sensory possibilities for a cold cell, a splintered plank, and an austere cross on a washed wall.

When Ivan saw me for the first time and realized that it was gold this madman clasped to his breast, he recognized the means for financing his escape. He had not been trying to help me when we first met, but to use the sausage on the stick to lure the gibbering lunatic close enough to snatch the pocketbook from his hand. When I revived, Ivan needed to devise a way to keep my moneybag with him; hence his idea that I take religious instruction. My habit of sleeping on the boodle made stealing it while I dozed problematic, and so he devised his desperate attack on the Turk-held monastery as a way of separating me from my goods.

"Desperate and foolish, as it turned out," Ivan said, clutching his side where the spear had entered him. "But I couldn't have you taking that purse to another church. If we could have found one whose doors were open, that is. For they'd have been only too glad to accept the donation. I say from some experience, they always are."

Ivan had, of course, snuck back into *Monastьirj na Krovi* later to retrieve the money, and had used it as the seed for his current bounty. Seeing how startled I was by all this treachery from a man I thought unimpeachably good, Ivan did point out that, for all his manifest faults, he had shown conscience. Never in his struggles to obtain my money did he contemplate murder, though many a man might have.

"You see the power worldly gold has?" he said, dropping into the mentoring manner of our original association, a ludicrous tone coming from a man who looked as if he might have materialized out of a genie's lamp. "A good man like I was—a monk who delighted in privation—turns from the path of self-denial and daily worship. And why? All because the flap on a pocketbook opens, and he's captured by one flash of light from beneath a harlot's skirts."

Seeing my surprise at the earthiness of his metaphor, Ivan laughed uproariously. "I'm sorry, Father. It's very hard for me to sustain suitable analogies in these, the latter days of my debauchery."

"Ivan . . . not that it isn't good to see you. But given what you've revealed to me about your irreligious character, I'm confused as to why you brought me here."

"Well, for one thing, you're all that's left of what was good in me. As insincere as my religious instruction was, it took root in you, and you have waxed in sanctity while I have waned."

I shook my head. "It's a lovely compliment, but I won't accept it. I have no way of knowing what impels you, Ivan. I can't presume to judge you."

"No, of course you can't, but I can. I'm a lecher and a drunkard and unrepentant about it. After all, it has come to pass, and so it must all be part of God's Holy Plan for me. But perhaps it's also part of the Plan that whatever good purpose I'm to serve will now be through you."

I sensed the business portion of our meeting presenting itself and said, "What do you propose?"

"That I repay your loan, with interest, and give you the church the Patriarch so covets. It'll be a fine one, I promise you, but not so fine the Turks will show up with wagons to haul all your ornaments away!"

There was a tranquil knock at the door, and two of Ivan's comely female servants arrived, carrying basins of gently steaming water on silver trays.

"Ahhh, what a delightful surprise!" Ivan said, sounding not surprised at all. "It turns out the good Father has stayed into the time reserved for my daily footbath. And these thoughtful girls have brought enough of their rejuvenating potions for two."

The girls set the basins down before us and then waited, expectant. A smell of cinnamon and less recognizable spices filled the air. Ivan smiled coyly. "Each one of my girls is an excellent masseuse, Father. It's a rough road you've had coming here, and the same road runs back to town. Surely the Lord won't begrudge you the feel of their tenderizing hands before your journey."

"Perhaps not," I said, standing to go. Immediately one of the girls looked more disappointed than was credible under the enunciated circumstances. "But I have business in the town."

"Indeed," he said, and a sadness crossed over Ivan's face that made his clothes look silly and him seem old. "There's a lot of fault and error in this world to rectify. I'm sure you're a very busy man." Then Ivan brightened. "Tell the Patriarch I'll be in town later this week to make the arrangements."

"Thank you, Ivan."

"Cosmas," he said kindly. Then he turned to the girls. "Oh well, more for me. Let's try one girl for each foot today, shall we? Father, if you don't mind, they're actually rather shy. The girl in the front room will let you out."

Chapter Fifteen

Watching my church's rafters rise toward the sky and then anchor themselves and sprout walls, ceiling, and floor, I felt the daily exultation I had witnessed in mothers and fathers as their small children learn to speak and walk. By my choice and in accordance with Ottoman restrictions, the building was a simple rustic meeting place, a dome-less basilica without apse or columns, made of hardy timber cut from the forest by my own congregants' hands.

In a cunning decree designed to make each new church into a reminder of their supremacy, the Turks had forbidden the exterior of any Christian house of worship from rising higher than the silhouette of an Ottoman soldier on horseback—a height of perhaps ten feet. Defying the spirit of this law while obeying its letter, we sank our floor four feet into the earth. This allowed the outside of the building to meet Ottoman specifications while giving the interior added height and a hint of grandeur. In a further act of muted defiance, we also carved a hidden dome into the church's interior ceiling, where our oppressors could neither see nor be offended by it. In this furtive manner did I consider myself a bold and unbent warrior in the service of the mighty Christian God.

The priestly sanctuary (where I would henceforth sequester myself from the flock to transmute bread and wine into the living flesh and blood of the Eternal Adversary) we separated from the larger hall by a rough-hewn but functional iconostasis—the wall where ornate and removable images of saints and martyrs would later be affixed. The walls and ceilings we painted with bible imagery, for decorative reasons but also to aid in the religious instruction of what was a predominantly illiterate laity by presenting hieroglyphics as a substitute for the cryptic mysteries of words on a page.

The nave of my church was a single room, where women and men could worship together, a practice that subsequently faded from the Orthodox tradition under the influence of the Muslim segregation of the sexes, but one that was still acceptable in a church of that time. Indeed, much of the hysteria that accompanies both the Christian and Muslim faiths on the subject of women and men was unknown to us as yet in that era and region, and even our male and female clergy were permitted within limits to commingle when their duties and obligations to the Adversary, the Patriarch, and the Holy Synod demanded it.

The building site selected by the Patriarch was neither fully of the town nor entirely of the forest. "The village will grow to meet you," his Excellency had said of the rural location. For this reason, and by my request, I was allowed three farm buildings, some animals that would bear milk and wool, and the services of a man to tend the land and beasts. This last fellow went by the odd name of "Nameless."

It must here be said that though the countryside had converted to Christianity centuries earlier, it was still in many ways an unblended mixture of religious and pagan biases. To most villagers, a purse carelessly set on a floor was still a portent of financial ruin. A spider in the house signified impending good fortune. To accidentally set an extra place at the table was to invite a demon to sup beside you. And so on. In the peasant's metaphysics, all manner of ogres, harridans, hellhounds, and other malignant entities had no trouble coexisting right beside the equally wonder-working Savior and the mysterious childbearing Virgin, His mother.

Nameless was a perfect embodiment of this contradiction of influences. A hulking giant, scorned by the town for what was thought his feebleness of mind, he was both dedicated to the Church and so superstitious that from his arrival in our region he would not pronounce his own name aloud for fear a witch would get hold of it and use it to work charms against him.

It is easy to make sport of such a person, but as the hub around which many spokes of outrageous speculation have turned for more than four centuries, I have had much reason to speculate on the role superstition plays in human affairs. I have come to the conclusion that there is a fundamental truth embedded in the compulsion toward irrationality and false notions. For what most people learn in the course of their daily lives is that they will often have little control over what happens to them. As long as they breathe, they will be at the mercy of larger forces—armies, diseases, governments, and even their own misunderstood emotions. So what is superstition but a way for common folk to give shape to the numberless invisible enemies any honest man will admit are always arrayed against them?

Lore and fable enshrine the inexpressible in fanciful stories, providing mythical tools for managing the pandemonium and chaos of being. And so it is that superstition becomes a needed consolation for some, in that it imposes coherence where there often is none. For when a bad thing occurs, a fanged monster that can be warred upon or guarded against is a far less terrifying explanation than the obvious truth: that some evil things happen to us for no reason at all.

Some, including Nameless, can even find this same appeal of explaining the inexplicable within religion. For as the Bible was a book Nameless could not read for himself, he saw no conflict in combining irreconcilable doctrines that to his illiterate mind seemed entirely compatible. If a priest called magic a miracle and a wizard a prophet, it was all one to Nameless.

In addition to the bumptious hodgepodge of his beliefs, Nameless was also as strong as an ox and twice as hardworking. Under his knowledgeable hand, our plot yielded cheeses, cream, butter, vegetables, and yarn enough to support our meager requirements, with some left over for barter or to give to the poor. While we could have easily lived as most priests do on the charity of the congregation, I was determined to set an example of sufficiency and thrift, and thanks to the husbandry of Nameless the parish soon buzzed approvingly over my frugality.

My church was still nameless, too, and the Patriarch did me the unheard-of honor of asking me to put a label to it myself—an enormous token of his favor. So on the night before the chapel doors were to open and the first mass in my new home was to be celebrated, I searched on my knees for the perfect patron saint for this new franchise, and even believed it was God's "holy voice" that brought a name to me immediately, and not the smell of dinner and my self-imposed restriction that I would fast until I had decided.

I would rather leave anonymous the poor but sanctified soul whose canonized title graced my nave, as I doubt he would be favorably inclined toward an association with someone of my subsequent notoriety. But to keep the paint on my self-portrait accurate and fresh, I will tell you he was one of the Fools of Christ, those God-infected beings who renounce life's fleshly compensations in the name of the One Truth and live as the birds do—that is to say, in filth and dietary uncertainty. Given my own past, this made him my perfect emblem. And so as I began my settled life as a country priest, I became known throughout the parish as the Lord High Protector of the Fool of Christ. He and I were two fools together under a new roof, and fool enough to think a bit of thatch, some earthen tile, and a cartload of lumber and masonry would protect us from anything more bullying than a summer rain.

Chapter Sixteen

As I mastered the art of sermonizing and could feel the congregants give themselves over to the persuasive power of my voice, I felt more alive than I had in any task since my earliest days as a warrior. The Patriarch sent approving words to me on a regular basis. It became clear he viewed even the great boon of my own church as a temporary roost in a longer climb, and that he was eager to find means for my further advancement. And so, with great satisfaction in both my own competency and the nobility of the task itself, I looked out at the years ahead and saw decades rolling toward me, all lived in perfect fulfillment, in a foreseeable routine of unimpeded service.

I settled in then to what I thought would be my life. I was good at it, and this mattered to me.

My hard-won equilibrium was to last all of nineteen months.

For midway through the twentieth, on a bright spring afternoon that smelled of lilac, I arrived back at my church from business in the town to find a group of twenty or so orphan children milling about in the yard, while Nameless tried to demonstrate how a horse is shoed. These wards of the Church—most rendered parentless by the depredations of the recently ended hostilities—were brought to us because our agricultural self-reliance had become so talked about and because the Church had plans to make productive citizens out of them, which in those days meant farmers.

Despite their merry cries and gamboling about, I barely noticed these waifs and strays as I hurried into the church to say a brief afternoon prayer. Thinking the chapel empty, the two nuns accompanying the children brought them inside to where I knelt, and their tiny voices were suddenly all around me. The goodly sisters apologized for the intrusion and silenced the youngsters, readying to leave.

"It's all right, sisters," I said. "'Suffer the children,' as the Book says." And then all the children came to me, babbling out questions about every detail of our sparsely appointed chapel, and I was quite overwhelmed by their disorderly interest.

The younger of the two nuns came to my assistance. "Children," she called, "now children, one at a time please, one at a time."

One of the boys pointed up at a mural painted on the ceiling overhead, where Heaven, the Blessed Trinity, and a variety of saints and martyrs gazed down on us with lordly disinterest. "What's that up there?" the child said.

Before I could answer, the young nun arched her long neck, raising her face toward the fresco above, and fully revealing her features to me for the first time. As her eyes searched for the sublime in our painted glories, a different Paradise opened before me.

It was Anya. I had found her again. And everything I felt the first time I laid eyes on her came back to me, redoubled by the secret portion of myself that had been yearning for her in silence since that first meeting.

"It's Heaven," Anya said, answering the child. And looking to me for approval or some elaboration on the remark, she saw my disquiet, became confused by it, and fell silent.

I somehow managed to get through what remained of the children's religious instruction without revealing anything of the ferment I felt, a task made more difficult by the fact that Anya's inquisitive eyes never left me. When the children went out to thank Nameless for his offices and to say goodbye to the animals, Anya contrived to see me alone for a moment. She found me waiting for her in the church.

"We wanted to thank you for a most enjoyable day, Father. The children found the animals delightful, and your servant is very sweet."

"You must come and visit us again," I said in a rush, "and soon."

She was bewildered by my agitation, and as she tilted her head in puzzlement, I saw for a moment the mournful and abandoned girl who watched after me as the Turks dragooned me into what had become my current life.

"I know you, sir," she said at last, coming nearer. "Forgive me, but I feel I know you."

"We've met before," I said, flustered. "Your parents. . . the town. . . the, er, Fool of Christ. . ."

"You mean this church?" she said, still confused.

"No, no. It was me. Uh, *I* was he."

She hesitated a moment more, and then at last recognized me as the babbling lunatic who staggered his way through the streets of the town in her youth. She could not have been more surprised if Lazarus and Moses had just walked into the room together. Her hand went to her mouth, and she laughed gaily—as heartfelt an expression of mirth as I had ever heard, so I could not but help laughing with her. And then, innocently and with no intent beyond letting me know there was nothing cruel in her amusement, Anya lightly touched my hand.

I don't know what she felt at that first touch—the turn of the grinding wheel, perhaps, or maybe some small fragment of energy that dislodged itself from my seething spirit and flowed into her. Her laughter stopped, and her hand pulled away as if she'd put it into a fire. Then she looked at me and saw at last what no mask of self-inflicted suffering was there to hide this time: the totality of my feelings for her. And as happens in both fairy tales and tragedies, in seeing the ardor in my eyes, Anya gasped and then tumbled straight down into the abyss beside me.

I would like to be able to tell you that Anya and I made unheeding love right there, to the distant sounds of childish laughter, under the watchful eyes of painted saints and martyrs who surely would have applauded the display if there was anything left of the reality of women and men within their hearts. We did not. Monastic celibacy and routine fasting were both required of me by the Patriarch's desire to see my advancement; for though I was a "white" cleric and not expressly bound by the harsh strictures of monasteries and nunneries in my low post, the highest offices of the church—including not only each bishopric but the patriarchate itself—all adhered to the rigorous denials of the flesh that still governed every order on the Roman side of the schism dividing the early flock. My vow of chastity, Anya's confusion over the sudden transformation of a neutered country priest into something more tangible, and the general uncertainty of our contending emotions all kept us from even acknowledging that anything unusual had happened. Instead, she mumbled another thank you and moved to go.

She was all the way to the door before she turned around. She looked at the floor, as if afraid of the consequences if our eyes met. Then, struggling to sound unemotional, she responded to my earlier invitation to revisit us. "Such a kind offer. We will certainly contrive a way to come to you soon."

And then she was gone. And I realized I should have asked her how many days it would be before that return, so I would know how many hours were to pass before I would be alive again.

Chapter Seventeen

A week went by. I neglected any responsibility that might take me away from the church during morning hours, and I waited. Finally, while I drowsed fitfully after another sleepless night of unquenched longing, there were childish voices outside, and I knew she had come back to me.

I dressed hurriedly and ran out to the yard, where Nameless was already introducing the orphan boys and girls to the wonders of mucking animal dung off the floor of one of the outbuildings. As Anya had proved so able in handling the orphans on their first visit, it had been suggested by her superior that Anya bring the children to us alone, a request she had acceded to, since obedience was among the first vows of her calling.

She saw me come up, and I could see that she also had not slept and that her heart jumped when I came into view. "Ah, Father!" she said, more brittle than she intended. "I have a few questions about today's visit. May I have a private word with you?"

"Of course," I said, and escorted her toward the sacristy.

"No. Please," she whispered, in anguish. "Some other place than the church. I have human matters I would discuss with you."

And so, as discreetly as I could while trembling in every limb, I led Anya into my residence through an isolated door that allowed me to come and go unseen, and we went into my chambers.

Anya and I turned to each other as soon as the door to my room had closed, and both were so eager to pour out our feelings in words that each spoke clumsily over the other's voice. "I have thought of nothing since—" she said, overlaying it onto my cry of "I cannot find the words to describe—" before we both stopped, abashed.

The effect of the exchange was so ridiculous that we laughed, and Anya's amusement was like a throaty melody in the room. "It seems that I have been anticipated," she said.

"For every second since we last saw each other."

Anya grew serious. "There's peril in this you know. We can't pretend there isn't. These feelings, if acted on, will change every aspect of our lives. And some of the outcomes are unknowable, and may be harsh."

I smiled then, so full of ardor I could imagine nothing painful would ever again be felt by anyone, anywhere. "Let it come then," I said. "For God wouldn't let us feel so much if he didn't delight in our experience of it."

She came to me then, her eyes unwavering as they looked into mine, and she shook her head. "Too easy," she said. "This isn't some holy emissary standing before you. Remove my smock, and snow-white wings won't unfasten as well and open inside your hands. There's just a woman here. Just an ordinary woman. And you—you are . . ."

She smiled then as if she would burst with delight, as if she wanted to shout in ecstasy looking at my face. "You are . . . extraordinary in every way! But still and also, an ordinary man. So no poetry, Father. Please. And no psalms. It's too easy to praise God or blame the devil for things they aren't involved with. If we take that path, before long we'll be wearing sackcloth and begging the clouds in your painted chapel to forgive us for something we did that wasn't wrong."

She put her arms around me, burying her head against my chest. "If we do this, it's because it's what we've chosen. Freely chosen. And then we go forward together, and we don't look back."

And there was no more reason for words after that.

Is the body a message or a messenger? What do we feel at a lover's touch, our own skin or our lover's fingers? Why do we cry out, as at a painful leave-taking? Why does such laughter come unbidden into our mouths?

In this tangle of skin, this maze of flesh, do I lose myself or am I just changing roads? And who, after so much glory, will rise from this bed? A lover? A husband? Dupe of the devil? An unchaste prelate? Or finally, and at long last, me?

We took our clothes off slowly, lingering over them, item by item, as if saying silent goodbyes. And then we looked at each other in the pale blue light that came in by my window. When all the black garments that had covered us lay piled on the floor, I went to her, and our hearts beat so hard against our chests we could have sheltered them between our fingers like little birds.

And then in caresses and sighs, we mapped passageways and tunnels to the undiscovered places inside ourselves. And we freed every prisoner we found there.

Chapter Eighteen

The road appeared straight to me then, but it was turning, turning, coiling like a snake, as it always does. Anya got permission to continue educating her charges with us; after that, I saw her three times a week. Since the town did not consider Nameless human and I was thought to be away at parish business in daylight hours, no breath of scandal could reach us.

Occasionally I would arrive late from duties elsewhere, aching for her, and I'd hear Anya's laughter lilting in the air like a song. I'd run to her and find her out by the stable surrounded by smiling children, all playing some clever game she'd invented on the spot. Nameless would be wearing corn-husk cow ears, or have a cat's cradle wrapped around his giant's hands, and he'd grin at me—a toddler's imbecile grin.

As Anya and I walked away together, I'd feel Nameless watching after us like a moonstruck calf. "He's in love with you," I'd say later as I took her into my arms.

"I know," she'd say. "How sad." And then we pondered nothing except each other, and stole our raptures where we could. Whatever Nameless thought of the hours Anya and I spent sequestered from his sight, he said nothing, and outwardly nothing changed between him and me.

Anya told me everything about her life. As I suspected, she had been severely mistreated by her parents from childhood—beatings and stranger harassments that the troll-ish father spent long hours devising. Adolescence came, Anya flowered, and a weird hysteria was incited in her keepers by her obvious beauty. Anything that could be done to mar Anya's appearance, her parents would do: dressing her in ill-fitting clothes, sheering and burning the ends of her hair.

Sometimes there were bruises on her neck and face, and her parents kept her in the house so others wouldn't see how she suffered at their hands.

Knowing nothing but her parents' hatred, Anya came for a time to think herself hateful. It was during this interval that she met me, in my guise as the Fool of Christ.

A boy came into the story after that, a smiling shepherd who'd known Anya since childhood. He was drawn to her by her sadness, she to him by his elation over everyday things, and it was as if together, in her darkness and his light, they had found the makings for one person. "It was he who taught me how to laugh," Anya said, and then her dusky laughter filled my rooms, as if memorializing the boy's achievement.

They explored each other tentatively, with no real knowledge of even their own bodies, and the slightest feel of hand on hand or lip on cheek was for each of them a kind of ravishment. They supposed they would marry one day, and they thrilled at the notion. But into this innocent world of private grace Anya's parents at last thrust themselves, catching the pair at nothing, reacting as though two coupling dogs had been found rutting in the street. When Anya stood up to her father, he beat her senseless, and she was kept inside for many days.

During Anya's convalescence, her father caught the boy skulking outside their house, and thrashed him so badly it was thought for a time the young shepherd might die. The lad recovered but wouldn't look at Anya when she spoke to him, and when he started grazing his sheep on the other side of the hill from the path where they used to meet, Anya decided she should accede to her parent's demands and join a nunnery—not, as they believed, to save her soul, but to be free of them both at last. Which in a way was the most soul-saving thing she could do.

All these slights and injuries Anya brought to me, the way a little girl might bring her grandfather a scrape on her knee. We took these broken pieces and fused them together, and Anya likewise found breakages to heal in me. In this way, we became so knit, so shared, so mutual, it seemed impossible that anything could ever tear us apart.

And then one day, there were raised voices in the yard below and sounds of a struggle between Nameless and others trying to force their way onto the grounds. Gate hinges groaned and snapped, then Nameless's heavy footfalls were racing up the stairs, and his voice was shouting in alarm. My chamber door crashed open, and there stood Nameless, tormented by seeing Anya and I together but determined to save her and me from worse things than the anguish in his agonized eyes. "DISCOVERY!" he cried. "DISCOVERY! HIDE YOURSELVES!"

But before we could do as he commanded, Nameless was shoved aside and there were others in the room: an elderly nun who groaned and wobbled at the sight of us and four brawny priests I recognized from the Patriarch's inner circle at the Holy Synod.

Hands that weren't lover's hands reached for us, wrenching Anya out of my arms. "No!" she cried, kicking and biting.

"Don't worry!" I shouted. "I'll come for you!" I screamed it again, but I didn't know if Anya heard me, because by that point one of the burly priests had carried her off and she was down the stairs and gone.

It took all three of the men remaining to keep me from going after her. It was only as they threw me to the floor and started forcing priestly vestments over my nakedness that I realized I was crying.

Chapter Nineteen

The Patriarch was reading a scrolled document as they brought me to him. He used the parchment as an excuse not to look at me, and for the first time in our acquaintance, when he greeted me, he did not choose to stand.

"What," he said, his eyes still on the paper. "Your friend Cosmas run out of foot salts? You couldn't take your comforts there, away from prying eyes, like every second man in the town?"

"I'm sorry, Excellency. I know I've failed you."

He looked at me then, and his eyes were full of laughter. "What? You? Don't be such a prelate about it. You've given me a mess to clean up, that's certain. It changes nothing. The Church still has plans for you."

"I love her, Excellency," I said quietly.

He froze then, in disbelief, and I realized it was the only time I had ever seen him come completely to rest.

"Come over here," the Patriarch said.

I went to him.

"Say that to me again."

"I love her, sir."

The Patriarch struck me across the face as hard as he could, making sure he used the hand that wore the heavy ring of his office. Sparks flew at the corners of my vision, and I tasted blood.

The Patriarch went back to his work, and spoke as if nothing had happened. "The girl is meaningless. In this case you have friends in high places. The All Highest! And I'm not talking about God either. I'm better at some things than God is."

"I'm leaving the Church," I said.

He smashed his hand on the table, and the inkwell jumped and puddled, staining the parchment in his hand. The Patriarch set the document aside carefully, then concentrated all his energies on me. "You're leaving nothing. I've invested a great deal of personal time in you, Father. You may be God's Fool, but no one makes a fool of me."

I turned to go.

"If you walk out that door," he said, "the girl is lost."

The threat was made in a tone so brisk and unemotional he might have been talking of tithings and legacies. It tore at me like a beast's claw all the same. I faced him. "What does that mean . . . 'lost'?"

The Patriarch hesitated, though whether he had qualms or was weighing the tactical considerations of revealing ugly truths aloud, I cannot say. "It could happen any number of ways. An abbess comes for a visit and hears a scratching sound one night. The next day, she swears she saw the girl bedecked as Satan's harlot, withering in her demon lover's embrace at midnight. Then a crowd gathers, somebody builds a fire, and that's that."

I swayed on my feet, finding his words almost incomprehensible.

"Or we preserve her reputation," he said, beginning to enjoy himself, "and ask our friends the Turks to jail her for excessive piety. And then they use the slow arts on her, until the only prayer she knows is one for death. Her prayer is answered, but slowly."

"You can't," I said.

"I can. I have. Or didn't you notice how our irritating friend the Boyar has never been replaced? Look at me when I talk to you!"

I looked straight at him, but he wore a face I'd never seen before.

I lunged for him then, my fingers reaching for his throat. But he was surprisingly quick and powerful for a priest, and my old warrior reflexes were dulled by soft years of study and piety. His clenched fist found my stomach, and I pitched forward, my chin striking the edge of the desk so forcefully that my jaws clacked together and a tooth split at the impact. Embers and tears swam at the margins of my eyes.

Then the Patriarch kicked me, his foot sinking into my side with vicious indifference—a mathematician applying a slide rule and abacus to a minor but vexing problem. He swung his foot again, I heard a rib crack, and red pain blistered inside me. He sneered at me as I went down, appalled and ferocious.

"I don't know what game board you thought you were playing on, Father, but this is chess, and I'm the king. You're less than a pawn, but maybe a bishop one day, because when we first met you made me laugh. But my first responsibility is to the Church, the worldly Church, as it exists here and now, with buildings and financial issues and clerics who think they're in love and Turks running around making my life miserable. Everything I do is for the Church's expansion and preservation. You will be an instrument of that great task because I require it of you. Or by God, I will destroy first the girl and then you."

"But why?" I gasped out, beginning to weep. "I'm nothing. Less than nothing. I'm not worthy of so much wrath."

"Maybe you are and maybe you're not. But the Church is real, not some figment in the sky. You know what a church in the sky is, Father? That's what the Romans had, after we took Jupiter and Hera away from them—no temples, no acolytes, no gods, just a church in the sky. That's what the pagan priests had, after we captured all the tree worshippers, tore the loincloths off them, and forced a Eucharist down their throats.

"Religions die if you let them, Father. It's a historical fact. That's why every fight I wage is a fight to the death."

Chapter Twenty

Shorn again, bereft and beaten, Anya was thrown back on the parentage that had rejected her so many times before. I stayed in the Church, exchanging my life for hers so that even greater harms didn't fall on her.

My body mended, but I stayed broken in more primary ways. As Anya vanished from my world like a reverie or an illusion, I myself sank into a perfectly functional death, becoming a ceremonial corpse in priestly wardrobe that waved and barked on cue whenever blessings were required of a thing in vestments.

I ministered poorly to my flock because I no longer cared what happened to them. My sermons, formerly a source of inspiration for the parish, became confused abridgements of things said better in a time when I believed them, and there was grumbling in the nave, though none of my constituents spoke what all felt.

In the first year after I broke with Anya, the Patriarch summoned me to him a few times and tried to resume our former friendship, as though there was no reason to taint it over a thing now firmly in the past. But he had ears everywhere, and surely heard of the dissatisfaction in the parish. Between that and my steadfast silence during our interviews, he soon judged me a broken man, and though he did not remove me from my offices, he found livelier cat's paws for his amusement.

The normal flux of life was overbearing to me. Mild sadnesses overwhelmed me, and even the smallest joy might set off a reaction that led me to think of greater happinesses now lost to me, leaving me weeping. It was only by narrowing my awareness to the most immediate concerns—a glass on the table, a fly bashing itself to death against a window—that I could stop the nightly dreams of

Anya from finding me and flaying me in my sleep. And so when she at last disappeared from my dreaming, I did not grieve her.

All these encroaching silences I welcomed, for it was only in silence that my own brain stopped thinking. And so time passed, and I moved into the shadows of my own life. I lived there quietly, without expectation, and looked forward to a span of forty years or so more where little would be asked of me beyond recited words long ago committed to memory.

One day I looked up from my silent table to see the worried face of Nameless standing at my door.

"She's sent me to you, sir," he said, and I could see the suffering the assigned task had cost him. "She wanted to see you just once more."

Then he told me of all the ways his story and the story of Anya had continued and even intertwined long after I had put a stop to the tale of my own life.

Shunned after she left the convent and with rumors circulating she had become some "prelate's whore," Anya returned to her village with no alternative but to live among the blows and buffets of her vile parentage. Her odious relations tired quickly of the torpor born of her grief, and also of the way the town snickered at them behind its hand. "It's time she fended for herself," her mother and father said, and so began readying to push Anya into the streets and be done with her.

But then a gentle giant arrived in clothes that were worn but clean and neatly cared for, and observing all the required formalities, he politely asked for Anya's hand. Such was Nameless, whose thwarted love was quieter than mine, but in the end more constant.

For Nameless cared not at all if the mob jeered at them—he had born their jests as lightly as a wind for all his years. He and his "harlot" are unwelcome in the church? Fine. He'll make a church of her footfall in the doorway, the line of her hand, brushing back long black hair. People turn from them in the street? It's a courtesy they do them, not an insult. For Nameless looked not on strangers but only on one far nearer to him, and the townsfolk but gave him a clearer view of her by stepping out of the way.

There were certain confidences Nameless didn't share with me during the headlong ride to his impoverished home, but I gathered that Anya had remained in a state of despair and mourning long after she came to him, and that she lay bedridden for over a year. He did not reveal their intimacies to me then, but so tender was his devotion toward her that I know Nameless wouldn't have touched Anya in all that time except to feed and care for her, nor would he have touched her after that without her consent. And so in a life of scorns and betrayals, Anya at last found a love that was safe and steadfast, unfeigned and true.

Now she was with child, and it had gone badly. "She's pale as a ghost, sir, and she cries from the pain of it. The midwife's there already and says my Anya may not see the morning. Oh, Father, what are we to do?"

I would like to say I felt the fellowship in that "we," for it was a simple man's expression of fealty and forgiveness and I was not worthy of it. But such was the deadening effect of the wasted years that I felt nothing. Just a vague curiosity about a woman I once knew and a man I used to be. To me, Nameless had always been a sort of pack animal. And so now he fed from my leavings. Well and good. Isn't that what a pack animal is supposed to do?

Still, there was priest enough left within the dull husk life had made of me that I agreed to go with him. We plunged by horse-cart at full gallop through trees that writhed in the wind like a Bible picture of tormented souls. Nameless lashed at the horse the way a demon might lash at the tortured spirits put into his hands for punishment, and the leaves that gnashed and clenched at the red sun over our heads stretched and whinnied in the dying light like sentient flame. This hell, though, was one mostly of our own making, so we inhabited it together and were its sole and only tenants—Anya, Nameless, and I.

A smell of cooking grease and stale Easter kulich came to me as we walked toward the fistful of bare thatch and branches that was Nameless and Anya's tiny one-room home. Inside Anya was lying on a straw bed, looking alarmingly thin for a pregnant woman and even more alarmingly white. A toothless midwife scurried into the shadows as we entered—a scaly crab wedging itself into the underside of a rock—and as I approached the bed I saw from the heavy beaded sweat on Anya's brow and the way she shuddered rather than trembled that the early stages of labor had already come upon her, and that she was momentarily between contractions.

When she saw me, her eyes filled with tears. "So," she said, her voice a dusky whisper. "You've come to me at last."

"Your goodly husband bade me do so, and here I am."

Anya smiled, and her lips were so thin and blue I could see the pale teeth glistening beneath them. "Church life agrees with you, Father," she said. "You've gained—in stature."

"You mean I've put on weight," I said simply. "Too much wine with my dinner." I took her hand. "While you look as though a little breeze might carry you off."

"Oh, weighty enough for all of that," Anya said. She laughed then, and her laugh was a memory of everything that was ever going to matter. "Though lightened soon if this good woman has her way."

An awkward silence came to us, one Anya and I were no longer quite large enough to fill. Her eyes searched my face a moment, perhaps looking in vain for the man she once loved.

"I waited for you to find me," she said at last, and Nameless looked away.

"Anya—"

"I couldn't imagine you wouldn't come for me. So all my life after I left you was temporary, a prelude only. A brief walk down a wrong path taken in darkness. Living like that, in a future that was never going to come into existence, it nearly killed me. And then this man here, this great ox of a man, came to me and patiently awakened me from that dream."

I looked away then, and she squeezed my hand until at last I turned and saw those crystalline eyes I had first spied on a rutted street in the town so long ago.

"It's taken all this time for me to forgive you," she said. "Not yet time enough, so I see, for you to forgive yourself. I would that you might find a way to do so. I will say a prayer that you do."

The birth pains came on her then. "You'd better go now, Father. It's time for this good woman to have another turn with me."

No sooner had Anya said this than her eyes glazed over in pain and her arms clenched, then started to swing and thrash. I stepped back. The midwife went to her work. A bed-sheet was put into Anya's mouth, and as the pain increased, she bit down on it so hard her lips began to run with gaudy blood.

I had been present at many births, and knew enough to recognize the dangerous signs of things gone wrong. I stepped forward, watched the midwife reach inside for the baby with some kitchen object—a wooden spoon—while Anya writhed in anguish. "You're killing her!" I shouted, and Nameless stepped forward, too.

There was a gush of squalling redness, and a baby appeared, gleaming like a painted devil. The midwife held the naked child in the air triumphantly. "A little girl!" she said.

Had things been well, Anya would have relaxed and her pains diminished at this juncture. Instead her movements redoubled in their fury, and the blood continued to flow from her. The sheet fell from her mouth, and the room was filled by the sound of Anya's heartrending shrieks.

I ran to her then, trying to staunch the deadly flow with my hands. "Tell me what to do!" I cried. "Tell me what to do to save you!" Blood was everywhere—my arms, my clothes, my face.

Then Anya shuddered, and suddenly she stopped crying out. "No," I said. "No. Please." Her eyes found me and then lost me again. And there was nothing in them anymore, just the merest suggestion of an unwelcome surprise.

Anya's face slackened, and it was the only unbloodied thing in all the world. As pale as the moon. As pale as a winding sheet. And then Anya, my darling Anya, trembled once and was gone.

When my senses returned to me, the room was filled with cries and moaning. The tsk-ing midwife, the squalling infant, and Nameless—a shattered man sobbing into his hands.

"We must to the church," I said quietly.

Nameless looked up. "To the church, Father?" he said brokenly.

"Yes. God owes me this. I've given my life to Him. He will return her if I ask."

"That's devil talk, that is," the midwife said, crossing herself. "I'll not stand by and hear it." She handed Nameless the swaddled babe. "I'll fetch my new goat in the morning. Make sure he gets his breakfast." And she was gone.

Looking at the baby nestled in his arms, Nameless seemed to feel all the more keenly the scale of his loss. He put his head down and started to sob again.

And I saw my chance.

Anya weighed nothing at all in my arms. She was a wraith, a shadow, a ghost. I ran out into the yard, lay her in Nameless's wagon, and thrashed the horse nearly insensible to get back to the church and the little painted nave that had played such a role in ruining our lives, before her body cooled.

I carried her to the altar, sobbing, caressing her, ranting at the rafters. "Lord!" I cried. "Trickster! Is this the reward I've gained by all my suffering? You've looked away from us for a moment, surely. Return your gaze, and see what devil's mischief needs amending here!"

I brushed the hair back from her face. "A little breath, sir, if you please. A little breath to animate her sweet face. To make her breast rise and fall once more in life's unceasing rhythm."

I listened, and there was no response.

"Demon!" I yelled. "Here in this house I made for you, I come to collect my voucher. To all your great miracles, add a lesser one. For though she and I went by different paths in the end, I can find no place to set my foot in a world she doesn't walk in also."

I waited an hour for some sign of life to return while Anya chilled against my touch. And then, certain I'd had my answer, I piled straw from the outbuildings against the walls and seats and set a wick to them. I held Anya in my inconstant arms until she melted and blazed in fattening rivulets against my face and chest. The only sounds were the roar of the flames and the curses against God that I was screaming.

PART THREE:
The Earthen World

Chapter Twenty-One

The light is the shadow. The shadow is everywhere. Everything.

It rises and falls, and I become ocean. It scurries and crawls, and I am insect, I am snake.

The shadow is hand; I am fingers. It is wall; I am stone.

It is the gate; it is the guard. It is the river; it is the dam.

I am the shadow.

Inside me, there are others.

"Who are you?" I say.

I answer: "I am Enoch. Keeper of secret script and lost things. I am knowledge forbidden but still known, actions not spoken of but yet taken. My way is the way of death in life and life in death. And I am hungry."

"Are you an angel?"

"Not angel and no longer man. My dispensation is long revoked. But some things are beyond even His power, and being a forever creature made by His hand, I am one of these. What was is, and so I am. I wait here in the grey spaces. I have waited here for you."

"Am I in Hell?"

"That place is not yet made for you."

"Heaven, then?"

"That place is not yet made for you. It may be that you are yourself its maker."

I hesitate. "What is being asked of me?"

"Petitioner, what is it you ask for?"

And then the shadow is Malaga, and the slain hundred, and two Turkish soldiers in the Monastery On the Blood. The shadow bends and twists, and every waning face withers once more, writhing into *the tomb beneath my priestly hand. As shadow I fall on battlefields; in cemeteries, I lengthen and crook.*

The shadow is Anya.

A charnel house. Run by an inattentive Madman.

It must stop.

"I want vengeance," I say at last. "Vengeance, and the weapons of war. I claim God as my Enemy forever. I claim God as my Adversary."

I am invaded then, ravished by fang and claw. Flesh tears itself away from my body and is eaten and then reborn as more flesh. I am destroyed and perfected, devoured and made whole.

I am in ecstasy.

"Take," I say, "and eat it. For this is my body . . . ."

"Granted," the voice says. "Your petition is granted."

I step out into the light.

It is like swimming in a lake of ashes.

I inhale spark and dust, and it nourishes me. Scorched timber and pumiced stone flow over my body. I wriggle within them, fishes in water.

Ears clogged by soot, I hear a sound like language. It welcomes me. It wants to teach me.

Then . . . fingers and sunlight and a face. I knew him once. I called him Nameless.

I blink at him. He blanches. "MotherofGodandGod'sBones!" he says. His arm moves: hand to head, hand to heart, hand to shoulder to shoulder. Faint memory whispers, "And they will know you by this sign. . ."

Nameless spits. "The smoke," he says. "They'll be wanting to see about it. We've got to get you away from this place."

I will remember later that my clothes are burned away and I am naked, that there is no hair left on my head. I will remember that the horse fled the fire and that Nameless carried me as if I was weightless for all the long miles. I will remember the outbuilding of his poor plot, the stinking straw that felt like luxury. And the dusky smell of Anya's blood, hanging in the air like a pledge or an accusation, and how Nameless washed her ashes off my skin, as gently as if he was washing his newborn baby.

Chapter Twenty-Two

In that dogleg theology of his, Nameless must have had a good deal of room for unexplained monsters. He had badly burned a hand dragging me from the ruined church, and knew exactly how fierce the fire I survived was, for he had seen with his own eyes how it consumed Anya's corpse so thoroughly that there was barely a bone or a tooth left. My clothes and even my hair had been singed off my body, and yet my skin was unscathed, and even showed the bloom of rosy-cheeked health. Here truly was the stuff of fiends and ogres and smiling demons that sneak through the half-open door and sit down beside us at suppertime.

But Nameless was unafraid. He arrived at the church as it burned down around me and heard me screeching oaths against the Adversary, my anguish raining down like ash in the air. Every one of my curses gave a voice to his own loss and sorrow. He would no more abandon me now than he would abandon his newborn daughter by the side of some untraveled road. We were allies, and his devotion was unbreakable. He would care for me and keep me safe.

I needed his care. For in addition to a pervasive confusion that settled on me and did not leave for some months, the whole physical world now coursed with new energies and textures. Breezes blew through the grass, and as the grass rippled, I felt it murmur and yowl. I could scent every man, woman, or animal within miles, and their smells were messengers. Ages, weights, heights, and even their general health and emotional status assailed me on the wind.

Nameless's few animals overwhelmed me with their general clamor. When they gaggled excitedly at mealtime, the sensations they generated almost made me scream. As in my breakdown after Malaga's death, I was unable to choose between the different stimuli, but here it was because the stimuli never ended. Infinities of impressions ceaselessly crowded in on me from all directions. Errant passions and impulses cascaded toward me from even the most common creature or thwarted undergrowth of scrub brush, so long as the thing itself had life.

By all other measurements I became daily more robust. My hair grew back quickly, but not in the stooped form of the bearded parish priest. As I healed, it was the dashing and mustached cavalier of ten years earlier that came back to life in me—an odd incongruity inside the worn peasant clothes Nameless borrowed somewhere and brought to me. My soldiering muscles, atrophied by the life of a country prelate, returned to their most glorious state and then continued to blossom with vigor, until I became a sort of idealized portrait of the man I once was, an unflawed statue somehow awarded the gifts of mobility and breath. Old, unfeeling scars began to throb, the dead flesh sprouting nourishing blue veins and then turning pink before fading away entirely. Soon my unmarred physique seemed in every way newly minted, and in my rude and animalistic vitality, I was stronger and even more physically compelling than I had been before.

Every organ of perception became slowly enhanced as well, and the five senses were joined by new faculties for which there were no human precedent. While still trying to make sense of the infinite stimuli accosting my unfiltered consciousness, my receptivity began expanding almost mathematically, so that, for example, I no longer simply heard Nameless clucking over baby Violetta when they came to check on me together, but also heard them through the barn's wooden wall and then across the half-acre of unproductive soil from which Nameless hoed and tilled his meager life.

Soon the stone walls of the farmhouse melted, too, and then I could hear them not just speaking but thinking—the baby a raw and open vessel for whom all things were equally fascinating and terrifying, the father internally constricted by grief and worry despite his outward fellowship and calm. I probed deeper, looking for scraps of Anya, supping on a husband's impressions of our mutual love the way a starving man might dine ravenously on a stolen dish of food. She was there with me, shy on her wedding night and frightened by the sorrow that still separated her from Nameless and everyone she saw. And he held her, and let her cry, and was grateful for even that small fealty.

When Nameless grieved for Anya inside his too-large bed, I wept with him. Not just for my own lost love, but for his simple animal awareness that, in a profound sense, there was something essential within Anya that she couldn't provide to him, having awarded it elsewhere. He knew me to be the cause of this unbearable distress, and this made his many kindnesses a sort of miracle. But so complete was his love for Anya that he could not hate her own love's object.

There was nobility in this. And something I would not have guessed at: that inside this creature I had taken for a sort of subhuman dwelt a love as profound and mysterious and limitless as any. A love more pure than my own, for Nameless could not have given his beloved up in the service of another man's abstraction the way I had. I know because I searched his heart. It was not in him.

Blended together in this fashion, we were in a sense one bridegroom. As I probed Nameless's heart gently like a lover's fingers, and seasoned the impressions made by his own delight and wonder in Anya with delights and wonders of my own, the broken and skeletal bones of our shared sorrow wore flesh and marrow again, and together we began to heal.

I started as a plunderer of his most intimate memories and finished by complementing and completing them, as a voice paired in harmony finishes a song. And within the song, which was a requiem,

Anya quivered and drew just enough breath for all of us to say a proper goodbye.

Chapter Twenty-Three

If my reputation has preceded me, you no doubt already have fully formed impressions about my nature and capacities. I warn you, Reader: what the world knows of me, is, for the most part, comprised of half-truths and outright falsities. If I am successful in this undertaking, you will be disabused of the worst of these fabrications and mythologies after a while.

But most important to your understanding of this portion of my story is something that has not been cited anywhere, in all the folktales and legends and writings that speak of me in so many languages and call me by so many names. This is that the special attributes I possess came upon me gradually, through a period of gestation and metamorphosis lasting many years.

In the popular mind, I struck a Faustian compact with the Devil in a forest clearing at midnight and then, wild-eyed and lusting for death, launched a campaign to claim every soul for my satanic master so that he might drag you and your children to perdition. This is not so, Reader; my Adversary is of another sort, and it's my belief that if you are human and mortal, this same Adversary wars ceaselessly on you.

You feel His touch each time you look in the mirror and spot a wrinkle on skin that was smooth the night before. As your children grow old enough to turn their backs on you, His handiwork is visible in your stooped and powerless anguish as they walk away. He's there in every fever. He stands beside each sickbed and leers with glee. If a child's breath catches in the crib, it's He who sometimes halts the baby's lungs and lets the infant smother. You throw Him by loamy fistfuls into the mouth of every open grave, and as life progresses and becomes little more than a series of unexpected goodbyes, you will slip and slide and tumble inexorably toward the Hell He has made for you.

His supreme conjuring trick is that in exchange for all these scourges and vexations, He commands you to worship Him and call Him generous and beautiful. And you do so, Reader, don't you? But if you could see Him as He is, you would shun Him. And if you then could look upon the confused and frequently panic-stricken creature I was in the first days of my transitioning, you would laugh at the idea of me as a comparably omnipotent fiend.

I was of course aware at all times that something remarkable was happening to me, but I had no capacity for judging the transformation's nature or what I would ultimately become when the process completed itself. In this moment of my life, I could no more tell you what to call the creature I was becoming than Nameless could.

What I did know was that I already possessed some powers I had been told from childhood were reserved to God, and bitter laughter came to me when I reflected on this sacrilegious evolution of my being. I had triumphed over death, the way the stories said God had when He rose from His tomb after being crucified on the Mount of Skulls. And like the stern and jealous God of the Old Testament, I was beginning to sense what was hidden inside men's hearts, even when they masked their true selves to others. But as these gifts flourished, I was also still myself. I could have walked by day if I chose to. If I looked into a mirror or a pool of reflective water, my reflection would have been visible and true. And because I was still something very like a man, all these wondrous changes both exhilarated and terrified me.

For many months, I hid from the world under a pile of straw in the outbuilding, grieving Anya and wrestling with my new self while Nameless kept my secrets. I stirred a bit sometimes, mostly at night, and terrified the animals whenever I came near to them. But for the most part, I simply lay there, mourning for what was lost and letting the new universes of sensation I had access to wash over me, while I slowly learned to master and control my responses. And as I hid myself, even the gossipy world of the town at last began to forget about the tiny apocalypse of an insignificant parish priest in a burned church, and appointed other men to chant over its gravesites and consecrate its wedding ceremonies.

Nameless noticed right away that I didn't eat and didn't seem to hunger. He accepted this oddity the way he had accepted everything since my strange rebirth, and simply stopped bringing me food. I cannot explain my initial absence of appetite except to say that perhaps the thing I became fed on the thing I had been, the enhanced being supping on the dwindling and vestigial man. But this self-cannibalism was not an infinite resource. As my head began to clear and my mind at last could focus, I started to feel inchoate longings—a suggestion of appetites so horrible that I refused even to consider them with my conscious mind. I forced these thoughts away from me, but they always returned, gaining strength from my efforts to suppress them.

One night I found myself standing over the child. She was well into her second year by then, a baby girl grave and solemn, as if she understood her many forms of loss. Her hair was coarse where Anya's was lustrous, her nose pert but bent like her father's. I had watched her grow in glimpses, for Nameless carried her with him each time he checked on me in the barn. Her eyes always sought for me and would not look away—so much like Anya in their endless blue and the totality of their attention that I had to turn my gaze from her.

I stared at the girl as she slumbered, watching her fingers twitch, seeing the tiny pulse of the veins in her thumbs, her arms, her neck.

She opened her eyes and looked at me. Unafraid. Not crying out.

"Violetta," I whispered, and it was the first word I'd said aloud since it rained fire and Anya melted in my hands.

Violetta reached out unafraid and touched my face, and I thrilled at the feel of her skin on mine.

A powerful urge came then to fall on her. To devour her softly and carry her away with me to some place where the world could never find us. Fatherly impressions gleaned vicariously from Nameless's experiences of the child churned inside me, and I suddenly believed with all my heart that Violetta was mine, mine and Anya's, the last vestige of our broken love.

I started to move toward the child in the crib. Lovingly. Bending forward, toward her soft skin, for a fatherly kiss . . . .

Just then, Nameless groaned, wakening. "Violetta?" he cried.

Nameless stood quickly and moved toward me, all aggression and terror, the very picture of the raging forest animal protecting its cub from an unseen foe.

By the time he was across the room, I was gone.

Chapter Twenty-Four

This narrow escape was the first manifestation of my new skill of transformation, for no sooner had I realized I was about to be discovered than a self-protecting urge to be elsewhere rose within me, and all but instantly I was a grey mist flowing under the crack of the door, and then floating weightless in evening breeze. Incorporeal, I felt the moonlight permeate my dewy skin, and I thrilled at all these fresh miracles, wondering, this time in exultation, where my strange journey would finally lead.

My euphoria quickly became dread as my thoughts moved to baby Violetta and my odd and hungering vigil beside her bed. What would have happened if Nameless had not sensed something amiss? Sensed it because he and I were conjoined now, after my ravishment of his memories of Anya and the access given him to my own recollections of the woman we both loved. What might I have done if Nameless hadn't reared up like a bear on its hind legs and stopped me?

I could no longer block the harrowing images of my strange new appetites from my mind, and so at last I began to understand fully the horrors available to my increasingly altered self. For I could see the very picture of my awful cravings as plainly as a memory, and what was worse, I was no longer entirely appalled by the impression it made. I knew exactly what I had wanted to do, what I desired with all my being in that moment before Nameless interrupted me. I would have drained baby Violetta until she shriveled into a childish husk, supping on her as easily as my priestly incarnation had drained the gilded chalices of the Fool of Christ of every winy globule of a Savior's blood.

I was becoming dangerous. Clearly forces were in motion now that none of us understood. All that was wanted was a catalyst, some unanticipated spark by whose uncertain light I could make my way toward a dark path I would never wander away from again.

Just as he had previously provided me with so much solace and comfort, so, too, did Nameless fulfill this additional requirement of my metamorphosis. Several weeks had passed—weeks of confused desire and wavering resistance—when suddenly my introspection was shattered as brutally as a rock shatters glass.

It came to me on the wind, the way so many things did then—a sudden burst of agonized energy so violent and unanticipated that my eyes watered from the pain it carried.

I recognized the timbre of the insubstantial voice that called to me.

It was Nameless.

He was dying. He was in a meadow near the woods.

I went to him.

It was one of those simple accidents of the fields, an event typical enough in character to be thought a commonplace in those times. Nameless had been hired to prepare a neighbor's plot for planting. The plough turned against a stone, and wedged itself so it could not be moved.

Impatient to finish his assigned task before the light died, Nameless got down on the ground without unhitching the horse and tried to pull the obstacle away. The stone resisted, so Nameless put the full force of his ox-like strength against it, and when the blockage gave way all at once, he tumbled with it, crying out as he sprawled across the furrowing soil.

Mistaking the exclamation for a command, the horse walked forward. The plough didn't stop until the blade had buried itself halfway through Nameless's spine.

He was alive but already in shock when I came to him. He recognized me, but my face, changed as it was from priestly days, reminded him of a happier time. "Ah! Father!" he said. "I was showing the children how to plow straight, and now look at me. Stupid Nameless! Made a mess again! You'll tell the sister how sorry I am, won't you? I couldn't bear to have her think I meant to disappoint her."

"You could never disappoint her, Nameless. She's far too fond of you."

"Ahhh," he said quietly, and was silent a moment. Then almost as a whisper he added, "But fonder still of you."

It was a warm night, but Nameless shuddered against an encroaching chill meant for him only. His face paled to a deadening grey and his eyes started scanning the tree line, looking frightened and confused. All at once, he began to cry. "Where is everyone? Why so cold of a sudden? Father?" I smiled sadly, too moved to speak.

"Father! We'd better—better get the children . . . ." His head lolled then, as if fighting off slumber or a memory. I took his hand, and my touch revived him a little. ". . . Get the children inside," he continued, "where it's warm . . . and they . . . can sleep . . . ."

I wanted to console him, to say all the bromides and aphorisms coined by the Church for use in moments like this one. I wanted to tell him that he was in the grip of Higher Power and was going to a better place, that there was a reward waiting for him there, that Anya would be standing in a doorway with a smile on her face and bright light shining all around her, while the smell of fresh-made pashka scented the air.

All these soothing blandishments should have come naturally to me, for I had said these things a thousand times in my former calling. But in my effort to calm him, I had touched Nameless, and I could feel the last of life fluttering inside him like a moth batting against the bars of a cage. And suddenly the sight and the smell of so much of Nameless's blood, oozing rich and black from his side where the plough entered him, was the only thing I could perceive. For if I didn't understand my true nature yet, the underlying urge to feed had been gaining strength in me for some time. And though I loved Nameless, and knew he had been good to me, hunger and my responses to it were all at once the only things in the world.

The old taboos and prohibitions had weakened in me, but they were not gone. I was still that much a man. I made a feeble attempt to resist the craving ignited by Nameless's blood, to reason with an irrational impulse, like a man who stands in the path of a river and chastises the floodwater as it overtops its bank and rages forward to claim him. I was so intent on my own pathetic struggle that I failed to notice that Nameless had already lost his. When at last and with a cry of rapture and submission I drank from him where the great wound seeped and bubbled, it was a corpse I ravaged, not a living man.

I filled myself as if there was no other food, as if there could never be another kind of nourishment, so hungry and insatiable that I noticed nothing but my own bliss until it was too late. The dead man's blood in my mouth tasted acrid and stale, and seemed to curdle everything it touched. Lips, throat, stomach—all scorched and corrupted, the way a draught of acid might have seared me.

I clawed at my face, roaring in agony, and ran off into the encroaching forest. Worse even than the pain that rippled through my neck, my chest, my lungs was the revulsion I felt at giving in to so perverse an inclination and defiling the dead body of the man who was my only friend.

And Nameless was gone! The full force of my aloneness struck at me like a club, combining with the overwhelming self-loathing I felt and leaving me anguished and writhing in dirt as I wailed out my woe. I still could not understand what was happening to me, but

I knew I wanted this tempest of exhilarations and horrors to stop. There in the forest, I begged whatever listened to make it stop.

And then, the living canopy of leaf, bole and branch began to wave above me in a sudden breeze, and the forest itself seemed to answer, for insinuating whispers were all around me. Calm. Stately. Noble. They proffered other ways of being, in an insubstantial voice that somehow had the power of an oracle speaking prophecy. And they said, "Be like us. For we are at peace, and we give peace. We move not until the winds move us. We do not weep nor laugh nor see. That is our role in things, and also our glory."

It was, in its way, a holy moment. For there was an era, Reader, that has mostly been scorned or forgotten since a frenzy of baptisms reimagined Europe, a time when men not only worshipped more tangible gods but also daily walked among them. These gods gave shelter and shade. Hatcheted to the ground and broken into pieces, they provided warmth and innumerable other comforts. Allowed to flourish unmolested, they seemed immortal, for they could live beside a man and then his son and then his grandchildren and their children, and when all those baskets of flesh were dust, these creatures would still burgeon and thrive.

They were benign gods also, with no cruelty or caprice within them. Such was their love of humanity that when variable man removed his affections and moved on to reverence other deities, they continued to provide their gifts to him and never resented his infidelity or refused to give what he still required.

Deep in the forest, I stood in the cathedral of these leafy divinities. And they wakened to me, the way all things now wakened to me, and they called me to them.

I asked them for respite from the animal urges that impelled me, and being benevolent, they answered me. No sooner did I hear their voices than I knew I would assent to everything they offered. I would unbecome—surrender the ghastly parody of skin and tissue I walked around in, relinquish all the jangling appetites that bred inside that riotous squalor of sinew and flesh like maggots on rotted meat.

As their generous gift flowered within me, the light began to fail, and everything basked in the day's last glow. A droning heaviness claimed my feet, quieting their desire to dash and flee, and soil seemed to flow across them like a purgative tide, anchoring me, giving me succor. My back arched, ascending toward crimson sky, and my torso widened and grew thick with sheathing bark. Two raised arms multiplied, becoming four, then eight, then outstretched dozens. Ten tendril fingers became scores. And every armature was so strong or so supple I could not imagine a need to set my limbs down ever again.

Worldly fevers cooled within me as my thinking simplified, and all the sparks and furies that drove me went silent one by one.

I could live with myself again.

And then Brother Willow and Sister Pine, being nearest me and therefore my mentors, joined me to them as their Brother Oak and bound me with their canticle. Together, we chanted it: 'We are at peace, and we give peace. We move not until the winds move us. We do not weep nor laugh nor see. This is our role in things, and also our glory.

'For we are trees.'

Chapter Twenty-Five

Oh, water in the ground! Oh, root! Oh, anchor to the earth that spins with the world and never runs against it! I sing thy wisdom, embedded and immutable, as I abandon legs.

Oh, verdure of foliage! Oh, leaf! Oh, stem! Gatherer of sunlight and food of insects! I sing thee also, you who are both harvester and harvest. I rustle in gusts and drafts as I abandon fingers.

Oh, glory of boughs! Oh, fibrous limb! Oh, branch! Shade-giver and nesting place! Let the roosting birds sing thy song—yea, and sing it for all the world, as I abandon arms.

Oh, rigid bark! Oh, armored sheath and covering! Protector and shield during the long winter's sleep! I sing thy strength as I abandon flesh.

Oh, oozing sap! Oh, juice of life! Oh, nectar! Quicksilver nurturer, you who brim and flow. I sing of sustenance, of light and soil and air. For see? The predator gasps and preys no more—

As I abandon blood.

There was nothing to do anymore, except be. Nothing to learn, and yet so many things to unlearn from my time among men—worry, remorse, grief.

'That's the meat you wore talking,' Sister Pine's swaying boughs seemed to say. 'You think about thinking as a way to avoid relinquishing thought.'

And Brother Willow's sagging leaves whispered in the wind. 'Hush,' they said. 'It's gone now. Let it go.'

So I let it go. Bit by bit and piece by piece, until there was no Anya, no Patriarch, no Nameless, only the real and ecstatic now, with dappling sunlight and the earth giving up its nourishing secrets to me.

As my awareness became limited to immediate things and the moment, ego and self vanished incrementally. All I wanted was for creatures to live on me and feed from me and take what was needed. If they feasted on my leaves, I thrilled at the sensation of dispersal and absorption as they chewed and digested me, and I reveled in it, even though each stem I lost reduced my capacity to nurture from sunlight. If something burrowed into my bark and clung there, siphoning off nutrients, I gave of my sap willingly, the way a mother might offer herself up to the baby who depletes her.

There were skirmishes in my branches. When the animals devoured each other, I accepted it as I accepted all things that are. Birds pounced on bugs or picked grubs out of my grooved covering, and I experienced the screech of protest from each life as it hurtled toward the void, but the sound could no longer reach me, and I was tranquil. I witnessed these predations with blank and unquestioning joy.

Once a beehive dropped from my branches and smashed, killing scores of its inhabitants and its queen. The agitated survivors swarmed a robin's nest I carried and stung to death the flightless chicks that cradled in it. I heard the birds' cheeping song grow shrill then silent and then the desolate call of their mother when she returned with food to find her babies dead. And I thought, how beautiful all these sounds are. How beautiful is the world. How beautiful are the bird alive and the bird dying, and the worms that will do their work, and the portion of all these that will become compost and then come alive again in me.

The first winter came as a great shock. There was a numbness of root and then a coldness of branch. Confused, I sent out a question to my brethren: 'Brother. Sister. What is this?'

'It is,' Brother Willow seemed to say, nodding in a gentle wind.

'Just be,' Sister Pine chimed in.

I felt something like fear when the creeping deadness moved into my leaves and I lost any feeling of the sun. My healthy greens became oranges then yellows then purples, and soon they were dead and brittle browns. My arms stiffened as foliage dropped from me.

'I'm dying,' I said.

'It's wonderful,' Brother Willow seemed to reply.

And then I was too tired to send a response, and a dim impression of Nameless nodding off in his final sleep came to me as I was overcome by a dreamless slumber. My last impression was of Sister Pine, who wakened all the year and so would never know dormancy. She was observing me with something like envy.

Chapter Twenty-Six

Spring came, and with it resurrection. I budded and roused, a woodsy Lazarus rising from an icy tomb. Summer followed, and all the while I lengthened and swelled and spread my arms further as they grew ever more strong.

Then Autumn came again, and there was no fear this time, but only my satisfaction in the rightness of the rhythm of all things. As my leaves transformed, I fluttered my rainbow hues to the keening birds that flew in arrow-shaped lines overhead, and I sang to them: 'Go to your wintering places! For see you here? The loamy soil is cooling, and soon there will be no grubs or worms to feed on. Take flight! Find other places to rest! I will wait for you, and will harbor you and feed you and nurse your children when you return.'

One blood-red day in this dying season, there were human voices and a vibration in the ground of running feet. A little one was being chased by two larger ones. Shrill voices called out "Demon!" and "Ingrate!" and "It will go badly for you!" Then the small feet were coming toward me, and then they ran to where I stood and stopped dead in front of me, as though entranced. I reached toward the intruder, and as I made contact with the small figure that was there beneath my branches breathing heavily from her exertions, I tingled with muted recognition.

It was Violetta. She had grown to four years old now, and she seethed with misery, felt bruised and hunted inside. She was running from something—some monster, a pair of monsters whom she hated. They were catching her. And she stared at my knotted vastness and yearned to bury herself in me like a weevil, to hide not just from her pursuers but also from all the perplexities of her shattered life.

With plodding tread, the heavier footfalls came near—two overweight nuns, puffing with indignation and misery. "Ah!" the first nun gasped. "There you are, you ungrateful little witch!" The other nun came up and caught Violetta by the arm, twisting it. She raised her arm and struck Violetta across the face with the back of her hand, causing red welts and tears.

"Charity has its limits, child," the woman said, and she flexed her hand resentfully, as if Violetta had inconvenienced her by putting her face in its path. "The next time you escape us, we may let you keep going, and then the other waifs will have your food, and where will you sleep? Here in the woods for all I care—you mark me."

The nuns dragged Violetta away, and as her cries filled the air and then diminished, there was all at once something unsettled inside me, some small particle of her misery that lingered and stayed with me.

I could feel Brother Willow chuckle indulgently at my distress. 'That's vestigial,' he seemed to say. 'Your former nature rising in you like gorge.'

Sister Pine seemed to nod in agreement, and other words seemed to flow from her. 'Remember our teachings,' she said. 'There is no sorrow. Only light to struggle toward, and giving. Shower the girl with bounty if she comes near you. If she sprouts wings, let her roost and nest. If mandibles harden in her mouth and she demands green leaf and stem, surrender these gladly. And always sing the song of the wind as she goes by. All these are tangible bounties, not some phantasm of ganglia and yearning, as men are prey to.'

I listened to their words and flourished with the warmth of their understanding. My delight in this wisdom was boundless, and all that they said took root in me and flowered. So I stretched out my arms in an open embrace, and everything that lived, including Violetta, was a part of me and was welcome.

The girl grew, and something there was that drew her to me again and again. Perhaps it was the faint outline of her father's memories held inside me. Perhaps it was her recollection of a mustached face hidden among the silage in an outbuilding, or of that same face gazing down on her with soft longing late one night when she lay in her crib, awake and undreaming. Whatever the reason, Violetta came to me as often as she could, for shelter and for what there was of my companionship.

She still ran away every time an unguarded door could be opened, and the nuns still chased her, but as Violetta's arms strengthened she learned to scurry up my side and hide herself in my boughs. In season, the density of my plumage was such that this made her all but invisible. She would put her arms around me, nestling her head against my branches, and hold herself very still while the voices of pursuit came toward us, passed us by, and then receded.

Soon, Violetta started sharing things with me, whispered articulations of an orphan girl's sadness. Parentless, she called me "Father Tree" and talked in a low still voice about desertion and confusion. Why had her father abandoned her to these cold and unloving women? Why couldn't she recall his face clearly anymore, and why was there no trace at all of a mother in her memories?

I knew the answers to all her questions—that she had not been abandoned but that an evil Enemy had abducted her parents. I knew Nameless and Anya had been taken by force to another country from which they could not return to claim her. I knew also that they had loved her, that this separation was not of their choosing, and many other things both of the past and from my own accumulated sorrows that could have consoled Violetta in her loneliness and misery. But I did not speak. I simply rejoiced at the feeling of the child cradled in my arms, as I rejoiced in the birds that lighted on me, or the moss that grew on my trunk. And if a draught of air came, I rocked Violetta in it and sang her the song of my rustling leaves until she gentled.

The years went by, and the nuns tired of chasing the adventurous and difficult little girl who always got away from them but always returned by supper. Violetta's visits with me became less frequent, but she still came regularly, and I watched her sprout toward womanishness, looking more and more like Anya, but with her father's long Thracian nose, broad brow, and coarse hair.

As she aged, Violetta stopped climbing in my branches, and instead sat with her back against my roots, staring up at the sky. She no longer spoke to me or called me Father Tree, and I could sense that she would have blushed if she thought anyone knew she had ever done such a thing. For she was at that youthful age of first blooming, when the young think they've matured into adulthood, and everything of childhood embarrasses them. Still, being what I was, I knew her thoughts, and while she was more accepting of the dull routine of orphanage life than she had been in babyishness, her mind still bent unwaveringly toward escape. She knew her moment would come to her if she watched for her chance.

And so Violetta waited, and all I knew of her grief was my own bliss at her nearness when she sometimes waited with me.

Chapter Twenty-Seven

One day when Violetta came to me, there was another presence trailing behind her, a stranger who hid himself in the scrub growth, coming close to us but not coming near. I reached out for this man, welcoming him with tree-like simplicity and joy, and for the first time found a mind that was so blunt an instrument I could not fully penetrate its thoughts. All that came back to me were some facts about his life. He was a man of twenty-three, and his name was Rusoff. He worked for the sisters doing odd jobs and handy things around the convent and orphanage. He had bad skin, and a tendency toward drink. He knew Violetta's name, but he had never spoken to her.

And he had been following Violetta regularly, at closer and closer distances, for almost two years.

Today Rusoff had finally taken the risk of following Violetta as she snuck off the grounds, and so he traced her to the woods and found her under an enormous oak, a tree so robust, so knotted, and so bent it was like an absurd variation on a human being. Rusoff looked at her, lying there in the grass, reclining against me, and he was fascinated by her pale skin, the empty blue of her eyes, the way her young bosom rose and fell in a rhythm that was like sleep. And I realized something, all in a flash, which was that Rusoff was in one respect like Violetta. He was waiting for some deliverance that in his case I could not understand or see.

Violetta came to me one day in agitation and clambered up into my branches the way she had in younger days. She rested her head against me, and for a long time she did not speak. "Father Tree," she said at last, "It's happened. God has answered my prayers. They're sending me to work in the fields. Next week I'll finally see another acre of the wide world."

She threw an arm around me, the way a child might hold her mother, and she started to cry. "Oh, Father Tree! What will these people think of me? What will they think of a rude country girl in rags, who's never slept in a room with fewer than twenty in it, who eats with her fingers and eyes every portion on the table hoping to snatch the largest piece? What will they think of someone who's never known laughter and who doesn't understand games? How will they feel when they see these hands at work, these hands grown rough and knobby as an old woman's from scrubbing convent walls and floors for so long on my knees?"

Her sorrow was beautiful. Her joy was beautiful. The weight of her in my branches was beautiful. Even Rusoff, listening in the bushes, was beautiful to me.

There was wind in the air, and I rocked Violetta, as I had so many times before. She quieted, and for an hour or so we again shared the wisdom of Brother Willow and Sister Pine. There was no clock ticking in our thoughts and no other place where we were expected. We could just be.

When Violetta at last climbed down, she stood just where she was on the day she first noticed the large oak that seemed to beckon to her from amongst all the other trees. She turned her head, as if I'd said something that puzzled her—or maybe it was my resolute silence that at last seemed so strange to her. The unflinching awareness in her eyes was so like Anya I felt as if both mother and daughter were there before me.

"I shall miss you, Father Tree," she said. "You, who have been so constant, and such a friend to me."

Then she turned away, and I knew her heart was lightened by her time with me, and I was glad. Just as I had been glad when I knew her heart was heavy and sad.

Rusoff watched Violetta go, and his eyes never left her. He wanted to follow her—he always wanted to follow her—but he did not trail her footsteps this time as she returned to the orphanage. Instead he rose from the place where he was hiding and came over to me.

I rejoiced at his approach, as I rejoiced in the presence of all living things. I undulated and swayed, encouraging him as I could to take anything I had, anything at all if it filled a need. And though Rusoff was not a leaf eater, and though he did not roost, it turned out I had one thing he wanted.

One of my lowest branches ran straight and thick as a man's arm, and as knotted as a sailing ship's tackle. This branch had died recently and had dried enough that it was more like a wooden staff than part of a tree. Rusoff looked on this dead branch in his blunt and unthinking way, and I could tell by his posture and the expression on his pocked and sallow face he had use for it.

He scrambled up my side, and his feet writhed along my bark like snakes, his fingers digging at my hide like saws and awls. He reached out, balancing, and I could feel him grabbing at the dead branch with both hands. Then he brought the full weight of his body down on me, and I snapped at the joint, and the severance was another kind of joy to me.

Rusoff looked at the heavy branch to make sure there were no blemishes of rot or weakness. He took out a knife, expertly shaving off the sticks and twigs, smoothing the broken tip till it was rounded against his hand. By the odd alchemy of my being, I felt the blade sinking into the piece of me he had taken, and each slice was like a caress. He swung the staff in the air a few times, and my heavy wooden head whistled, low and throaty, and I was like a night bird rousing to prey.

Then Rusoff turned and, without saying a word, set off for the convent. And I thrilled at the sound of his receding step, and I thrilled at the thickening light, and I thrilled at the little piece of myself he had taken along with him.

Chapter Twenty-Eight

There were other sensations as Rusoff smoothed and varnished the limb he had taken from me, and then it slept for three days in darkness. When he reached for me in the corner where I lay hidden, I could feel the excitement thrumming in him, and his nervousness and emotion also thrummed along my sides and edges as he took me into his hand.

Violetta went about her day, and Rusoff managed everything so that we were always near her. When she kneeled among the others at morning chapel, we sat and watched her from the shadows of the sacristy. When her face turned toward the altar and she raised her eyes, we sighed in unison, a sigh both of his frustration and my uncomplicated ecstasy.

Violetta did her chores, and we contrived to always be near her. She rubbed her hands raw with scrubbing brushes and scalded them in tubs as she worked on the convent's laundry. She seemed to have no friends, for the sisters did not allow the ones in their care to talk except at meal time, and even then they watched over their dour world so closely that any sound like laughter died in the air.

Once or twice, Violetta caught sight of Rusoff, who would be polishing a doorframe somewhere near her or putting grease to a hinge. She made no sign of acknowledgment. Her eyes looked at but through him, for he was like the walls and windows to her—an object observed since childhood, a thing that had always been there.

And then, toward the end of day, when he found Violetta alone hanging out the wet washing in a corner of the grounds that was hidden from view by a mold-slick garden wall, Rusoff approached her.

"Missus," he said, "umm . . . Miss."

Violetta started violently, for to her it was as if one of the paving stones had suddenly decided to speak.

"Sir?" she said, half-alarmed. "Uh . . . Mister Rusoff?"

"There's word about you're leaving us," he said. "Is it true?"

"Aye," Violetta said, and she couldn't help smiling at the idea of her escape. "I'm going to work in the fields. It's very likely I'm to stay there with a family that needs a hand sowing its land and taking in the harvest. It's likely I won't come back."

There was something odd in Rusoff's reaction, so she hurriedly added, "Not that it's any of your nevermind, sir." And Violetta turned back to the bedding and black robes she was hanging on the line.

"Ah, but there's where your wrong, mistress," Rusoff said. "For you'll not be parting so casual, to roll them hips at other men, and flash those witching eyes. It's long years I've given to this place for love of you. And today I'll have my due."

Violetta started to whirl on Rusoff, intending to run him off. But before she rounded, he swung his polished piece of branch with considerable force against the side of her head, dazing her. He came at her as she dropped, swinging the cudgel that was also a part of my body again and again, now against the body, now against the arms and the hands.

I felt every blow from its other side, tasting Violetta's bruising skin as it kissed the place where Rusoff had fashioned me into a knobbed and insensate wooden fist. And when Rusoff pushed Violetta against the stone wall so that her face struck against it and she chafed and started to bleed, her terror could not reach me, for all I heard was the psalm of Brother Willow and Sister Pine:

'We are at peace, and we give peace. We move not until the winds move us. We do not weep nor laugh nor see. This is our role in things, and also our glory.'

Then Rusoff strangled Violetta and took her maidenhead from behind and by force, and I was there at her throat, exulting in the drip drip drip of her unbelieving tears, which were a kind of nourishing rain, tasting of my old loves and of lost possibility.

I would have been grateful that all this tumult of meat and sweat was beyond me now, had I a capacity for such gratitude, but there was none inside me. Whatever a farm dog's tail feels when it's wagged in happiness was what I felt, and when Violetta finally screamed, I heard her but could not listen. My ears were stopped by other musics, and if they heard anything in those days, it was the slow and immutable tick-tick-tock of a clock set to arboreal time.

I did not see Violetta for some months after that, though listening to eternity as I did then, the span passed in a breath for me. Snow fell and melted; water became ice and then water again. Like other woodland creatures, I slept and awaited the spring, and then wakening, I spread my arms and blossomed, as if saying, 'Shelter here, ye creatures of air, and you, leaf eaters, come and be welcome! Acorn-devouring squirrels, sup upon my limitless bounty. For this is my body, which has been offered up to you.'

In my memory, there is next a flurry of motion—garlands of cloth, strewn over branches and bows, a sudden spray of dying flowers. Human voices bark and snap, and then are raised together in horrible harmonies of godly abasement I dimly remember from my time suited in skin. "Marriage" and "matrimony" are words that rise above the din, the way the loudest scream might rise above the other noises of a house fire.

I sense Violetta near me and know what I can know of joy again. My mind reaches out, caressing her, offering her what is communicable of my strength.

She has need of it. She is indistinct, a veiled whiteness, shading toward red. She walks with arms outstretched in supplication and pleading, a childless pieta, abandoned by her Redeemer, and cradling instead the unseen but still palpitating figure of an uninterred grief.

But no—she is not childless, for all of that! Puerile breasts are swollen with the milky residue of undelivered life! My Violetta has supped from the great procreative feast, has learned the first steps of the great dance that changes unformed matter into new things that walk and grow, swim and fly and crawl, and all the while still cries out, lusty-voiced: "More! Make more! Make More!"

Oh, for a wind to swirl my arms, that they might descend and enfold her, my sometime daughter, the child of my one true love!

Farmer Rusoff was there too, dressed in what passed for finery within his meager world of material and spiritual frugality, as cold and unreadable a thing as always, though I perhaps felt something swollen inside the smallness of his soul that might have been a kind of gloating. The "good sisters" were on hand, smelling of spoiled sweet meats, so cross with titillation and horror that I turned from them, and would have trembled, revulsed, had I not forsaken the realm of pulp and brawn for branch and root and tree.

The last man on hand came parceled with the airs and graces of a bishop, though he was but a simple country priest—my successor as Lord High Protector of the Fool of Christ, in point of fact. I ransacked his essence in vain for some faltering sign of life's vital forces, but he was all sealed corridors and bricked doorways, with perhaps a small and impotent flame twittering against the generalized gloom in some abandoned corner of the glistening basement where he believed his sanctity had been successfully confined. This fitful smolder was all the illumination to be found in the man; so cold and cheerless a tomb had he made of himself that even the rats had fled.

So there they were—the grieving Violetta, the smug Rusoff, the appalled she-demons of the nunnery, and a sanctimonious altar boy—enacting scripted rituals of matrimonial delectation and godly consecration. They thanked the Eternal Foe for the earth, the sun, the air, begged His forgiveness for the frailty of the riot in their profane and sensate tissues, which should have been their glory. They were unworthy, unworthy, unworthy and so they begged His mercy, mercy, mercy on them all.

In ornamented language they cried out "Lord!" and "Father!" and "Omniscient and All-Powerful One!" But their prattle, when it reached me, sounded but the one word: "Adversary, Adversary, Adversary." And if the Foe was listening to their supplications, he did not answer back.

The Lord High Protector made a blessing on what all agreed was an ill-starred and iniquitous marriage, and everyone but Violetta inwardly congratulated themselves for their generosity in rising early of a Saturday and witnessing such a union. Then Rusoff marched Violetta off like a brood mare on a leash to await a foaling, the "good sisters" rubbing their vulpine hands in anticipation at the prospect of another child who was sure to do better under their blameless and sanctified tutelage.

Chapter Twenty-Nine

Violetta lost the child one hot summer night, when she was so heavy with carrying it that she was slow getting Farmer Rusoff his dinner. My cudgel-self was wielded and struck at her, and the blow that took her last chance at happiness came to me, in the enclosed pergola of my foliated stoicism, as the gentle brushing of a winged lip.

After that, I was with her most days. She came to me for a weeping place, chafing her face until it bled against my unyielding hide. "Father Tree," she said, "only you know the contour of my sorrow." A child herself, she mourned the loss of childhood, convulsing in grief over her own young loins, first ravished, and now sown with salt. She rued freshly the departure of her slow-witted but loving father, wakening for a moment my own buried remorse, and then sobbed for the mother who had exchanged her life to preserve Violetta's own.

She even grieved the odd and piteous Stranger who had lived in the barn once, hadn't he? The Silent One, the muscular Watcher with the grave and improbable mustache, who haunted her childhood even after he departed from it. And when she dreamed of a tender man, whose quiet fingers would touch her patiently but in a slow ferment of expectation, it was some decrepit remembrance of the Stranger's face she would see.

But the foundation stone of her grief was always the lost babe, and she caressed her sorrow in disbelief, the way she had caressed the blue-faced almost-boy whose olive-pit hands would never hold hers, whose worm-livid lips would never taste the milk now curdling within her, beside her already curdled heart.

Perhaps it was because I had known her in my human form, when feelings governed me as they do all human things. Perhaps some buried trace of Nameless and his unquestioning and dog-like devotions still drowsed inside me. But gradually, like tentative spring air warming an immobile waterfall, the profundity of Violetta's feelings began to penetrate the barnacled shell of my ringed satiety and quicken the imperturbable husk within, where feelings began to flow. I doted on her, as I doted on all things, only perhaps a bit more (yes definitely a bit more!). She was a melody to me (melody? made of sinew and flesh?), and when she wept among my roots as if begging them to become arms to hold her, for me all was harmony, tranquility, and love (what do you know of such things, Father Tree Father Tree Father Tree . . .).

Then my love for her began to differentiate itself from other qualities, a string on the instrument going slowly out of tune, until it became the only sound audible. Could I be tranquil in the face of her torment and still call my feeling some form of love? Was my self-sufficiency in the face of her anguish in any sense an act of devotion?

Soon, under the influence of her despair, I was champing at the periphery of my disengagement. When restless suns threatened her pale skin as she lay insensate after crying herself to sleep, I shifted my mighty bower imperceptibly to protect her by a cunning positioning of leaf and shoot and sprig. On the rare nights when Rusoff strayed from the tavern long enough to pillage what could never be his by marital right, I sent spore to her on the wind, entering her through flared nostrils, bringing enchantments and the musky residue of all the lovers that might have been. And she quieted, until Rusoff rolled off and pushed her aside, his brief but violent business brought to its inevitable conclusion.

Over time, so as to go unnoticed, I molded my roots to take her shape, so that when she lay with me, she lay membrane close, as in the womb. My bark I thinned until I could feel her breath, permeating; the crooked tangle of my bulbs, tendrils, and tubes I gradually smoothed, then straightened or curved, as the demands of her comfort needed be.

Brother Willow and Sister Pine took note of these developments with the same impervious circumspection they had schooled into me. They moved not until the winds moved them; they did not weep nor laugh nor see.

But being of their tribe I sensed a subtle disarrangement, presenting itself in their more immature growths, high up, where proud tops seemed to grab at the sky. The birds sensed it, too, and left their roosts to spend what remained of the dying summer in mating and song among my joyously expanding branches, pleasantly fatuous, as only birds can be.

At times, Violetta's grief seemed to leave her. She once murmured, "Beautiful," when, as she rested against me, we watched rosy-fingered dawn come up across the fields. And there was even momentary laughter when the antics of a particularly hard-headed quail chick brought it into unexpected but harmless head-first contact with Brother Willow, and then with me.

But the sunlight grew short, and the nights began to cool, and I felt my jointed arms stiffen in a forewarning of winter sleep. The first yellowing leaf felt like a betrayal, and so I covered the mutinous one with others more loyal, preserving for her the illusion of my unblemished verdancy for one more darkness and one more dawn.

Then came a profusion of red that could not be obscured, followed by still more yellows and sprightly swatches of purpling greens. It was my peacock season, but it gave Violetta no comfort to see me adorned in rainbow vestments. The bond between us had been her silent salvation, but she was not strong enough yet to face another leave-taking.

She still returned to me, day by day, but stood now at a distance, looking on, impassive as Brother Willow or Sister Pine, as one by one the adornments that had been her sanctuary flared and sickened, browned and died.

My last impression before dormancy ripened, and I went unwilling to my winter's rest, was of Violetta, curled weeping below my naked bowers, searching in vain and with both hands for some nesting place among roots piled high with the dead fronds of a curative summer that had failed to cure.

Chapter Thirty

There was darkness. There is always darkness. Something wounded, scrambling against my snow-flecked flanks.

Thin legs. Skeletal and spidery. Lighter than remembered. More desperate, but more sure.

Violetta is climbing. She is carrying something. Deliverance? No. More fibroid. Less true.

Then, sudden thrashing weight in my cruciform arms. I carry its slightness, laughingly. Still drowsing, I reach out for her. She is near but no longer touching. There is writhing movement but no breath where breath should be.

Becoming sentient, I see tearless eyes, gone staring and sightless. A whitening tongue lolling against a cheek.

She is dying.

It is pure and radiant joy to have her near.

Trees have no word for self-murder, though we have abetted self-murder and every other kind.

The mob lynches innocent men accused of wizardry among our branches, and we but bear witness until the corpse rots, then go on as before. Put to the torch, we spew flame so blasphemers and heretics can give uncoerced voice to the Glory of the One True God. Men are beaten to death with our severed branches. Sharpened into spears, we atomize every variety of brain and leg and heart.

And what was I, as an unthinking mallet in Farmer Rusoff's hand, but a silent conspirator in the massacre of a blameless soul?

Only once, in the long and unwitting history of tree folks and their dull complicity in every form of slaughter, only once in the senseless abattoir that is the collaboration between us and the human enthrallment to all forms of butchery, has one of our number chosen to intervene. That epochal moment came on a snowy day in the dead of winter, when my sharp hide bit through an abraded crust of January ice and then bristled, severing the rope Violetta had thrown across me in my sleep.

Let us say that by a favoring chance, some errant sprig or branchlet cut the slipknot with the precision of a surgery. Let us say another favoring chance caught her in my leafless winter boughs and then delivered her branch-to-branch, as if by light-fingered rescuers, who passed her lovingly hand to hand until she nested safely at my snowbound feet.

Farmer Rusoff found her there in an hour or so, breathing weakly, half-dead with frost. The unmistakable impress of her action was raised, like the mark of a branding iron, on her otherwise pallid throat, and Rusoff's confusion and befuddlement were great enough that, for the first time, I was able to feel his thoughts.

He did not feel pity for Violetta, or anything like the remorse he owed her. No, his thoughts were of the town. What would they think of her ungodly act, and would the taint of it extend to include Rusoff, too? They might be shunned and mocked and scorned, even more readily than they had been as adulterers mired in the Devil's own filth.

Better she had died from the rope or the fall, he thought, for at least then he might merit the womenfolk's meatpies and pity. And so he began looking about for some stone big enough to finish the job, when suddenly Violetta's eyes opened wide, and the startled and guilt-struck face of Farmer Rusoff was the first thing she did see.

She took in the dead forest, the slate grey sky—her unloved world. "Still here," her lips whispered, blue and trembling. And then she rasped out her sorrows on the hard earth one more time, and even Rusoff was moved, at least enough to stay his hand, if for no greater reason than out of a fear her living tracks on the ground might make it look like murder to the townsmen.

Chapter Thirty-One

During Violetta's recovery, gossips liked to sneak out and stand before me, outraged and titillated, murmuring that through blind chance the rope was a cheap one and had broken not once but twice. But the rope was a good one, product of consideration and a carefully worked if desperate plan. And Rusoff knew it, for I saw his sense of amazement and wonder when he fingered the place where the baleful chord had fallen away, sliced clean.

I wish that I had happier stories to tell you of poor Violetta from this point, but there are not many grace notes in her subsequent history. In those times, we had "personages," and only the glories and forfeitures of the illustrious were recorded and made into poems and saga and song. But what of poor Violetta, who lived her life wearing rags, born unnoticed and destined to die the same, and all within the unguarded gaol of a few broken acres so insignificant they didn't have a name. What of Violetta and her stern and incontestable destiny? Why say the stars move to Clytamnestra's agonies, but not to Violetta's?

She was guilty of nothing beyond a sort of idiot perseverance in the lot assigned to her, and that makes her blameless in all. What fault can be found in an organism with no lexicon for freedom in not having a vocabulary for being free?

The life I brought her back to was little changed, except in one respect, which was that Rusoff feared her now, and he would follow her at a distance sometimes to make sure she was where she should be. He did not watch her with compassion, but in trepidation that she might bring added shame to him by the manner of her dying. Still, this gave her enough of a scrap of control over her situation that after he next tried to take her, and she came at him with a secreted carving knife, she was no longer required to speak to him, and he never laid a hand to her again.

There was increased scorn in the town, of course, which was to be expected from such godly women and men. This augmented the certainty of Violetta's solitude, and might be thought by some as an enlargement of her curse. Violetta did not see things in this way, for she had given up on everything by that point, and when she at last took a lover, it was not so much from passion or even loneliness but as a final flicker of righteous anger against her fate and a need to know the touch of something other than Farmer Rusoff's horned hand.

Her lover was a brusque and querulous Captain of the Guard, but physically as much like the Stranger in the Barn of her childhood as faltering memory and grasping chance could make him. She was docile and unreachable in his presence, and when he broke things off by leaving her a handful of coins and a curt note she could not read, she seemed relieved rather than aggrieved. Still, when they made love beneath my branches, there was a small subsisting echo of life's great pageant in her hollowed breast, and once or twice, after he rolled away from her with a grunt and went quickly to sleep, she nestled against his splayed and unguarded arm, taking by stealth the comfort no one in her brutish life would give her freely.

You might well take umbrage at my own role in all of this, and so I give inventory. Lost mostly in a tree's dream of permanence and connectivity, I yet offered her dappled light and intermittent shelter from wind and rain. My roots were a bed for her, as I have told. When children of the birds, nested in my arms, at last broke through albumin and nothingness into sunlight, their first peeping songs were for themselves, for her, and for me. And despite her loneliness, she was not alone, for I fed the nut eaters and let Violetta watch in amazed silence as evening fell and phosphorescent lichens came alive, drawing luminous succor from my dark skin.

Small compensations, you say, but I say no. These are profound gifts, and amid anything other than human travails, they would be healing profundities. But in the end, alongside the accumulation of betrayals that the self-proclaimed Crown of Creation too often inflicts on innocent others of his tribe, a tree is but a tree.

Chapter Thirty-Two

And so the world turned, and Violetta grew older as I grew taller and stronger, and we were never parted now, except by the night, or by the unyielding mandate of the frosted season. As I dreamed away each winter, she waited beside me, swaddled in hirsute borrowings of animals more suited to the inclement weather than she. And from time to time, I would struggle up toward a near-wakefulness, if only to feel the ardor of her unquestioning allegiance to such a wearied and barren traveler as I.

Farmer Rusoff still kept to his periodic watch, a despairing old man, friendless but still holding to some half-remembered prospect of acceptance within the town. As time went on, and his thick hands began to slender and twist, his back stooped, and he developed a palsied shake originating in the left hip that made him seem to prance as he walked. The children of the town took to mocking him to his face the way their parents had mocked him to his back. And when the children scampered away from him, they laughed the harder if he shook his fist at them in an age-enfeebled caricature of his former passions.

He was desperate in his loneliness, afflicted and bereft, and now when he witnessed the bond between the aged Violetta and what by all appearances was an unthinking oak, his attitude was no longer one of puzzlement, but of envy.

One spring day the warming sun came up and she was not there. Bees hummed lazily at their rounds, drifting from blossom to bloom, and she was not there. Grasses swayed in the gentle wind, young sheep on the hillsides bleated and scamped, trees shed their winter skins in shards on the moist and living ground, and still she was not there.

A week passed, and then another. I remained watchful for some sign of her, but none came. I sent spore on the wind, but no sensation of her fragrant lips returned to me.

Soon Brother Willow and Sister Pine were whispering to me in dreams: 'She has forgot you, Brother Oak. This is as it should be. For we are trees. We move not until the winds move us. We do not weep nor laugh nor see. This is our role in things, and also our glory.'

At that time, a visitor to the forest would have seen a strange sight. The fertile splendors of spring were everywhere apparent—new life jostling on all fronts, from river bottom to the tops of the tallest trees. In the midst of all, I, the mightiest of the oaks, clung stubborn to the last edge of winter. What there was of young foliage, I had inhibited in partial growth on the first day I failed to see her, and there was the purpling of annual demise in my every stooped and half-formed leaf.

Such were the colors of my grief.

Then Rusoff came to me, his yellowed and rheumatic eye glinting dully with an imagined triumph. "I have her now," he hissed. "I have her now, Father Tree. She will not rise from her bed again and turn her back to hearth and home, and the love of the man what puts food on her table and fire in her stove. She will not stand beside you and count the numberless stars, or the blades of grass, or chart the fall of the sparrow, or whatever passes for conversation between the likes of you and she.

"She's caught her death," he cackled. "'Twas on the way to see you in the misty morn when she caught the chill. There's no mistaking it, she'll die sure. And then I'll take what remains of my good right arm, and a few sharp tools, and make of you an oaken casket, so you and she can rot together in the mold and damp, and be food for worms, as all betrayers and seducers should be."

He sidled toward me, and his odd, prancing walk was festive, but his aspect was all self-pity and mock-tragedy.

"She had no love in her heart for a good man, whose only sin was his over-fondness for a faithless wife. She gave all she had of fidelity—" and here he choked back tears "—to a fooking tree."

Then he spat at me and hobbled away, and where his saliva touched me, I did not feel clean for a week.

Chapter Thirty-Three

Rains came, cleansing the surfaces of things, but unable to scour the abscesses in all our damaged hearts. Other things grew, culminated, and began to recede, but I remained half-formed and immobile, as if by refusing the rhythm of seasonal life, I could stop time and keep her alive long enough to make her recover.

My arboreal clock was broken and past repair. Blithe eternities were no longer available to me, and every instant was an agony of watchfulness, diminishing hopes, and solitude.

One night there was a sort of vibration. An emanation in the darkness, much as the Gnostics say the soul makes departing the body. A low tone, a shaking of branch and leaf.

Then I heard Rusoff's cry in the distance, and broken footfalls nearer.

With her last strength, my love was returning to me.

Did the unconcerned weeds and grasses sense her faltering gait and take pity on such wretches as her and me? Did unthinking stones turn in the dust so that she would not stumble, knowing that to break her stride with their usual intransigence would have been, to Violetta, a lethality?

I cannot say. But somehow she came to me, with less of life's force left in her than it takes to power a flea.

How can I name her beauty for you in that moment? Brittle as a bone, dry as a stick, her grimaced skin pulled as tight against recessed cheeks as the drawstring on a miser's purse, she yet radiated defiance. And though too weak even to raise her hand, her trembling form beneath the half-eaten moon was a brandished fist, shaken in the unblinking face of the Baleful Adversary.

A fist that said, "Take what you will. I choose life. Sicken me, abate my flesh until it feeds like maggots on itself. Make of me a walking necropolis and dwelling place of diseases. I was and I am. While I draw breath, your victory is incomplete. And I will live on, in one I loved's memory."

And so she has. And so she does.

Things moving quickly now. She is falling (I am breaking her fall). She is in my arms (my arms). I hold her aged head, aim it at the stars. I am rocking her to her final sleep.

Rusoff in the clearing, his odd gait complicated by a long axe on which he leans heavily. He cannot bear to face us, and so sets to against my broad and uncomplaining back. The blade bites deep—a thing I sense, but don't feel. For I am with her. I am all and totally there with her. There is only her and me.

I would like to say that in those last moments, Violetta found her happiness, but happiness if it ever came to her was dew on a field, a baby chick returned safely to a nest, or cool water from an unexpected stream. No, the last emotion that flickers across her face is rage. Rage against every squandered moment, all the cruelties and distractions that moderated her pathway until she was steered into a thicket, the edges of which she could neither traverse nor see.

And all the while, Rusoff's blade nicks and cuts and spits and stings, and my back splits, and black sap runs.

Then Violetta's transfiguring face calls out in one last ache of something remembered or felt. And I decide to answer.

I cannot fully describe the next moments, for they were a whirl of sensation of a type that had become unfamiliar to me. Please keep in mind that though Rusoff's misperceptions about the source of his dishonor gave him more strength than an old man should have, he was no mortal danger to me. My body had grown so vast through the years that his tiring hand had no hope to fell me, or even to penetrate beyond a few easily repaired strata of my indefatigable bounty. I was unlike other creatures of the wood and could have healed myself in an instant.

I chose not to do so. For what the axe at my back instilled with greater force at every blow was not ruin and devastation, but overpowering emotion—something unknown to Brother Willow or Sister Pine, but quite familiar to a once-man like me. For we are men. We move not just when the wind moves us, but unceasingly. We weep and laugh and dance and see. That is our role in things, and sometimes our only pathway.

And so to the waning crack of the old man's tiring axe, I give roaring answer, becoming radiant and alive, splintering and emergent. I shed my oaken self, the way something amphibious might shed an unwanted skin, and lunge again for that ravaged shore where humans clench and beach themselves, gasping for one more breath of life-giving air. Bark and shards and acorns fat like black accusing eyeballs rain down, and I am leaning, leaning toward Violetta for our first and final kiss.

Violetta's last air gushes out against my lips. Then her eyes grow wide as if looking past me, and her body liquefies in my hatcheted hands, spitting red hot bones into the hissing night, as if the very stuff inside her is eager for leave-taking.

Amazed at his own strength but puzzled that a tree could scream out its crumpled deathsong so loudly and still stand, it was then that Rusoff came around from his coward's placement to meet me face to face. He fell to unfleshed knees in a supplication he owed another, with cries of "Vourdalak!" and "Murder!" and "Woe is me!" and other things that were not language.

And woe indeed I meant for such as he.

Chapter Thirty-Four

What followed is not, upon reflection, my proudest memory, and is in fact the precursor to subsequent events I would undo had I the methods. For Farmer Rusoff's expression was a kind of perfection—an absolute of terror— and I see looking back at it the mirrored aspect of my worst and most vindictive self, given unmeasurable power over human life and death, and ready to wield it with the petty ferocity of an omnipotent child. Red hatred pulsed at the corners of my vision, for I recognized in Rusoff's babbling and fear-struck countenance that he looked upon my petty imitation of Another Not Myself, one whose image and likeness I had so struggled to unbecome.

In wakening the vilest and most murderous being within me, Rusoff had brought me, as irresistibly as a falling star is pulled through an atmosphere, into the unwavering orbit of the Great Antagonist. I was once more if momentarily His Other Begotten Son, and when Rusoff's screams became guttural and subhuman, it was not an axe-wielding farmer but the Adversary who stared back at me through an old man's rolling eyes.

So I reached toward the hapless farmer, using strangely elongated and stick-sharp fingers. His blood sprayed; the whites of his eyes turned grey and then were just viscera and sockets. And though I looked down at Violetta, and screamed "Defiler!" against the heavens with such fury my ex-brethren the Willows and Pines seemed to sway in cautious answer, and though Rusoff had no face at all when he at last fell from my grip and I realized that unleashed emotion had made me again into something like a man—as I ran into the snarling and gleeful woods, I could not escape the feeling that it was not my own perfidious heart nor the chattering night creatures all around me that drew me forward, but rather the Adversary who clutched at my arm and took me by the hand.

That night was my Gethsemane. Reawakened to the capricious gifts of mobility and to animal impulses that were but dimly remembered from my earlier periods of human life, I became overawed by sensation, feeling giddy and alight. Three score and ten years of rooted gravitas and fecund tranquility lay in splinters beside poor Violetta's cooling corpse, and I could weep for her now—for her long but unfinished life.

And so I wept, for every caress she never felt, my own chief among them. For the bludgeonings fashioned from my own body that Rusoff used to enforce his will. I wept for the misguided piety that held Violetta enthralled by an existence that was not worth leading, left her enduring sorrows as a kind of penance for crimes of which she was the object, not the perpetrator. Most of all, I wept for the sad joke that awaited Violetta's ethereal soul: the torturous realization that all of happiness she was ever to know was behind her now, that she had squandered the only chance she would ever know to be truly free.

Where Rusoff's blood and flesh still clung to me, I licked and bit at it, discovering in doing so that my transformations from man to Wood Demon and back again had taught me the trick of shape-shifting. When I craved for a particularly sanguinary Rusoff morsel on a portion of the shoulder beyond my tongue's reach, I was suddenly rewarded with the feral and flexible form of a raging timber wolf, and dined rapturously before returning to a more recognizable figure.

I sensed that an infinity of other shapes jostled beneath my skin, and my delight in their multiplicity made me overlook a disquieting detail: that where the blade-splintered oak caught my arm as I emerged from it, I was bleeding, and would soon have a new and lasting scar. I, who had seemed impervious until now, was injured, if mildly. It seemed of microscopic importance, but would grasp for me like a hand from darkness later on.

At the edge of the wood, I saw firelight in the distance, felt something evil ravening in my throat, and turned quickly away from the discontinuous beacons of the motionless town. A beckoning luminance still seemed to hover before me, and my cravings were only heightened by the voracious symphony of night sounds. Wandering the bug-thick woods, listening to the predator's chirp and squeal and cry, I thought how easy it would be to simply accept my strange new otherness and spread myself, like a wind-borne malady, across and through and past the slumbering village that snored and gasped and dreamed beneath my glance. Dreamed of lost happinesses and impossible reunions, of childhood's forgotten games and the milk-white skin of neighbor-house bridegrooms, of illicit partnerships clutched in sweating conjugal ecstasy on somebody else's straw bed.

How easy to become like the night-world that writhed and blinked and bit and sang. To join in the dark dance and simply claim that which had become mine by divine right: the bright red blood of every woman, man, and child that twitched and waited in restless reverie—there, within the limits of my considerably expanded reach.

I could claim them as a kind of prey. The way a mosquito claims a wrist. The way a flea claims a leg. The way a grave claims a corpse. I could, with no more energy expended than a dead leaf carried by an autumn wind, consummate my strange new relationship to mankind, drifting through cracked peasant lintels and splintered farmhouse doorjambs, floating above the sweet new grass on the floors of clandestine haylofts where prohibited lovers slumbered, each in the other's forbidden arms. And I would declaim, in a soft voice whose authority would be magnified by the unnatural fact of my ice black silence:

"Dreamers, keep dreaming. Of arms and legs and sky and flight. I come bearing gifts. The waking world, the world of toil and woe, of betrayal and hardship and death, all this I take from you. Let us together quench the slow-burning fire the Adversary left you to die in, abandoned, the way a drunken potter abandons good clay to crack and fail in the kiln.

"Newer hands have plucked you from the fire, and they rejoice in your steadfast shape. I here give you my one unblessed commandment: thou shalt not wither and wilt. The Adversary has been pulled down. The chains are broken, and there will be no leave-taking. Mortality—carnal, earthly mortality—has itself been made mortal. And you and I and a thousand others like us are now and forever the sworn, implacable, and in all ways triumphant enemies of time.

"We are imperishable. And we are one."

Such thoughts teemed within me as I listened to the forest's rapacious incantation, and they filled me with hunger and dread.

The time was soon, but not yet. The mortal noose was slipped, but the impress of the rope had left scars and fibers. And so I hung my head, uncertain and terrified, as though the scaffold still rested beneath my feet, and the short drop and long dangle remained as my all too sure human culmination. I had escaped the pen, but I was still God's well-trained cur, able to feel the leash, even after it had slipped forever from my one time Master's hand.

I was as yet unready.

As I stood there, teetering on a precipice I would later plunge toward, it was then Violetta said, in a voice untarnished and true, "Husband, come away from there."

And stepping away from the brink of something still undisclosed, I knew Violetta was telling me exactly what I had to do.

PART FOUR:
Strange Blessings

Chapter Thirty-Five

Clearly, my touch had communicated my—what, my affliction? my gift?—my supreme otherness to Violetta. But how?

I thought back to the moment when she staggered toward me, insensible. I remembered her weakening breath, her feverish sweat, a tasting of salt. Abashed by her beauty in her moment of final repose, I bent forward to kiss her, becoming lips again, and tongue, and teeth....

Teeth. And taste. Salt. And something more. Then torchlight, and the gibbering old farmer with his oaths and imprecations, crying "Demon!" and "Vourdalak!" and "Woe is me."

Even now, down the long centuries, I shudder as I wonder: as I cradled Violetta in half-human arms, what exactly did Farmer Rusoff see?

It took me three nights to find her. Three nights of Violetta's coquettish scampering and cries for rescue. Three nights, in which she exulted and wept and evaded me, while all the while she was haunted by ghastly premonitions of a new self previously undreamed.

A dry well is a gravestone for a bright prospect, overrun and gone to seed. Since wells don't dig themselves, they are the product of human hope, embarked on in the belief that with a bit of muscle, a strong spade, and the right divination, the life-giving stuff is there in the ground for the taking, and everything will be possible later on.

In our optimism as we dig, we erect whole futures on aqueous foundations. Water will raise the crops and slake the beasts. Water will wash gold into the pan. Water will cauterize the wound, scour blood off the newborn, deterge the farmer's dung-flecked shirt, and sterilize his body when he dies.

And then a spade turns against the hard reality of nature's masonry, and all that expectation becomes another hole in the ground.

Still, only a knave abandons a dry well without filling it in. They are a hazard to anything that runs and jumps and crawls, and more than one dry well has broken a leg or become a skipping child's accidental sepulcher. And what was Violetta if not a kind of child—something newly born after a long gestation in other vestments?

I sensed her, watching me, low and indistinct in the withered grass. "Husband!" she said fretfully, and I accepted this appellation gratefully, though her voice was graveled and thick, as if speaking through something half-swallowed. "Husband—glak—why have you been so long—glak—in finding me? Why—glak—did I sleep alone so many nights before at last—glak—you took pity?"

Her raw voice grew reverent, remembering. "Your kiss—glak—was ravishment—glak—and I am transformed and made new. Artisan, it's your handiwork—glak—Would you like to see it?"

I stepped to the mouth of the dry well eagerly, but she skittered deeper into the gloom to preserve all she now owned, which was her secret. Blood red eyes moved beneath me, but that was all of her that was available to my sight.

I was impatient to be near her. "Come to me, Wife," I said. "From this day forward, let us never part."

But she grew sulky, wanted wooing. She fluttered then, in a kind of virginal ferment, and her voice grew petulant and shy, and even wistful, with a kind of homesick longing I would not have thought her capable of, given the lineament of her former life.

"Tell me, Husband. Was I beautiful—glak—as a young girl?"

"The handsomest woman on earth."

"And as an old crone?"

"More handsome still."

"And tell me, Husband—glak—What beauty do you find in this?"

And then she skidded forward, and up into the light.

It is hard for me to do full justice to the presentation Violetta made for me then. Imagine if you will a beautiful toy in the hands of a capricious child. He tears the stuffing from it, removes the ligaments bone by bone, then turns the unfortunate and now gelatinous effigy inside out, and treads on it with his heel. Moving on to other atrocities, this homicidal child leaves behind him a sort of rounded ball, made randomly from the inversion of a dummy's face and arms and trunk and legs. That was Violetta's mein, coupled with improbably long and carnivorous teeth that gnashed when she spoke or even breathed.

But there was more, and ghastlier still.

From my bloody time in the soldiery, I recognized the fleshy shapes that everywhere dangled from her like tumorous fruit as fully functioning organs of the body. But whatever horrid force held them to their unnatural placements was inconstant. For more than once, a bit of stomach or liver or intestine lolled off to one side, detaching itself in a thin strip from the tissue it was a part of, and then tumbling free.

I could have broken this monster's heart with just a repressed shudder or a partial gasp. Those red eyes were ferocious, but it was the ferocity of Violetta's learned habit of self-hatred that I saw in them, and her fierce need to at last believe in something that would not leave.

The latter part was easy, for my love for her was undimmed. I spread my arms, saying, "Wife, come to your husband." And with a guttural squeal, my strange bride and offspring was in my arms. And never more comfortable and unashamed were any two lovers in meeting.

Chapter Thirty-Six

Our days passed in tutelage, for no one was more qualified to advise Violetta on her changing aptitudes than I. We slept not, supped for pleasure on beasts of the field, and were tranquil and contented.

One night, when we had made a dinner of a hapless doe found dead and bleeding in some huntsman's trap, she looked at me, her scarlet eyes aflame with new cunning. "I am," she said, "—glak—very hungry."

I indicated a shank of faun dragged back to our home in the dry well for later use. She shook her flapping head, saying, "Where can I get me—glak—some Rusoff meat?"

I had told her of the old man's violent end, and how I'd supped on bits of him afterward, thinking it would please her. Now I regretted it bitterly. Every day, she asked for a taste of this unnatural sacrament, and every day, I explained again what had already been explained. It was like educating a difficult child.

"There's no more Rusoff," I'd say patiently.

"—glak—Why?" came the daily reply.

"Because Rusoff is no more."

And then she'd cry out, "Waaaaaah! But who has—glak—more right to pick her teeth with his burned black bones than me?"

I could formulate no answer for that. Because, of course, no one had more of a right to pick her teeth with Rusoff's burned black bones than my poor Violetta. But by an accident of timing, it was never to be.

Today came a deviation in our established ritual. I said, "No more Rusoff," and waited for her reply, then faltered when none came.

I looked at her. She was watching me with an oddly observant air I had not seen before.

Thinking that like a bad music hall actor she'd missed her cue, I tried my next gambit. "Because Rusoff is no more."

"Yes," she said, all brooding petulance. "I know that." And then suddenly fierce: "But there are OTHERS."

She shouted this last, and in the deep hole where we'd made our nest, her voice reverberated like a clap of summer thunder.

My heart thumped. I waited before speaking, but did my best to do so offhandedly.

"Others? There are other Rusoffs?"

"Other PEOPLE." She began to rock, agitated, and I could see she was expressing thoughts that had been a long time forming. "Husband—glak—don't play the Fool of Christ with me. I have seen you at night—glak—walking the edge of the forest, watching the village like a general on a parapet planning his next campaign. Like you—glak—I hear them breathing in the darkness. Like you—glak— the dewy animal musk of their cream-white bodies is a perfume to me. The one distinction is that where I hunger, you thirst."

Then, as if to lighten the mood, she invented a gruesome little song:

"You wants the juice—glak—I wants the meat. Let's get together and EAT EAT EAT!" And she grew so animated in her movements that a little piece of kidney or spleen dribbled free of her face and went rolling, hitting the bottom of the well with a moist and distant impact of blood on dust.

I grew very serious then, because while I loved Violetta, my love was not unqualified—unqualified love being the province of schoolboys, balladeers, and others who walk in dreams. "Violetta," I said, taking her by what I took to be her hands. "Is our deviation from life's servile path to be a blessing or a curse? We alone have stepped outside the great stream that wears a groove in every human monument until that monument crumbles. You and I, solitary beings among all men and women in all their death-plagued history, have slipped the bonds. Have we made this escape only to fashion new chains of our own devising?"

I shook my head.

"I will not play at God—take life capriciously, bring sudden unheralded endings to incomplete beings, and send them as supplicants to the Source of their indenture. That is the Adversary's way, and we know him for a cruel entity. But what are *we*, Violetta? That is the question we must answer. What are we?"

"You," she said, quietly fierce because confident her words would wound me, "are some plaster saint—glak—setting up shop in other tabernacles. I—glak—am the one thing only: HUNGRY!"

And with that, at a leap she pulled free of me and was through the dry well's stony and unclosing mouth, then crashing through the bushes before vanishing into the night's silence.

Chapter Thirty-Seven

Mayhem followed, of course. The same transformation that would have left me a mute piece of livestock if Nameless had not shown pity on me was working fresh changes on poor Violetta. I reach for some metaphor for her predicament and see the livid corpse of her dead child as she described him to me. Violetta was unfinished in the same sense, and like a child in the womb she was also caught in the daily and profligate grip of terrifying exponential change. But she was incredibly dexterous for something not fully born, and had a whole life's half-remembered impressions to draw upon for guidance and motivation. Each day there were new capacities, undreamed of during mortal life. Each day, she became a little more like me.

And who among us might not wreak similar havoc if given such mischievous toys?

The village began to awaken to unmotivated screams—not at daybreak, but in the middle of the night. Cows lowed and walked the dirt pathways in their sleep, and the milk spoiled within them. One or two times after midnight, when the candle had burned down but had not gone out, meek little men who were foolish enough to sit alone in their studies at the mischief hour found it hard to concentrate on their accountancy books and had the beginnings of pleasant daydreams more vivid than life itself. Each woke with a start to find the first seam of his crisply laundered pants stained crusty white with a fluid his rather pitiable and failed body had all but forgotten how to make.

How do I know these things? I know them because I was everywhere in those days. I was the spider who dangled unnoticed down the wall. I was the gull from the Black Sea whose cry sounded so much like a startled child's hysterical laughter that young mothers, upon hearing it, would turn to see if their wayward boys were still beside them.

The rats in the field, the barnyard creatures who bleat and roost, I was them all. If it had eyes, I saw with them, if ears, I listened, always straining for the gravelly "glak" of Violetta, always hearing it, if at all, too late.

The sheep started dying first. Their carcasses would be found in odd and disconcerting contexts—having plunged *en masse* off a cliff, for example, or drowned themselves in orderly two by twos while a mountain shepherdess burbled and shrieked.

Next the cows took down barns and trampled fields heavy with new crops while farmers cursed and beat them, adding pathos and comedy to the repertoire. At this occurrence, I could not understand Violetta's line of attack. She seemed to be sowing terror for its own sake. How were the dim farmhouse creatures she afflicted a better repast than a roasted faun and a husband's arms at twilight? And how was all this leading her to her much-craved "Rusoff meat"?

When the dogs rebelled, I sensed her method, for her control over them was half-hearted before becoming complete. For three days, there was a piteous wailing and howling, mad barking, and a frothing of mouths. Then the animals quieted, and as on a signal, they went for their masters and wouldn't stop rending and tearing until every single one of them had been put down.

I knew it then. She was experimenting, using the lower animals as a gymnasium for the strengthening of her ever more powerful mind. Violetta had become a kind of paranormal vivisectionist—devising procedures, testing nostrums, before moving on from the animal kingdom to the real object of her processes:

Man.

But where among thousands of possibilities could she be expected to strike?

Chapter Thirty-Eight

And now, as my insular life with Violetta comes to its end, and I seek her under rocks and floorboards, our canvas broadens to include brushstrokes my hand had only a tangential share in painting. I must depart for a time from my own piece in all these strange comings and goings, and enter into the thoughts and feelings of those I knew and loved, and of people less close to me. This will, I fear, be a continuing aspect of what remains to our exchange on these topics, for it is at this moment of Violetta's escape and my pursuit of her that our forced entry into the wider world took place, bringing enmities to us and more benign affiliations that cannot be described accurately from a single vantage point. All of the curses and blessings to follow flowed from our contact with others. So to know my real story, you must also know the stories of those I hated and loved.

As this account was taken up as a work of instruction, I hesitate before crossing this particular threshold. For Reader, it is not so much a conversation as a monologue you and I are engaged in, and with no means to gauge your responses, I fear the impact these digressions will have on your faith in me as honest arbiter. You may ask, as the readers of newspapers and other mundane commonplaces do: by what means does he ascertain the form and color of these events? Some impure magic of his condition? And if so, coming from that dark source, is anything he says in this voice to be trusted?

I answer these questions with ones of my own. By what necromancy do you know a friend is cross with you, even though he showers you with honeyed affections? Which weird art makes you feel the pains of a lover's day as keenly as if they were your own, even to the point of becoming confused about their origin? What charm or enchantment allows you to look at an outsider and immediately know if they are a threat to you, as well as subtler things about their motivations and personality? Why do you cry at the sufferings of an unfamiliar child?

The answers: Empathy. Observation. Extrapolation. And, in the case of those you love, your familiarity with the inner world of the people closest to you, allowing you at times to assume their characters more vividly than they themselves do as they move through their overlooked lives.

Now envision these faculties amplified a thousand fold, and you will still have only a dim imagining of the range and acuity of the impressions available at all times to a mind like mine. A stranger jostles me on a footpath, and the darkest place in his heart is illuminated as by torchlight, making me shudder. An old crone taps the ground with a stick, and the rhythm, if I let it, will tease a coded message from the stones, telling me in every detail of the hope and disappointment of her wedding night and her heartsick joy in the son or daughter who came thereafter.

I can tell you what a sleeping hunting dog last got his teeth into, and how he felt as he made the kill. I can hold a weeping baby in my arms and see what he'll look like in a dozen years, or twenty-five, or forty. A horse-cart passes me on the road, and I know what the horse dreams of.

Please understand that I do not claim omniscience. These are capacities only, and you will see as this account of my life continues where I stressed the wrong detail in the moment, or threw my focus to something that deserved less prominence, often with calamitous results for myself or for those I loved. But where our story moves freely between my own perceptions and the perceptions of others, you must think of me as a diligent biographer who, having had access to the figures I write about, has gleaned from them, often without their knowledge or willing participation, the most accurate details of pivotal events, and then organized these same so that you may understand clearly the relationship between causes and effects.

So to your natural inclination to shout "He could not possibly know that!" I reply he could and he does, both in the same way you know the teeming population of your own daily story and by other means unavailable to the likes of you. If you remain open to these mysteries, you will find them among the least incredible aspects of what remains to our story.

But we can tarry here no longer, lest Violetta make good her escape. There are other human signposts from my wayward journey I must now introduce you to.

Chapter Thirty-Nine

In every village there are those who are neither loved nor hated, but tolerated. If they are fortunate, there are no other tangible obstacles to their happiness. They have loving parents, or at least parents who are not unloving and cruel, and while the other children do not invite them to form up when they raise their angel voices for a round of "And the little man's hatchet will chop you up," they are also not the object of other songs expressly invented to ostracize and tease them.

These persons are not comely or over-intelligent, but if their good luck holds into adulthood, they have no obvious warts or blemishes and any lack they suffer in intellect merely dulls their sensitivity to quiet rejections. And if the indifferent fates are kind, and conspire to absolve these simple folk completely from the thousand abuses conspiring fates usually perpetrate against the undefended, said creatures live out their lives without expectation, but also without undue remorse, and so pass an unnoticed span.

Such a one was broad-faced Donka the milkmaid, whose life of udders and fingers, slop-pails and horse-carts, was neither burdensome nor carefree but just heavy enough to hold her in place.

Hers was not the feeblest mind in the village, but it was among the most accepting. She accepted that at church service people did not turn to greet her, because she also knew if she stood beside them they would not move away. She accepted uncomplainingly that she would always smell of cow dung. She accepted that she was prone to fatness, and that this attracted a certain boy who would not have been her first choice if she were prone to thinking in choices, and she accepted she would be his one day if he turned to her, as she expected, because she owned three cows and he could do no better.

But inside Donka, there were secret spaces, as there are in most things. Pockets where she allowed herself to graze on hidden grasses and even, in her own way, to dream.

These were not dreams as you and I might know the term. She was not empowered in them to slaughter whole armies, nor was she sexually charismatic, and neither did they revisit on her some embodied phobia learned in babyhood to leave her quivering in her sheets. Donka's dreams were simpler than that, and less self-servicing. More like the fleeting impressions a dog might have of a day well lived: some warm air on the face, a hearty lunch held down, grass between toes, and a scent of red flowers.

And sometimes, there was a boy—a rather austere-looking and frail youth, with a cloth sack at his shoulder and barley grains in his hand. He was solemn but soft-faced as he patiently strewed the rich black furrows that were Donka's world as she imagined it in sleeping.

These were peripheral impressions only, for Donka never looked at the lad directly, though she was sure he would be beautiful if she did. He merely appeared at the edges of her vision while she gazed on something, like a butter-churn, that was more indicative of her actual life. But even when she couldn't see him, which was often, she would sometimes hear the quiet "chick" of his hand among the kernels in the sack, and a sound of barley germ kissing the fertile soil like soft rain, and this made him enough of a presence in her inner life that she even gave him a name, calling him the Sower.

Like everyone, Donka was appalled by developments in the town and was sure the Beast of the Woods was at the root of things. For hadn't old Rusoff's head been carried off into the underplace, from whence those nearest the forest still heard it screaming? Hadn't

Violetta the witch lady, whose warm bones had been found in the dirt like the skin of a snake that's shed it, hadn't Violetta, the crone who had been trying to charm the Beast out of the oak with her licentious ways for nigh fifty winters, so they'd say, hadn't mad Violetta the sorceress been seen riding her broom of skulls just before the trouble started, and with the Beast of the Woods hopping on his one great leg beneath?

If pressed, Donka would have admitted to some dispute about the nature of the relationship between the town witch and the devil she'd called forth from the great tree they swore still stood but with a gaping hole in it where Hell's doorway opened. Unimpeachable sources said the Demon followed Violetta as she flew, but others just as trustworthy swore that it pursued her—a not inconsiderable point, since smarter people than Donka said the unholy pair would be far weaker and easier to defeat in enmity than in allegiance.

But the main details were unimpeachable and multisourced—screaming head, Hell's doorway, broom of skulls—and it was all trouble that was beyond Donka's capacities of understanding anyway. So she busied her days with what chores could be accomplished with hands occupied by crossing herself every three minutes. And though she thought the church elders a little too frightened-looking for men of faith confronted by Hell's own (for what was faith's use if not for confronting Hell's own?), she waited with her characteristic docility as religious men burned their incense and searched their Bibles (and other Divine Books less commonly known) for something that could be taken for an answer.

When the cows mutinied, Donka took it as a personal affront, for hadn't they been fed and emptied by her hand for many a long year? She was not an old woman yet, but she was a woman, and with her parents in the ground and her whey-faced suitor still undecided, she had put all the gentleness of what was ultimately her truly gentle soul into the little pats and slaps and strokes she gave to the three animals whom she never named but simply called "Cow," one and all, because it was easier for her to remember.

When the creatures began walking in their sleep and could not be wakened, Donka was patient with them, saying, "Cow, come away from there," or "Cow, don't you know sleeping is a laydown activity?" Fences came down and had to be put up again, but she was a large woman, with her father's broad palms and thickly industrious fingers, and she was indulgent of misfortunes as long as they were small ones. After all, she herself was sleep-disturbed lately, what with the sheep dying off, or (some said) being carried off by the Beast of the Woods. It was the least she could do to indulge Cow, Cow, and Cow if they needed to modify their behavior during such abnormal times.

And then one day all three beasts gave Donka the whites of their eyes when she came to them, and then bucked like unbroken horses—one so violently that Donka was sure its heart would stop, a worry that made Donka cry. Other dairy folk slaughtered their stock quickly, out of a fear that what Donka prayed was a passing fever had in fact opened a portal to the dark place and thereby represented a permanent contamination. From the plots nearest to Donka's, she heard the hideous whine of cows being lashed and beaten, then the mortal thunk of an axe hitting a skull, and then total silence.

Except for the sound of Donka's own compassionate tears.

She could not have done such a thing, not only because there was too much of kindness in her, but also because she could not imagine her life or livelihood without the three creatures that on some days were her only companions. Then the fever passed, and Cow, Cow, and Cow gentled and returned to chewing their cud and switching at flies with their tails. Donka saw that, despite their days of madness, they had not completely destroyed the barn her father had built for them with his own hands, and she took this as a sign that all her years of small tendernesses had not gone entirely unrequited.

Chapter Forty

Meanwhile Violetta prowled the woods and fields and paths and streets, and I prowled after her. Initially, she was easy to track—a pancreatic dollop here, a splotch of stomach there, and sometimes something unidentifiable that could be nothing other than part of her. But the texture and constitution of these grisly signatures was changing, becoming mealier and less moist. And then I stopped finding them altogether.

I reached for Violetta with my mind, as I had done ten thousand times in the forest where she grew and aged beneath my branches. She was taller now, and the lineaments of something more human were beginning to make their appearance, which made her even more a patchwork creature than before. Her inverse skin had begun to pucker and turn in on itself, which is to say, it was struggling to attain a proper orientation. And there were the beginnings of a cartilaginous replica of the boney frame she'd lost in transformation—an improvised solution her body was generating to solve the problem of supporting her increase as she grew.

I was startled by the confusion of desires and impulses I found within her—drives toward safety and vengeance, deliverance and liberation, escape and relief. And always there, like a malignant background sound, was her fierce hunger for just one bite of "Rusoff meat."

As proof of the growth of her gifts, when I made an attempt to see the world through her eyes as a means of locating her, blackness came down on me so quickly that I stumbled under the weight of it. As I pitched forward, I heard the sound of her voice, gravelly still, but more like the Violetta I remembered, saying, "Husband—glak—you have been a poor provider!"

And that was the last contact I had with the only creature in all the world perverse enough to escape from my own equally perverse capacities, until she favored me with more substantive proofs of her intentions.

Chapter Forty-One

Donka had no dogs. They had a tendency to make the cows skittish, and skittish cows give limited milk, which was of course a threat to her good fortune. But few animals other than man have as broad a vocabulary for suffering as dogs do, and there came a day when the sounds of canine distress were unmistakable throughout the town. This disturbed Cow, Cow, and Cow afresh, which seemed unconscionable to Donka given the recentness of their deliverance. As nearly every farm had some sort of a hound, the noise was and remained for a time almost deafening.

Some lessons had been learned this far along in the continuing crisis. What there was of an economy locally was based on barter, and though dogs were not productive animals in the way cows and sheep were, they were often workers—herders and guardians and huntsman's helpers—who earned their keep and were an essential part of any calculation of a man's net value. Dogs were also, as in other places, much closer companions than the barnyard stock, offering their characteristic unknowing consolation when any of life's many troubles arrived unannounced.

And of course there was the example of the cows to consider. Those dairy folk who'd killed off their animals were now unquestionably ruined women and men, while those who'd waited for the fever to break were greatly enriched. After a decent interval to ensure their cows were giving out honest milk again, they might charge twice the former price for their corner in a supply of milk and cheese now so dear it would barely keep the babies alive until winter.

By and large it was decided that the most newly infected species would be spared another pogrom, but this did not mean that the town's dogs were safe. Such delicate calculations of profit and loss were only applied to one's own animal, not a neighbor's. Indeed, it quickly became the accepted custom to regard a strange dog, or even a familiar one that belonged elsewhere, as the bearer of an unknown contagion, to be dealt with ruthlessly.

Such were the poor beasts' discomforts that they frequently slipped the leash or vaulted the fence, and it became a not uncommon sight to see a capering dog, already exhibiting the most pathetic signs of agitation and distress, being chased through the town by a mob and then cornered, flayed, stoned, and burned by the goodly folk.

So it was not an altogether unlikely occurrence when an afflicted wolfhound appeared one day at Donka's gate—though on consideration, *afflicted* might be too strong a word for a lithe, strong animal that held Donka's gaze when she looked at it. It should be said this disconcerted Donka more than it might have upset another, since when she favored the humans of the town with a glance they rarely glanced back. But having gazed upon the creature, Donka decided she was comfortable with looking at it again.

She was impressed by the way the hound seemed to emanate calmness, first to the cows, who began lowing drowsily, and then to Donka herself. And the truly remarkable thing Donka might have noticed but didn't, on account of her unexpected reverie, was that the hound's soothing influence did not abate when it reached her. It continued past and through her and into the hills beyond, so that first near Donka's plot, and then just past it, and then farther away, and farther away still, and on and on in a widening swathe that eventually included the whole of the local landscape, the dogs fell silent.

It was but a moment before Donka's natural kindness asserted itself. "Dog," she said, the name Cow having been applied elsewhere, "night is falling, and you're in danger of your life! Quick, hide in the barn and I'll do my best to protect you."

At that, it was as if by her broad-faced and docile goodness, Donka had been put to a proof and had been affirmed, for the hound lost its attitude of watchfulness and came to lick her hand. Again, there was a pleasantness in this that Donka found soothing, so soothing that it seemed entirely right and appropriate when she heard sounds articulated that she had previously known only when she dreamed them into being: the familiar "chick" of a sensitive hand among the kernels in a planter's sack and a noise of barley germ kissing fertile soil like soft rain.

"You've done well with him," a man's austere voice said, and Donka found that the sound of it set something aglow in her woman's parts. "He's usually not so accepting of strangers." It was amazing that Donka could hear the lad, for not only did he speak as softly as dew forms, but all the dogs of the town had suddenly erupted against their masters in a frenzy of gnashing and tearing, causing an unfamiliar phrase to form and then vanish in Donka's thoughts: "Rusoff meat."

She curtsied but did not glance up. It was ingrained in her from a thousand slumbers that she should not look at this boy directly. But the stranger had another thought, so he took her chin in his hand, and with surprising strength for such a frail-looking youth, he turned her eyes until they met his, and he held her there effortlessly.

"How will you call me?" he asked.

There could be only one answer. "Sower," Donka said hoarsely. And then she turned her gaze slightly to include the butter-churn within it, if only to have a view of him as she remembered it and be sure it was he.

"Sower," the stranger repeated, as if committing it to memory. And then he took her hand and placed it on an intimate part of his own body, and though this thrilled Donka so that her neck flushed and her breasts heaved, the Sower seemed entirely sincere and curious when he said, "Tell me, Donka. What are these man things for?"

Then Donka turned toward the house without releasing his hand, and the two went in together, and neither looked back.

Chapter Forty-Two

I had long suspected that the faculty for breaching the gateway of another's thoughts as if overhearing conversations implied the ability to place things in the mind as well. The common burglar does not leave behind a gemstone of his own when he robs a house, but there would be nothing besides his own increased likelihood of penury to stop him from doing so. Violetta was a prodigy. She not only understood this duality but implemented it, at a stage in her development where I had been naked and mute, and baffled by grief.

It is probable Violetta bloomed quickly in this area as an act of self-protection. To any who didn't love her, her outrageous appearance would have been a cause for panic, and so she had an immediate need to cultivate such skills if she were to retain an absolute freedom of movement.

A passerby who witnessed Violetta's initial encounter with Donka would have seen a very different figure taking Donka by the hand—one not completely recognizable as the monstrous Violetta of the well, but only less unsightly if the eye of the beholder declares it so. By a deliberate accident of timing, much of the village was engaged in fighting off their suddenly feral canine companions when Violetta was so exposed, and Donka—well, she was lost in a dream of her own devising.

And yet I will not say, as some do who have come to know of the twilight world, that it was a "spell" Violetta put upon poor Donka. For spells belong to the same realm as Violetta's reputed broom of skulls—that is to say, to lore and superstition, and not to fact.

In her unenacted dreams and her placid acceptance of the idea of their unattainability, Donka left a portal open to what was most vital inside herself, and believed it safely enclosed. Things so strong gain power in darkness, and if Violetta used this power for her own ends, this is no more casting a spell than a young girl casts on a rich old man who knowingly throws away his fortune on her just so he can relive on better terms a thing lost to him. Theirs is a tragic collaboration, as was the exchange between Donka and Violetta. Thus do the little unhappinesses we learn to live with arise to undo us.

Violetta had unhappinesses of her own to exorcise, and hungers greater than the one for "Rusoff meat" to slake. I had underestimated the impact of the many sorrows of her former life upon her new self, believing her main predicament to be one of adjustment to bizarrely unfamiliar conditions. In fact, her primary aims were of different origin, and almost predictable given her former circumstance.

She wanted, above all, to know love, and from both sides of the male and female division.

I, of course, believed that I had already provided this to her, or at least that I could over time. But though she accepted our unnatural union explicitly and called me Husband, and though my hands had been the first to hold her in infancy, she had never really known me in my human state (for remember, even as the Stranger in the Barn, I was already imperishable).

Donka was as human as a human could be—kind and fleshy, pliant and docile, and as accepting as quicksand of anything that wished to sink into her arms and vanish. Had I known of her sooner, I would have known also that in so many ways, Donka was the perfect object of Violetta's intentions.

It was Violetta herself who would turn out to be so very ill suited to her own purpose.

Chapter Forty-Three

We must imagine their lovemaking as, above all, filled with tenderness. Discarded and rejected, undesired and despised, they shed their many bitternesses like so much laundry, and each in the other's eye is beautiful.

Violetta, feeling things as a man, is amazed by her own ardor—so different from her old yearning to be claimed. There is so much Donka beneath her hand (yet not enough, there could never be enough), and Violetta is greedy to know every freckle, every mound, every pore.

The music of moans and sighs, the protean vivacity of hardened teat and reddened throat, the gooseflesh and little white hairs raised by a breath or a touch, all this comes to Violetta as both natural and wondrous. She will never be in greater harmony with herself than in these moments, yet she apprehends them as fleeting. For so much of her life has been lived as an exile, awaiting a return to such a place. Violetta is a product of old wounds, and she could no more remove them from her psyche than a fish can pull a hook out of its mouth.

For see? There, outside the window, the world is all flux and movement. Stars wheel, skies move, the ground cools and then heats again. At each hour, something sleeps and something stirs, and for every lover melted in willing arms, another rises from a bed or puts on a shoe.

For Donka, this moment of sweat and grunting is the realization of a celibate's dream of desire. Though her passion is as great as Violetta's, her awe in discovering her own body in another's is tempered by her unexpected grief at the loss of a mystery.

What Donka had believed in was a kind of absolute understanding attained through a mysterious configuring of bodies, and in her heart of hearts she had even convinced herself that lovers can vault over the wall of separation between creatures and feel everything as one—each coupling a commingling of thrust and retreat, each caress felt as both the electricity of fingertips and the ravishing of the skin beneath.

Now she knows the hand that gives pleasure feels what it feels, the pleasurer remaining inscrutable to the pleasured, and though twin pulses indeed beat faster, they beat in syncopation, not harmony. She and her Sower are together, but in a profound sense, Donka is alone, and knows in this moment of sublime communion that she will be alone forever. And so Donka has lost something along with maidenhead that is as irreclaimable. She will never again dream this dream freely, or without reference to the austere and frail-looking boy whose long white hands needed holding as much as they needed to grip.

Farmhouse pragmatism is a proven palliative for such melancholia, and if this endeavor is new to Donka, she has witnessed it in a hundred barnyard variations. In those brutish encounters, each took what was needed, unconcerned for the other's bliss, and the empty eyes of the beasts always terrified Donka, who would search there for some intimacy and find only immediacy and disinterest.

In those moments, Donka feared some evil truth about a journey she had not yet taken, and now here she was, safely embarked and arrived. And so gazing down on Violetta, whose need for Donka was palpable even in repose, Donka thought: Here is a lover who looks in my eyes and will hold me until daybreak. There need be nothing more. For if Donka had learned anything in life, it was to count blessings and make do.

If there really is anything that sets man above the animals, it is this: an altruistic responsiveness to another in the moment of his most tender vulnerabilities.

And so night passed, and Donka and Violetta were inexhaustible, even as they tabulated wonders against wounds, and memories against longings, in that human way that can be almost comical. And as one by one they lay down the defenses life had given them but which proved such insufficient fortifications after all, I at last had my opportunity of finding them. For unlike Violetta, I never relax my vigilance, and unlike Donka, I understood that despite the night's glories, mortal jeopardies remained.

Chapter Forty-Four

I will leave Violetta and Donka a while among their transitory splendors because it is the way I want you to remember their union—a union that, whatever its faults, became a real one, as you will see. Also there is another story I must tell you before cooking you a dish of fresh horrors. But fear not. There will be horrors enough in later portions of the meal for you to lose your desire to feed.

So what was I doing during the weeks leading up to Violetta's meeting with Donka, and the strange intimacies derived therefrom? Searching, as I have told. And in that process, learning about the limits of "unlimited" powers.

As the days passed, and I pressed at the margins of my energies in fruitless pursuit, I came to know my capacities better than before. I have said, for example, that I became all manner of creatures in the chase. This is a true fact. But slowly, almost imperceptibly, the balance of my manifestations began to favor guises of night-flyers and seers-in-the-dark.

At first I suspected a reaction to my four score years in the forest, where I basked in brightness all the day long. But then my vision began to bleach under long exposure to hot sun, and my pallid skin to wither and flay. Headaches soon followed, and once, when I flew two circuits along the river's edge in the unremarkable aspect of a finch chick, I retched and was overcome by a chill—sensations so alien to my recent experiences that before I became incapacitated, I had no idea what was happening to me and feared Violetta had developed some new skill to torment me.

My recuperative powers being what they are, I improved quickly enough to speculate about what had happened. From soldier camps and battlefields, I recognized the symptoms of sun sickness, a disorder the Bulgars were more prone to than the Turks. The Ottomans I served under were dark-skinned, and always contemptuous of Thracian men, calling us "pink babies" and "pale horses" for our tendencies toward consuming more water than they did and requiring more shade.

Perhaps there was some essential connection between skin coloration and tolerance for daylight. And since I had reassumed human form, my own complexion had grown ever more pallid, to a point where I now consistently used a small amount of my transformative talent to maintain an appearance of natural color. I realized to my sorrow that if my theory held, I must soon say goodbye to the day forever, save perhaps for those oblique and reflected beams that occur in the last moments of twilight. In the meantime, I confined my daylight investigations to densely shaded areas of the forest, where sunlight barely penetrated, though like as not I would assume incongruous night-flowering shapes even in these sallies because the forms now suited me better.

By contrast, the compensations of the night grew ever more seductive, until in a momentary state of enchantment, I actually considered abandoning my search. This happened in the tree-thick forest, where I retired after two full and fruitless days in the town— my longest uninterrupted search there—but still without sign of Violetta.

I returned feeling uncharacteristically worn. The night sounds were singing, and I could not stop my ears. Come away, the obsidian hunters seemed to say, and learn to move with the swift silence of the moon. We will provide for you. Listen to our instructions, and you will never hunger or thirst again.

Hunger and thirst. Another call to feeding. Rousing myself from reverie, I thought of Violetta, and her "Rusoff meat."

I knew I was a monster to the townfolk. I wondered more and more if I would recognize it when I became a monster to myself.

Chapter Forty-Five

In the middle of the search, when the cows were afflicted and the dogs yet to become so, I found myself in a small forest clearing. I recognized it instantly as the very spot where I had served as Lord High Protector of the Fool of Christ, not least because, to my dismay and wonderment, there were ruins of another place of worship on the exact spot where my own sorry temple of priestly illusion once stood.

By this point in the region's history, the Ottoman yoke had been closed over the people's throats for close to a century. Because he did not kill every cross-worshipper he laid his eyes on, but instead favored tithing and taxation punishments that left all non-Muslims on the verge of penury, the Turk has been adjudged by some who never knew his lash the most tolerant of masters. But masters are only tolerant when they are unafraid, and the blistered icons and shattered nave told of rulers threatened enough to enforce their will by violence, and cunning to the point of leaving a ruined church as a warning to those passed over by the Angel of Homicides, that he might return for them in future incarnations.

I wondered about the fate of the cleric who presided over the unholy marriage service between Rusoff and the young Violetta, for this was surely his church, and the Turks rarely left a priest behind after they'd broken his crockery. And then I heard footsteps, or rather, a kind of dragging of feet, and I saw to my surprise that it was he.

The years had been either very kind to the Good Father or spitefully cruel, for he had achieved a span of a century—and who can say whether such decrepitude is a reward or a punishment? The air he breathed seemed scented with the sepulcher, and his feet did not so much walk as slide, as though a floating ghost were set lose among the wreckage of its former world. His vestments were a masterpiece of mismatched patches, and you could trace the decline in his fortunes by the cheapening cloths.

I could not resist the opportunity to bait the old man and so stepped forward arrayed as a tradesman, saying, "Bless me, Father, for I have sinned."

The priest started, then judged me harmless and recovered himself, saying, "Father no more, I fear." Despite greatly reduced circumstance, he had lost none of his lordly graces. "Though Father enough for these ungodly parts, I dare say."

"What happened here? What is this place?"

His laugh was sour and short.

"Why, see you not? This place is a monument to man's beneficence and grace. See there? There is where the godly Turks removed a bit of roofing that obstructed the Lord's view of his flock. He sees us better now. And there? Those charred and moldering remnants are the stacidia chairs that tempted the slothful to worship God without sacrificing comfort. And so, by the torch, piety has been safeguarded.

"The strong door that stood there kept the beasts of the field from worshipping beside their human brethren, and it has been knocked down in the spirit of Christian brotherliness. These oaken candle sticks have not been beheaded and broken but rather given tonsures in the manner of the Christian friars. And these lordly icons—"

His voice cracked when he looked upon the overturned effigies, too large for his frail hands to lift, though whether he reacted from age or emotion I could not say. He harrumphed to cover this display of frailty, and I heard ashes shift in his lungs.

"The Pasha's legions took to the road with fire and sword," he said, losing his mocking tone. "I beseeched my onetime flock to carry the painted saints away and give them refuge in the barns and fields. I was rebuffed. Catastrophe befell and then passed, and I pleaded again for enough assistance to reorient the holy ones from the blasphemous postures you find them in. As with our Lord on his cross, not a one would help me, the serf always fearing to touch even the leavings of his master's cruelties."

It was a moment before he reassumed his more jocular voice. "Or so I thought, in my ignorance of theology. I know now it was excess of devotion stayed their yeomen's hands. For, inverted and kissing the ground, how much better do the saints remind us that the fate of all men is dust and clay?"

"But surely these catastrophes are years in the past," I said, intrigued by his impiety. "Why speak of them with yesterday's bitterness?"

The priest laughed his arid laugh once more. "Yesterday's bitterness? Yesterday was the least bitter day I've known in these sour times." He gestured at the upturned icons. "I came today to tell my last remaining friends about it. Yesterday the townfolk came and asked my help in the current crisis, and I had the luxury of telling them that the devil had a better chance of enlisting my aid. So there. You see? You know nothing of my yesterdays, stranger. And why shouldn't I hold them close, with my store of tomorrows so depleted?"

"The crisis in the town is real. I have seen it with my own eyes."

"As have I. They herd sheep in the hills yonder. I saw two of the unlucky beasts rise up on their hind legs like mad horses, then beat their heads upon the stony ground until their hearts stopped."

"Then why did you turn down their request of aid? Surely your God is strong enough."

"He may be. But then there's I myself to consider. And I have prayed for catastrophe, and worse things, to befall the villagers for many a year. Which is not very like our Lord, I know. But sometimes, even priests are past redeeming, though they do live long enough to take delivery on an answered prayer."

Just then I heard a footfall and turned to see a sight so pitiful it haunts me down the centuries. A Roma woman, a gypsy in fetid rags, entered the ruined church and approached us, carrying a small child in her arms.

The mother was dark, but by some oddity of lineage, the little girl had the flowing white curls of a picture-book angel. The child looked to be napping, but was unconscious, having received some injury of the woods now weeks old. Her right leg was swollen and gangrenous, and it seemed certain she was in her last sleep.

The mother's fierce protectiveness overlaid such profound grief that the combination of her emotions almost unmanned me.

"Fazzir," she said, in the accents of the hills, "I have come for your blessing. A demon is in my daughter's leg, and he will not leave her. Please, put your hands here, and we will cast him out together with prayer and songs."

I could sense the priest shared the common revulsion against the Roma, and waited for him to turn the poor wretch away. He defied expectation in a most noble fashion, and I realized the years had in fact changed him from the self-satisfied prig who presided over Violetta's undoing.

He took the woman's arm gently, careful not to disturb the girl. "My dear," he said, gesturing at the rubble, "this is a church God has fled from."

The woman shook her head with an anguished smile, showing blackened and irregular teeth. "No, Fazzir, no. He is here, he is here. We need to make talk with him. Draw his eye. He is not watching. He would not take my daughter, after his snake make her cry so long. You guide his eye. He will see her. Take the demon."

The priest's face seemed desolate and old. He stroked the girl's hair, waved away a fat river fly that had landed on her lips and been crawling there unimpeded. Then he said softly, as if to himself, "Perhaps God wanted his little angel back."

The effect of the platitude was startling. The woman shook her head vehemently, her voice raising a half octave in her fright. She assumed a posture of desperate haggling over a price.

"No, Fazzir, no! What does he want with poor Roma girl, when there so many fine childrens in the town? Those childrens smart. Dress fine. Go to heaven, like where they live. Not Roma girl. Not Roma girl."

Afraid her words were not communicating in what was for her a second language, the woman nodded at the priest, then at the sky beyond. "You . . . Him . . . talk. He will see you. He will save us."

The ancient cleric stared at her for long seconds. Then he looked at me and said softly, "Help me here, won't you?"

And we took hold of the girl together, and we laid her on the altar, which was the only dry and level place, and he and I lit candles for her—two unchurched priests, preparing for a conversation with someone who was at best half listening.

Chapter Forty-Six

They were three days praying together in that fetid skeleton of a chapel. Three days, during which the dogs of the town began their ceaseless howling while the cleric worked the beads and burned incense, and the Roma woman spat, made poultices of mud, and played her assigned roles in his priestly rituals as she understood them from her own magpie awareness of Christian custom.

Using my tradesman's guise, I pled business elsewhere but promised to return to them if I could. In fact, I rarely left the spot, except to fruitlessly pursue Violetta for a few hours at a time, though the priest and the poor bereft mother would not have recognized me by the form I took in watching over them.

It was during this interval that I discovered the nuances of my relationship to crucifixes and crosses, a detail with which I began this account. The cleric wore a large rosary around his waist in the manner of his calling, and fixed to it was a carving of Christ in His death agonies. These disturbed me so little that I even brushed against the bauble once or twice while helping the old man carry and settle the girl.

But at some point, the holy father decided more godly energy was needed, and he fashioned a substantial empty cross out of two mold-crusted beams and placed it in the nave in a position of honor. For reasons I have described elsewhere, this sight affronted me, so much so I turned and fled, only to reapproach from a different placement that changed the view.

The girl continued her slow decline, and gradually the Roma woman's eyes deadened, and she stopped her spitting and stamping, until she was as still and unblinking as the fractured icons strewn about the chapel floor. The priest noticed her fatalism, forgave it, and continued with astonishing energy to pray over the child, going without food or sleep for the final day as the drama headed toward its denouement.

Gradually, the cleric's voice grew hoarse and then faded, though his lips still moved in prayer, and the only sounds were the distant bay of Violetta's hounds and the catch of the little girl's breathing as it slowed ineffably, minute by minute, a keyless clock winding down toward silence in the absence of the clockmaker's hand.

"You were right, Fazzir," the woman said, without raising eyes that no longer left her daughter's face. "God is not here. Only the demon."

The priest blanched. "You—you mustn't."

Her single laugh was dry as death. She did not look at him. "*I* mustn't," she said.

Then she reached into a pocket of her ragged skirt, withdrawing a single black and pockmarked onion—probably the only food she owned. She held it out to him, a householder paying off a grocer.

After hesitation, the priest took the offering. He was impoverished himself, and doubtless believed he had performed her some service, and I will not judge him for it.

There has been too much weeping in this story, but that is man's lot and none can change it. Left alone with her daughter, the Roma woman reverted to her own tongue and expressively cursed the heavens, wailing and lost. She shook her fist, slapped the girl's face as if she would force the life back into her, and again brought an unseen ogre in the rafters as near as he can come to tears.

It was to no avail. For the girl's condition was indeed changing, though not for the better.

Within minutes of the priest's departure, and as though relieved that she would not have to disappoint the cleric to his face, the child sighed—the only sound she had made—and commenced the unmistakable process of her dying. The agonized mother recognized the signs, and ran from the church in high agitation, crying "Fazzir! Fazzir!" until her voice receded and was gone.

And then all was distant howls, labored exhalations and encroaching silence.

I dropped from my hiding space, monstrous in my rage, not bothering about what shape I took. Breathing out gusts of winter, I sundered the cleric's makeshift cross, hurling it down among the toadstools in icy shards.

It had been long years since I had spoken to the Adversary, though He rarely left my thoughts. When words issued from me at last, it was not prayer but a voice from the lower world I hurled into the sightless firmament.

"What?" I screeched. "Unholy and deaf as well?" In a single leap, I was at the altar, rubbing against it with my broad and scaly back, scraping marbled wounds into it with the ridged musculature of my horned hands. "Bear witness," I cried to the Great and Silent Listener. "See here a thing self-created and beyond Your greedy grasp! Behold, an answer to unanswered prayers!"

I gathered the dying girl to me, saying, "Never fear, little one. There will be no more unannounced departures. We will fight Him. Corpse by corpse. Death by death. Until the epoch of vassalage commenced when a conjuring carpenter shirked the tomb ends in a God's capitulation." I kissed her forehead, savoring her blood, and turned yellowy eyes skyward. "See now, Adversary? Your corner on immortality is broken. She and I and the others like us inhale the rot You birthed us in and exhale fecundity. And so there will be more of us. An army someday, blessed by other consecrations. We will rise from all the unsealed tombs and pull Your peerless corpse down from its illegitimate throne, baptizing worlds in a Tyrant's blood, incarnadine."

There was a sound at the door, and the elderly priest entered, then groaned in fright. I smiled through wolfish teeth, genuinely glad of his company. "Regard me, cleric," I said, with savage glee. "The herald you called for is come."

He held his crucifix before him—a predictable gesture for such as he. "That charm has no power here," I cried, grabbing the beads away from him and holding the priestly trinket before my face, a child tormenting a doll.

"See how impotently he struggles?" I turned to the miniaturized godhead itself. "Climb down for us now, Little Usurper. But as always, we speak and He does not hear."

And then, with an energy born of terror and outrage, the old man lunged at me, crying "Get thee behind me" or some other bromide of his vocation, and my work was nearly finished before it had begun.

It was mentioned earlier that among the bits of clerical debris in the ravaged nave were decapitated oaken candlesticks. Genuinely fond of the old man, who had been kinder to the gypsies than he might have been (if still ineffectual after the manner of his calling), I was afraid that in my present form I might inadvertently do him grievous harm. I leapt away from him and stumbled, the way an overconfident harpy might trip scrabbling after easy quarry. I landed on three of the jagged oaken sticks, and all perforated my side as easily as a skiff goes through water, causing considerable pain and much bleeding. Examining the injuries later, I saw a matter of inches was all that separated me from a mortal hurt, despite my proud boasts of immortality.

Fortunately, thanks to the hellish rattle of my sudden distress, the goodly father did not press his advantage but rather turned and ran from the nave, in a much-quickened variation of his strange and ghostly walk.

Taking the child in my arms, I kissed her tenderly on the forehead a second time. And Reader, I will not turn you away from the real truth of the matter with descriptions of her transformation that are bound to appall you; for she was in all ways beautiful, whatever her form.

Then I heard a sigh behind me, and it was the Roma woman, and she said, "Take me with her. I would rather believe in a demon than in nothing at all."

And so I claimed her. And afterwards, I carried them to the dry well, where they made little cries of "Husband" and "Father" to me, and they trembled in expectation and dread over things forthcoming, whose shape could not be guessed. I bricked them into the ground there for safekeeping, but not before we'd piled their bones on the shattered altar, like relics of a religion yet to come.

PART FIVE:
Scars and Markings

Chapter Forty-Seven

The night quieted as the last dog save one finished his span at the sharp end of a farmer's pike. Bereft of sheep, unsure of their stocks of milk, their barns razed and their bodies mangled by creatures that had lived beside them in peaceable husbandry for decades, the folk took stock of their position. They found it sorely wanting.

As the animals rotting in the streets and burning on makeshift pyres already knew, the first inclination of the town's dread was to attack what was ready to hand in a frenzy of bloodletting. As yet they had but a dim notion of the nemesis arrayed against them, or of measures that might defeat it, and so their savagery was more contained than they might have wished. But the parameters of their awareness were about to shift, bringing hope of fresh carnages to come.

For into the town rode an ancient cleric on a borrowed steed: a donkey stolen hastily from an unattended neighboring plot. Later on, during the brief interval when the townfolk believed their troubles ended as a result of this goodly father, there was disorderly talk of erecting some monument depicting the deliverer's unlikely arrival on ass-back, and comparisons were drawn to the Christ and his affinity for donkey companionship, dating back to the Nativity. But initial impressions of the eccentric, ruddy-faced, and defrocked priest's arrival were that he came to offer much needed levity during dire times, and so he was greeted by anxious townfolk who nevertheless found the intestinal fortitude to laugh at him behind their hands.

All this changed when the priest launched an elaborate and slightly embellished depiction of his encounter in the ruined nave with the Beast of the Woods, and gave them his observations of

213

tested means involving cross, crucifix, and three shafts of oak by which he felt sure they might triumph.

The goodly father could not have done the townsmen more grievous injury if he had arrived on a black horse, breathing fire, and swinging a mile-wide scythe.

Chapter Forty-Eight

Violetta was not disappointed with Donka but with love itself.

Bitter though her track had been, Violetta woke in Donka's arms to realize that she had nourished a single illusion through the famished years: that love, when it came for her, would convert her to something better and make her suddenly new.

Not convert the way her own talents did, outwardly and in a dumb-show spectacle of thunder and blood. No. Violetta had hoped for softer transformations, more lasting and true—for some measure of respite from the aloneness coiled around the impermeable opacity within her.

And so it was with a sense of betrayal that, just before the first light of day, Violetta opened her eyes and greeted not only tender, uncomplicated Donka but also the one person she least hoped to see—herself, essentially unchanged.

Her frustration found voice in the return of her menacing "glak."

"Glak—Is that it then?"

Donka rolled over, heavy with sleep. "What, my love?"

"All this raggle-taggle jingle jangle.—glak—Lives ruined. Temples pulled down, babes put to the sword. Over what? A little spasm."

"It was beautiful," said Donka, imperturbable and coy.

Violetta rubbed her arm anxiously. "Was, was, was!—glak—We live in a world of 'is-es,' missus. 'Is-es' and 'ams,' ma'am.—glak—'Ams' and 'is-es.'" She hugged herself, as if an early frost had blown into the room, presaging a long and frozen winter.

Donka smiled and said nothing—her learned response when people said things that she did not understand.

Outside the window, the cows lowed, and Donka turned toward the grey light, her naked fullness revealed as rumpled bedclothes shifted. This awakened appetites in Violetta, but not for more intimacies. Rather, she felt the hard and forgotten pull of her still unsated craving for "Rusoff meat."

To her credit, Violetta struggled against the animal call to mischief, though her heart thumped and she tasted her own saliva in her mouth.

"We must have breakfast," Donka said. "I'll cook—"

Violetta struck out at the bedpost, at last awakening Donka to her lover's turmoil.

There was a long moment of quiet. "Have I said something wrong?" Donka said meekly.

Violetta ignored her, and would not look on her. "There's nothing here for me to eat," she said quickly, sounding unconvinced. "Glak— I'll take my meal in the town."

There was an expectant silence between them, bridged, if at all, by the affinity between Violetta's solitude and Donka's simple hope that the night had not been an ending but a beginning. Then at last Donka said, "I'll see you off," and they clothed themselves and made their way into the yard.

Had Violetta been a less mottled compendium of impulses, things might have ended there, in a sort of horrific caricature of a not entirely untypical romantic situation. Violetta would not be the first lover to hurry off guiltily once base need was satisfied, and Donka would not be the first maiden of the farms to learn too late to rue the gentle stranger on the road.

But as the moment of parting came, Violetta was conflicted, as she was about all things. For this single night was not the sum of her feelings for Donka. For weeks and from the shadows, she had observed Donka's gentleness with the animals, her patient and diligent management of her property and affairs, her unexpectant pleasure in immediate things. Inside, Violetta's heavy heart cried, "Tell me your secret, gentle lady. For me the world is a cauldron of woe. You walk as if between the raindrops, and I am drowning."

Then reaching into Donka's dreams to see what languished there, she found the Sower—not just an austere vision of gentleness for Donka to cherish in the silent hours, but the very picture of a being in balance, something Violetta herself so yearned to be.

She knew the failure to do so was a lack inside herself.

And so Violetta paused at the gate, still turned toward the road, but saying, "Lady . . . if I have taken something from you, I am sorry."

Donka's forced gayety was pitiable. "Return it to me then, when you pass this way."

Violetta turned toward her but could not raise her eyes. "My path is wayward," she said slowly. "Wayward and unpredictable.—glak— That day may never come."

Then Donka held out her arms, persisting in this posture of openness until Violetta looked at her, and said, "Then I will be the fixed foot of the compass and wait until the circle rounds."

Staring at her accepting lover, Violetta's face grew fierce with— what, despair? Desire? Something forgotten, some item reclaimed or lost?

Or with the unnatural hungers of the Hell I blessed her with?

I cannot know. But crying out as though she could fight some powerful urge no longer, Violetta hurtled toward Donka. And that is where I made my fateful entry into this misbegotten tale.

It had seemed for many days I had become a tree again and would spend all eternity watching for Violetta, and waiting. Then Violetta unlocked the barred door inside herself long enough to let Donka pass, and watchful for my chance, I slipped through and found my way again.

I had been spying on them for an hour, my share in Violetta's sorrow leavened by my fear for the risks innocent Donka faced. For Donka was all love and trust and simplicity, but inside Violetta, I felt the hot hunger redden and glow and rise toward flame.

As she leapt at Donka, I bore down on them from above, crying, "Wife! Stay your hand!" I might have kept them apart, but just then, the forgotten wolfhound Violetta had used as the vessel of her seductions plunged at me from the shadows with a ferocious yowl. Slowed by my injuries from the church, I failed to dodge him, and while the beast kept me but an instant before I crushed him against my chest, it was just enough delay to stay my hand.

Violetta hurled the amazed Donka to the ground, then turned to me, her eyes covetous and yellow. The idealized features of the gentle Sower were blended into something feral and diabolical, as slowly, slowly, Violetta assumed her own still-appalling shape.

"Aaahh—glak—Husband!—glak—So young in expectation, and yet cuckolded—glak—already! See this tender morsel I have found you?"

Donka whimpered. With confused gentleness, Violetta ran a taloned finger through Donka's hair. Then the Sower's noble voice spoke through Violetta a last time, saying, "But how could you not see her? Her beauty is a torch to fire the world."

Then Violetta looked up at me, grinning. "And here you are, my thirsty husband—glak—come to claim your marital share!"

I spoke soothingly, so as not to add to her distemper. "Violetta, this woman has not harmed you. To hurt her would be unholy and wrong."

Violetta laughed. "Unholy.—glak—There's that hesitant priest again.—glak—Wherefore do things like you and I speak of holiness, and you with so much new blood on your fingers?"

Violetta spat, something black and squirming.

"Holiness—glak—" she said dreamily, quietly distracted by Donka's frightened loveliness. "The very word . . . scalds my tongue."

Then Violetta drew a trembling breath and bit down on gentle Donka's pallid shoulder so forcibly that when I could bear to look on it, neither flesh nor bone nor sinew remained.

In that moment that sealed so many of our destinies, I can see everything. The dumb amazement on Donka's face, gouts of her blood on the infertile soil, the docile incomprehension of Cow, Cow, and Cow, the dead hound asleep in gore.

And Violetta lost in the attainment of her carnivore desires, snuffling and chomping, a pig over a slop-bucket, in ecstasy.

I realized then that my gifts are not passed easily like an infection from carrier to carrier, but only through purpose and method or else directly from me. The lore that has accrued down the centuries would have it otherwise, in an improbable mathematics of contagion that, if accurate, should see my like conquer a world in a week.

Would that it was so, but it is not, and here's the proof: bitten with ravenous caprice by Violetta, Donka was dying. And rapidly.

Still she managed words, though the pain it cost her I cannot imagine.

"What, lover," Donka said. "Tired of me already? But didn't I watch the moon rise in your arms? What was all that chaos of bodies and words?"

Violetta's blood-crusted lips shivered when she looked at her, and "Oh! Oh! Oh!" Violetta said. Then taking a form still more hideous, one that was no known animal in this world but perhaps the most reviled of beasts in the next, Violetta shrieked, so loud the cows bolted, and then she disappeared into the wood.

I went to Donka and took her hand. "Donka, your wound is grievous and will do for you soon." Her eyes were already visionless, but she nodded once to let me know she understood.

"We are godless creatures," I said. "We pride ourselves on living beyond the reach of His long grasp. It is a gift to us, but might be a curse to some."

She nodded again.

"I can remove this sentence of death, but the cost is irredeemable. You will slip from God's sight. And the possibilities told of—all those bright fairy tales of angels and trumpets and the Savior's warm embrace—if these things are as promised, they will be lost to you. But if you stay my hand, you will go in moments to learn a thing I can never know, in a place where nothing is certain except that you will never again see the likes of your lover or me."

She shifted, trying to raise her head, though she could not. "What? Never?" she said, quiet but in disbelief. "Never to see my love?"

Donka was a swimmer then, fighting the current that would drag her out so sea, and the agonized war I watched within her as she pit her failing strength against its pull I will not describe for you. But her voice gained strength and conviction as she spoke.

"I would leave my house, forsake my stock and livelihood for those sweet lips. To lay encircled in those bright arms, I would seek my home in the fields and feel sheltered even though skies stormed. I had not searched for such a one, believing the world held nothing for me of more than common value. A God who would part us now, after so much unacknowledged longing, is not to be worshipped but cursed."

And so gentle Donka, who said "yes" to whatever life placed before her, at last found something to defy the world for.

She tasted of the milk that had passed through her hands and the grass her feet had walked on. And afterward she bade me lead her cows to a neighbor's farm where she knew they would be well attended to. We watched them chew the new grass in the rising light, as gentle Donka placidly accepted the changes my kiss brought to her, just as she accepted all things she encountered, save one.

Chapter Forty-Nine

Afterward I took Donka to meet her new family—for family we were, or rather, three children in a nursery watched over by a widowed father. We lived ankle to shoulder, stacked like fruit bats along the overcrowded walls of the dry well, among a rotating population of vermin. As in any brood, each of my globular beauties had a personality to complicate our lives with.

Nastya, the Roma girl snatched so dramatically from the Adversary's grasp, was a fearless adventurer, always ready to plunge. She had not been chastened by her experience of the snake that took her life, but she retained an abiding phobia of slithering things. Petra, Nastya's mother, had been beaten down by the uncertainties of Roma life and the hatred the Roma provoked in the wider population, and so was chronically fearful—a nervous type. This combination of temperaments was touching to observe. Where in life the mother fended for the daughter, those roles were now reversed, the daughter protecting the mother from imagined hurts and slights.

Nastya would pester me with questions night and day:

"Father, why did the snake want to kill me?"

("Because he felt threatened, dear, and there's a lesson in it.")

"How come I can see in the dark now?"

("Why were you taller when you were six years old than when you were five? Some things just are and have no reason. Best not to question it.")

"Will the man who dug this well be mad at us?"

("No, because he didn't want it, so it's ours now.")

"What happened to my real father?"

("Uhhh . . . Petra, Nastya needs a word with you.")

"Father, can we go outside?"

I never had to answer that question, because at the mere mention of the outside world, Petra would blanch and tremble, saying, "Waaaahhh! Don't make me go back out there where all is toil and people are cruel! I want to stay in this hole! Nothing wrong with a nice hole! Why won't you stay with me in my hole?"

Petra would shake feverishly until Nastya came and put arms around her, saying, "It's all right mother, I won't go anywhere without you." And so, one by one, in such little reassurances, a daughter began the lifelong process of repaying a mother's thousand kindnesses.

Donka meanwhile was just plain and simple Donka—patient, serene, accepting of things as they were. She would not even shift in her placement in the well unless given a reason to, and was as content facing the mud as with her back to it.

A typical conversation between the three might go like this:

Nastya: "I wonder if it's raining up there. Do you think it's raining?"

Petra: "Why would you want to know such a thing? We live in a well. Rainwater can seep in and fill it up, and then we'll be cold and damp all the time! Aa-choo! I'm sneezing just thinking about it!"

Donka: "Rain is nice. Dry is nice. Damp is good."

Petra: "Waaaahhhhhh!"

Despite Petra's crying, life in the well gave me needed time for reflection after the mad whirl of recent events. The slow healing of the injuries I received during the priest's attack on me in the shattered nave kept the matter of the oaken candlesticks in my thoughts. Why this strange vulnerability among so many possibilities?

I thought back to the only other injury I'd received since my rebirth, also from oak, when I tore my arm breaking free of my verdant prison to embrace Violetta. Clearly, blending myself with the tree—or breaking my bond with it so violently—had given oak timber potentially murderous authority against me. Discreet experiments made when the girls were resting using other types of wood from the forest showed no additional vulnerabilities.

I worried this weakness would adhere to the others. They were different from me, but also changing rapidly. I kept this worry to myself, but devised a simple test by bringing an oak switch into the well from the forest, and then summoning the girls to my side.

"My darlings, you know your father loves you, don't you?"

To this they could all agree.

"And you know he would never purposefully hurt you, don't you?"

Nastya and Donka nodded yes, though worrisome Petra the Skeptic at first began nodding, then stopped, grew puzzled and said, "Why would he say such a thing to me?"

I reached for Petra quickly, knowing that if she saw the others in discomfort, she was likely to flee. The oak sapling broke the membrane of her forearm as easily and precisely as a pin might have, though she reacted as if I had severed her leg at the knee.

"Owwwww-howwww! He's done it, hasn't he? I've been good! I haven't misbehaved! Why is he trying to kill me?"

Donka and Nastya gathered wondering around the small injury.

"She's bleeding!" said Nastya.

"It's very pretty," said Donka.

Then Nastya put her arm around Petra and held her till she stopped crying. When she had made sure Petra felt loved and secure, she harrumphed, and with a hard question in her scarlet eyes, looked up at me.

"I'm sorry, Nastya," I said.

"You should be!"

"But Nastya, don't you remember, back when Petra was all there was, sometimes, to care for you, she had to do things you didn't like?"

I could see her childish mind struggling to remember her former life, which was returning to her in increments, but remained sketchy.

I steeled myself, knowing the best way I could teach her was to revive an unpleasant memory. "Like on the day of the snake," I said carefully.

She clenched at the word and shuddered. But she didn't panic as I feared she might. She stayed beside me, and kept thinking for me.

"She told me to stay in the wagon," Nastya said slowly.

"That's right," I said. "And you disobeyed her, didn't you? Because you wanted to feel the long grass between your toes."

Nastya nodded guiltily.

"This is like that, my darling. If I'm to protect you, I have to know what I need to protect you from."

There was a wordless interval. Then Nastya held her arm out, and Donka and Petra scurried over to watch as the oak stick gently pierced her, making a small wound from which I delicately pulled it free.

Nastya whispered to Donka, "It doesn't even hurt." And then I noticed that contented Donka was smiling up at me.

"Donka, do you want one, too?"

She nodded vigorously. And so I learned in this amusing way of a mortal peril I had communicated to all three.

My other concern was over my pretty chicks and their appetites. Was Violetta's carnivore taint one of the distortions of her personality, or, like so much else, was it communicated to her through me? Could I expect her "sisters" to follow her wretched example or to stay the endearing little balls of fanged sweetness they were? To avoid the possibility of another escape, I kept the dry well sealed at all times with a stone too heavy for the girls to lift, and waited for some indication.

It came in the following conversation:

Nastya (looking up toward the surface): "I wonder what's out there."

Petra: "Out there! Out there has nothing to recommend it." Then licking her lips, "Except it's where the meat lives."

Donka: "Meat is fine. Meat is good. I am so hungry."

It was one of the quietest conversations they ever had. But Petra's enhanced interest in the outer surface and the fact that Donka had just made an assertion that went beyond the affirming echo of whatever was said to her was like a scream in the enclosed space—a scream for blood.

Three days later I watched sweet Donka, without so much as a change of her blissful expression, break a hapless field mouse's neck and then swallow the creature at a gulp. I knew I would have to solve the problem these nascent urges represented before the girls matured much further. This led to a secondary set of questions:

Why wasn't I similarly hungry? And could my untroubled appetite be expected to last?

Chapter Fifty

And what of Violetta, you may well ask. Didn't I also fret and worry as I had before, and didn't I pursue her?

It is not to my credit to say it, but I did my best to put Violetta from my mind. For the fact is, she had worn out my patience. Her violence, while understandable as a reaction to her earlier circumstance, was not only reckless and destructive but in the end a self-indulgence used to set her needs above the needs of others. For it is a permanent aspect of human relations that the most vivid among us are often allowed too much space on life's stage. Uncomplicated Donka, whose life Violetta almost ended, had as much a right to happiness as she.

I still loved Violetta, but there were three little ones to take care of now, and she had already matured past the point where I could control her, or wished to. I had enough responsibility on my hands. What befell Violetta could no longer be a part of my calculations.

Until one day as I brooded about the future and the girls were keeping still, there was scratching on the heavy stone above us, and I knew it was she.

"Husband!" she said, her speech more human sounding than the last time I'd heard it. "Husband!"

Frightened like kittens by the unfamiliar noises, the girls came to me and buried themselves against my chest. "I am here, Violetta," I said.

"I've no home and no one to love me. Please let me in."

Her fingers scratched like rakes against the boulder, and the long scraping sound caused little bits of dirt to rain down through the dank air.

Despite the pleading in Violetta's chameleon voice, I was not moved.

"Tell me, Violetta," I said. "How have you made your way? Is there a villager left you haven't eaten, or have you given up your interest in 'Rusoff meat?'"

Her voice grew arch, and with the subject turned to eating, little telltale "glaks" found their way into her speech.

"I steal.—glak—Pies left on windowsills. Chickens from the spit. Bread-pans from the oven. I eat cats.—glak—Snatch the ploughman's lunch where he leaves it in the shade. Anything—glak—that goes lost in the town, if it fits in a mouth—glak—that is my handiwork."

Then Donka whispered, "I know that voice."

I hushed her and returned my attentions to Violetta.

"You are reformed, then," I said. "You have curbed your former appetites."

"Aye. Curbed them all but one."

And then Violetta cried, so piteously that the girls started to whimper from terror, or perhaps sympathy.

"She would have waited for me," Violetta said. "And I could have hurried on, and learned myself a little better in life's hard schooling, to become worthy of her devotion."

As if from instinct rather than memory, Donka cried out confusedly, "Sower?"

At the sound of Donka's voice, the transformation in the despairing creature above was startling. Furious wailing, gnashing, and rending seemed to surround us in the echoing pit, and the great stone overhead jumped and danced as Violetta writhed on it and kissed it and swore eternal love to it and hurled her body against it. From the dry well's insecure walls, vast clods of clay peeled away, and I thought Violetta's anguish would bury us.

"What?" she cried, regaining some of her senses. "Carried off? Hidden from my sight? Husband—glak—remove this rock and let me see what fresh horrors you've made!"

Then she threw herself against the unyielding barrier again, and I was a long time waiting for this fresh rage to subside. The girls were terrified throughout, which only strengthened me in my purpose.

"Violetta," I said at last. "The harm done to Donka came from you, as you know better than anyone. Now that Donka is in my care, I won't allow her to become the further object of crazed appetites and pointless wrath."

The pleading came back into Violetta's voice then, and Donka moved against me at the sound of it. "But I am reformed, Husband.—glak—Let me in, and see how mightily I've changed!"

"If you are truly reformed, then set another's happiness above your own. Return to your life among pilfered pie tins and filched cats. If Donka is ever ready for you, I will send her to you."

Then Violetta went silent. But I could sense her sitting on the rock, dazed and blinking, like the traumatized survivor whose house and family have been carried off by a fire, or rising water, and who sits bereft, wondering what to do with the even greater catastrophe of her own unbridgeable solitude.

It was in this protracted stillness that my heart broke anew for her, for I could feel the stratagems that swirled inside her—to beg or threaten, barter or demand, redouble her attack or her pleading. She analyzed every option, knowing none of them would roll the rock back if she were the one on the other side of it.

She was not to blame for who she was, but we live in a world of behaviors, not motivations, and the girls had to be protected from her.

Then Violetta did the most astonishing and unexpected thing she could do. She laughed, as if her many burdens had suddenly grown so light that they floated above her and no longer needed carrying. And in a voice grown girlish, as when I first met her in the woods, she said, "But my love breathes. It breathes!"

And then I heard her lightened step move away from us, but I had no time to reflect on this odd farewell, because Donka was crying, and so required my attentions.

Chapter Fifty-One

I f there was ever an idyll in this gruesome era of my life, it came in the months following this unhappy reunion. The girls grew and became outwardly like idealized versions of the creatures they had been in life, except for a certain suppleness where lack of bone left the joints unsupported. I rolled the stone away from our cramped quarters in the dry well, and we walked again in the upper world. We were careful to stay in places where the woods were so thick I could go about by day without fear of sun sickness (this was not yet a concern for the Women, who were newer in their skins than I was), and where the path-abiding townfolk would also be unlikely to follow. Not far from the dry well, I found the perfect spot: a place where the treetops grew so thick they blocked much of the light and the shade killed off the little growth beneath. This domed clearing became our refuge.

This wholesome interval was made possible because I was able to devise methods for safely slaking the girls' growing appetites. Like a scientist, I performed this wonder by ratiocination, using step-by-step analysis to clip the evil flower of unnatural appetite before it bloomed fully within them.

I felt sure the key to the problem was my own lack of hunger, which, once deciphered, might be communicable, like the other aspects of my gift. And so I retraced everything that had happened since I emerged from my oaken refuge and decided to make my way among more perishable beings.

In all that time, I felt an overpowering echo of Violetta's cravings only once. This was after I slaughtered Rusoff, tasted of him, and then contemplated the town, whose many folk seemed laid out as on a banqueting table before me. Poignantly, it was Violetta, not yet subject to the ravishing impulses that matured within her, who took this dark enchantment off in revealing her altered self to me.

A like occurrence came when I had a more enfeebled sensation of hunger after I returned to the woods from two uninterrupted days searching for Violetta in the town. This impulse was easily subdued and could not have overtaken me.

One logical explanation for my satiation since was that, unlike Violetta and the girls, I had feasted repeatedly. First Rusoff, then Violetta, then each of them in turn had been meal to me. If this were the answer, my present equilibrium wouldn't continue indefinitely. My appetite would waken soon, and I shuddered, thinking of Violetta and reflecting on what the urge to gorge myself might bring to the surface.

I catalogued the other characteristics that made me distinct from my charges. Foremost was the odd manner of their gestation—the skin and organs inverting themselves, the livid shedding of red-hot bone, and then the compaction of their bodies, until they became like reversed travesties of an unformed babe, kicking and twitching in its mother's womb.

It made a certain sense for a still-forming creature to assume this shape, and I had also observed that in many ways, Violetta's skills as a changeling were more undisciplined than my own, though I was in all ways by far the stronger being. Perhaps the absence of inelastic bone gave Violetta added flexibility, while my vigorous and still-living skeleton gave greater potency to me.

The other distinction between us was my span living with Brother Willow and Sister Pine in our foliated cloister. At least one vulnerability from this time had passed to the girls through me. But were there also uncommunicated benefits accrued from my time in the forest as Father Tree?

I had the answer then, and it was so simple I was surprised to have squandered a night in thinking on it. For Reader, never let yourself believe that the gentle forest doesn't sup on dust and charnel, like you and me. Down in the moist soil, where long roots dig and thrive, whole cemeteries of bugs and worms and larger creatures are dissolved into fertile muck, to be reborn as leaf and flower. This marvelous resurrection is all the more a wonder for being so common as to go unremarked upon. The very ordinariness of the rooted world's many splendors blinds creatures that crave sensation from seeing them. And so we come to another of man's limitations.

Both times when carnivorous hunger wakened in me, I had left the forest for the town—in the initial instance, for the first time since taking up my rooted vow, in the second, after I left the forest for an uncommonly long span. And so I realized: my proximity to the forest soil where I once rooted and branched was what slaked me, and this was a skill the girls could assume by their first act of transformation, as soon as that power was available to them.

So with the patience all parents must know, I taught the girls a game to take their minds off their stomachs: how to root themselves in the earth like a sapling and turn their leaves to the sky. To avoid introducing fresh difficulties, we limited this exercise to imitations of the oak, and watching them assume the shape that had been my refuge was like seeing an old friend. The forest performed its tranquilizing magic, and the girls emerged momentarily serious from each glimpse of the eternal their oaken selves afforded them. The nourishing earth helped in their growing, until they were two women who called me "Husband" and a radiant girl who called me "Father," and they no longer needed to metamorphose to sustain themselves, for their bare feet took nourishment directly from the ground they walked on.

And so unknowingly, in this gentle way, I bequeathed to my darlings a second potentially fatal vulnerability.

Chapter Fifty-Two

There came a day, as I knew there must, when a pair of yellowish eyes made themselves known to me. They were as large and lidded as a camel's, but they peered at us on independently maneuverable stalks, like an insect's. This allowed the improbable creature connected to them to survey Nastya, Petra, and myself with the left eye, while keeping the right one trained on the true object of its interest, which was Donka.

I felt an odd surge of paternal emotion as I walked over to the log where Donka sat, patiently appreciating the industry of some ants.

"Husband," she said as I approached.

"And I will continue to call you Donka, so my three girls don't become like Cow, Cow, and Cow to me."

Donka laughed, always bemused by references to her former life. Then she grew serious.

"Your four girls, you mean."

"You see her then?"

"Oh, yes." She flushed a bit, and I realized she had been trembling since I approached her.

"And you know who she is?"

"Of course I do." Her eyes held me steadily at last. "Love of her was the reason I came with you."

"She's only just started watching us. If you'd like I could—"

I had expected some astonishing display on Donka's part, but I was the startled one as she threw her head back, roaring so loud with laughter that Nastya and Petra came over to share in the joke.

"All this leisure is making you indolent, Husband. It's near a fortnight since those motley patchwork eyes began watching me."

She laughed again at my embarrassment over my lapsed watchfulness. I turned to Petra and Nastya. "Did you know this?" They nodded and giggled. "I wanted to go play with it," Nastya said, "but mother wouldn't let me."

Then gentle Donka touched my hand. "It's how I know she's harmless now, Husband. Had she been a threat to any of us, you would have seen her right away."

I sighed. "Well, now that I have spotted her, what do you want me to do about it?"

Donka stood, with an imperious decisiveness I would not have thought her capable of. "You can tell her I'll be walking by the brook in an hour's time, and that she can accompany me if she agrees to stay silent, walk no closer than twelve lengths behind me, and vacate my presence when I turn back toward this place."

I was abashed by Donka's uncharacteristic firmness of purpose and said, "Is there anything else, my liege?"

"Yes," Donka said. "No more masks. Man, woman, or fish, let her come to me as she is, not as she thinks I would like her to be." Her eyes flashed. "You can use the hour I've given to settle the matter or to drive her off for good if she doesn't agree."

Chapter Fifty-Three

It's one of life's little tricks that passionate fealties mark us permanently but are based in situational intimacies. What child doesn't find a "best friend forever" living in some neighbor's house by the age of three? How many moonstruck lovers have taken a knife to a tree-trunk to memorialize connections that will outlast the stars?

The child matures, the neighbor family moves away, one of the pair of lovers grows fickle and finds some other knife, some other tree. But down the days, under the right moon, or overhearing a certain kind of childish laughter, each partner will remember the one lost to it, sometimes in pain, sometimes with a smile. The names carved on our hearts are more stable even than forests; while we abide, they endure.

So it was between Violetta and me.

My love for her did not wane, nor had the less wholesome stimulus of my pity. It was an accident that saw me bring her into the world; by an accident I became her confessor of the woods; an accident made her the first to follow me across the parched but liberating landscape that led us both away from the Adversary. All her life, we had bumped against each other like battling puppets, until our bruises made it impossible for us to touch. But I never lost my feeling for her, and I know she never lost her feeling for me.

So it was with trepidation, but also with genuine affection, that I approached her among the weeds where she'd hidden herself. I found her gnawing on a dead stump in nervousness, her great arachnoid mouth spitting splinters and larvae at my feet.

"So, Husband! You've found me out at last." It was the voice I remembered from our final days in the forest, the voice of Violetta, grown old.

"Yes, Violetta. How have you been keeping yourself?"

She laughed tiredly. "Not well, I'm afraid, as you can see. My mind wanders, and I find it hard to take a pleasing shape or even remember what pleases anyone who isn't me. Is this form beautiful? It lets me scurry and watch, and the meat I crave when I wear it allows me to avoid the town, which is murderous and has grown tired of me."

"And what of Violetta? Do you remember what she looked like?"

"Oh, yes," she said, her great wings chirping in agitation. "She was quite the ugliest of the bunch until I made modifications. Would you like to see?"

The long stalks retracted and eyes blinked in her head again. Black fluttering wings became pallid arms, and Violetta—my young and beautiful Violetta—was before me.

The modifications she spoke of were plain enough: her face, her arms, and all the skin she showed me was cross-hatched with thin, patiently applied scars, like the markings on a badly plowed field.

I took her hand. "How—Why would you do such a thing?"

"I learned it accidental. I was carrying off a pig when the pig farmer spied me. He didn't run like they all do, but drew a bow and held his ground. 'Oh ho, little man,' I said, using my most terrifying voice, 'brave or foolhardy, but either way you bleed. Reconsider the game. The play is not by hands but by feet.' His arm shook but he released the arrow—it was the shaking saved me. It split my shoulder, and it lodged there. I have it here."

She held it out to me.

"An oaken shaft."

"It was," she said. "Indeed."

"What happened to the farmer?"

"I would have killed him. Ohhhhhh, I wanted to.—glak—He was plump and tanned and would have tasted sweet."

"What stayed your hand?"

She smiled at me, her eyes moistening, as if I should have known the answer. "Promises," she finally said. "And anyway, it was a boon. It gave me a way to mark the absences, day by day. And running out of pelt to scratch, I returned."

"Donka is not as she was," I said.

Violetta's breath caught and she gripped my fingers, afraid I'd come to send her away. "She will see you," I said hurriedly to dispel her fear, "but has conditions."

Violetta nodded.

"You must not speak to her. You must walk behind, not nearer than twelve lengths. You cannot return with her to this place when she decides to leave. And you must come to her as you are now, not in a shape invented to please her."

Violetta listened to the terms with eager assent until this last, and then she moaned wretchedly. "But I have marred myself for love of this girl. What chance do I have to be near her, looking like this?" And in the twinkling of an eye, she was the Sower again, but with the agitated mien and voice of Violetta. "Please let me go to her in the form she dreamed."

"She will not have you under any other terms. I'm to send you off forever if you don't agree."

Violetta groaned, seeing no choice. "And ten paces behind. You said ten paces, yes?"

"I said twelve lengths."

Grumbling nervously, Violetta agreed.

What followed was the strangest courtship I will ever witness. Donka went for her walks by the brook, day after day, with the expression of someone who daydreamed in her solitude. Behind her, at the edge of the proscribed distance, monstrous Violetta, a monster no more, walked with such diligent concentration on silence and furlongs it was comical to see.

Violetta didn't speak, though she seethed with the desire to do so. And though her yearning to caress Donka was palpable, she did not draw close. Indeed, to my eye, she maintained a slightly greater separation than required of her, so as not to violate terms accidentally.

On the first day, when Donka turned back toward the place where we were waiting for her, Violetta shivered in a momentary fright that the verdict had gone against her and this was all of Donka she would see. As if noticing Violetta's discomfort, Donka hesitated in departing. Then she voiced the only words she said that day, still without looking at Violetta.

"Eleven tomorrow."

And when the puzzlement on Violetta's self-scarred face turned to rapture as she realized this was not an hour of the clock or some strange numerological comment but an instruction about the narrowing of the expanse that would walk between them the next day, I confess I turned away to mask an emotion I didn't want Nastya to see.

She saw it anyway, of course, my evasion drawing her to me.

"Is everything all right?" she asked.

I gathered her in my arms. "Don't worry, little one. Everything is just as it should be."

PART SIX:
Across a River

Chapter Fifty-Four

I spoke true, but only of matters within our strange little family. Violetta's arrow could have been a fortunate chance for the farmer, but I doubted it. His odd combination of craven and brazen behavior made the choice of wood seem considered. This meant we would have to avoid the town. But my blundering had made it all but impossible for us to leave.

The oak is a mighty but particular piece of vegetation. Finding favorable soil, it's the strongest and most thriving tree in the forest. But transplanted elsewhere—even as a sapling—it dies, unable to accept the smallest variation in the loam it nourishes itself by.

My precious ones and I were bound to the limits of this forest as surely as if enchanted to stay within it. We would feel its soil between our toes and stay peaceable, or else take our chances elsewhere in the multisurfaced world, with its swarming supplies of "Rusoff meat."

Still there was room for optimism. Violetta had abandoned the hundred petty torments she inflicted on the town after her injury, and her campaign of pilfering and pranks was stopped months ago, if the teeming scratches she marked the days by were reliable indicators. The townsfolk weren't aware of the other women, thinking of them, if at all, as carried off and devoured. And human eyes had not seen me since I encountered the old priest in the shattered nave.

Distilled to its essence, our security depended on one simple question: were the villagers plotting against us, or were they satisfied they'd driven us off?

The pig farmer who shooed away Violetta was a man of standing in the community, not prone like some to swagger and boasting. There was persuasive evidence of the truth of his account. The halfcaten pig in his yard spoke for him, as did scorch marks on a fencepost where boiling blood from the Beast of the Woods had scalded it.

In the days that followed, what remained of the villagers' livestock stayed grazing in their plots. Unattended stewpots behaved themselves, their fatted meats and boiled carrots lingering long enough to disappear down farmers' throats at suppertime. The folk's troubles seemed ended, and they could be content.

But they were too conditioned by listening for monsters not to hear them. Every dog that howled, each wheel that broke against a rock in the road, every worn out crone who took to her bed and didn't rise again, all was evidence that subtle forces still ranged against them.

His counsel vindicated, the old cleric was now a hero of the town. His lordly airs, which had been mocked for years, suited his new station. Indeed, some now thought him a modest man, given his manifest greatness.

Aware a man of his years had just a little time to consolidate these gains, the cleric didn't rest on his laurels. Reinstated by acclamation to his priestly role, this noble father used the pulpit to reawaken his flock to the corruption he'd always seen in them, inveighing at every opportunity against invisible snares.

"The body," he said, "is a stinking pit the soul stands mired in. Look to the Lord's example: penned inside a festering cistern of blood and meat, He did not resist the cruel Roman hand that would release Him, but welcomed it. In so doing, He alone gloried over the stinking animal His noble spirit was fastened to. His life passed in perfection, uncorrupted by things of the flesh, unblemished in its purity.

"How many of you in the town can say the same? How many of you can pass from one sun to another without a daily lechery? We assemble here, here in this holy sanctuary. I look out from this godly perch, and what do I see? With the words of Our Lord on their lips, young men turn to glimpse at preening girls, the one pretending it's not a mound under a dress caught his eye, the other demurring, as if she doesn't welcome such attentions.

"The gluttonous lose their place in the psaltery, dreaming of dinner. The greedy reach into the tithing basket and jingle the coins it holds with a clenched and empty hand for appearance sake. And this is only what I see, with my failing eyes. How much more relentless is the unblinking eye of God?"

Then, pounding the pulpit with his hand, he moved on to the theological implications of the Beast of the Woods, where his expertise was unquestioned.

"The unnatural occurrences of these past months are a punishment and a manifestation. You conjured this demon, not some witch whose bones you burned. With every covert leer and night-soiled sheet, each slothful impulse that slowed you on your way to the fields, by every inattentive moment of your wholly distracted lives, you built this monster, limb by limb, and brought it among us.

"Some of you breathe safe now, because this thing has stopped stealing your table settings. Fools! Your stolen souls he will not relinquish. And while he lives, his sins accrue to your immortal part, blackening it. His every corruption corrupts each of you, and salvation is dead to you."

Under the constant pressure the priest's oratory exerted on popular opinion, it was only a matter of time before a volunteer militia took to the fields, armed with oaken swords, staffs, and pikes, and with arrows like the one that proved so successful in routing Violetta. By ingenious means, they blended with resin the pulp and oak dust left over from the manufacturing of their weapons, and painted ropey fibers, making nets they hoped might snare the Beast.

For his demonstrated courage, the pig farmer was made captain-of-the-guard.

The fight, the townfolk all agreed, needed to be taken to the enemy.

Chapter Fifty-Five

On the day when two lengths of distance between them was to be reduced to one, Donka skipped over the last stage of the ritual, taking Violetta by the hand and saying, "Well done, my love." They walked arm in arm for hours then, talking so quietly no one else could hear them, and in this way they were healed.

They separated themselves from us after that, but we still saw them regularly, and when I imagine their life together, I hear a glory of sighs.

Meanwhile Petra had adjusted fully to her new state, and resumed her mothering responsibilities. A good thing, too, because energetic Nastya remained both a frustration and a delight. Our admonitions to stay away from the town only made her more curious about it. As a Roma girl, she'd ranged with her people, and had no impression of village life. Petra would pantomime a snake's fangs with her fingers to persuade Nastya that the village wasn't a place where she'd be welcomed, and Nastya always shuddered, and always acquiesced.

One evening, Petra started to build a fire. We had no need of it, as we felt discomfort neither from warmth nor cold. But autumn was coming down on us by then, a time of migration for her people, and some nostalgic impulse drove her to seek the torch's sheltering crack and roar.

The common hearth is where the Roma's history is preserved. Aloud, the tribe remembers its kings and knaves, tells tales of witchery and folly, and passes on anecdotes of the family dead.

We were all gathered—Violetta resting against Donka, who stroked her hair; Nastya, picking at dirt and covertly kicking bugs and dry leaves into the blaze to watch them spark and burn; myself, patiently moving the logs to keep the fire lively; and Petra, whose sad eyes stared into the flames, but saw something more distant.

Then Petra started to sing, solemnly at first but with gathering emotion, a song in her native tongue. Nastya, the only one among the listeners who understood the words, stopped fussing and put her arms around her mother, quietly singing along. Though the lyrics were enigmatic, the longing Petra communicated stirred inside me, and in the others, because it was already a part of us all.

Petra sang for her own people but also for all the dispossessed who travel unmarked roads. She sang of the abandoned and the forgotten, of trackless deserts only partially traversed. The slap of the reigns, the turning wheel of the horse cart, tired hooves pounding the endless dust, the fluttering of scarves wound around nose and mouth to keep out the choking sand, the twitching of the driver's eye as it nervously scans the horizon for some sign of water—all these hovered above the fire in Petra's voice, like a vision of a past or a destiny.

I looked at their faces. Donka and Violetta, who had found a home in each other. Nastya and Petra, whose bond had transcended death itself. And me, more alone than the others perhaps, but in my way, bridegroom to them all.

Stateless ourselves, we pulled closer to the burning kindling, and I wondered again if the time was approaching for our own exodus to lead us all home.

Chapter Fifty-Six

Catastrophe, when it came, proved an able tactician. It struck at us through the one least able to defend herself.

We didn't sleep, but we did have periods of stasis where we were more vulnerable. With the town's intentions toward us unclear, I grew concerned. Rather than recline on the unprotected grass, I dug additional catacombs into the dry well and insisted to Petra and Nastya that we take our comfort there.

Nastya the adventurer complained bitterly. "There's nothing down there but dirt and bugs," she said. "Up here we have dirt, bugs, trees, grasshoppers, squirrels, rabbits, thorn-bushes, toads, wild-flowers . . . ."

I let her go on like this for some time.

Finally out of breath, she said, "Aren't you going to stop me?"

"But it's so educational. I had no idea this forest contained trees."

Nastya had been a good girl for a long time. She never lost her curiosity about the town, but she also never went near it. It was only when the town came to us that she couldn't resist taking a look. For one day, in late afternoon as the sky edged toward twilight, vibrations in the ground roused us in the dry well: slow hoof-beats and the churning of laden wagons. As these dull thumps and mechanized squeals grew closer, lesser noises differentiated themselves—booted human footsteps, and swords and scythes chopping at brush.

There were too many of them for me to read them all clearly, and they were diffuse in their thinking. Some of them were hungry. Some thought of women. What came through strongest in the jumbling of impressions was that they were all frightened, and they were all bored.

Being Roma, Nastya knew the sounds the intruders made. She turned to her mother and made an exclamation of recognition that was immediately silenced. Nastya quieted, but there was puzzled yearning in her expression. These were the noises of home.

The interlopers hacked their way into the domed clearing that was our sanctuary. Then their wheels stopped and I heard excited shouting, and suddenly their minds sharpened and were considering only one thing.

I knew I needed to get close enough to ascertain their plans.

It wasn't exactly a camp the villagers found. There were no signs of appetites slaked or bodily needs met—no compost, no chicken bones, nobody had dug a latrine. There was indeterminate evidence of foot tracks, but there were no bedrolls or canvas tents. Still, as they carved their way into the remote and gloomy clearing, their huntsmen's eyes immediately sensed a disturbance.

The rocks weren't right, for one thing. Nastya had turned most of them over to see what lived beneath them, and many of the stones were moss-side up. After much cajoling and wheedling from Donka, Violetta was learning to be an earth-eater, but she still lived on bugs and grub-worms when she came back to us, so several stumps bore deep scratches and chew marks, like they'd been attacked by a monstrous bear.

Then the villagers found something they could easily understand. It was weeks old and had consumed itself almost completely. In a cluster of rocks where the enormous creature they thought they pursued might have set up his kitchen, they found unmistakable evidence of a campfire.

This meant a creature of industry and intent. Coupled with the other oddities, they knew they were on the right track.

All eyes turned to the pig farmer. With perhaps an hour or an hour and a half of sunlight left to them, there were critical decisions to be made. Did the evidence suggest the monster once camped here, or perhaps that he still did? (The consensus leaned toward the former.) Should they set a trap, post a guard, or return to the town with their findings while the sky was still light? (The consensus leaned heavily toward the latter.)

I watched their deliberations from a carefully chosen branch where the sun couldn't find me. The pig farmer took his command authority with utmost seriousness. He pointed out that the moon was waning, and this meant the Beast of the Woods would be in a weakened condition. Also, they'd had a dry, hot summer, so the Beast's coat would be thinner and easier for them to pierce with their special-made weaponry. On the other hand, they'd made three left turns in the woods today finding this place, and that argued against staying, as the Beast could benefit from their carelessness. So there were many factors for him to consider, and he was not about to have such an important decision rushed.

And then Nastya was in the domed clearing, asking these men in her language why they'd come and were they Roma, and everything afterward is a blur of movement and tragedy.

Chapter Fifty-Seven

Here's what had happened. When the wheels of the villagers' wagons rolled by, the moist clay in the newly dug catacombs began to shift from the tremors. After I went out to get a look at the trespassers, there was a minor mudslide at the far end of the tunnel—a very loud noise, falling from above into the far edge of our quarters. Petra feared a reconnaissance party might have stumbled on an unprotected entry point. Assuming a fearsome aspect, she admonished Nastya to stay as she was, and went to take a look.

But Nastya heard the call to adventure. These were men in wagons. Maybe they were Roma. Or maybe they would tell her about the town; she was forbidden to go there, but surely not forbidden to hear about the goings on in such a place.

So she clambered out of the dry well with an outlook of absolute trust and went out to meet pack animals far deadlier than any snake.

Having heard the priest's story ad nauseam, these men knew of the angelic Roma girl the Beast had carried away. They immediately assumed Nastya was the precursor to some kind of an attack, and they formed up into two ragged and confused units of twelve men each, scanning the area for other signs of movement and drawing their weapons on Nastya, who gave a little scream of fright.

There was still too much sunlight in the clearing for me to attack without consideration. In the millisecond while I calculated the distances from shade to shade, a deafening roar filled the air, and Violetta reared out of the brush and charged the villagers, armored in scales and claws.

When I recall that moment, I see the villagers' lines quiver and break as Violetta runs at them, the cowards of the group making themselves known in the usual way. Two have the presence of mind to make a run at Nastya using their netting imbued with wood pulp. The rope holds as it grabs her, yanking her off her feet, and deep scratches appear on Nastya's skin where the chord chafes as they carry her off.

Violetta roars toward the child and into range of the villager's first line of defense. Of the eight or so men who have held the attack stance, three are archers. Two of them fire wide, but the pig farmer is unwavering this time. His oaken shaft finds its mark.

Then, without so much as another sound, Violetta is tumbling toward them, and her body is skidding on the ground and going still. With a sigh of air, her fearsome form shrivels. It's the arrow-scarred corpse of an old woman that lands at the villagers' feet.

They know her. Violetta, the witch of the woods.

The second line falls on her with oaken swords, in an act of pure butchery.

And now it's my scream and my fearsome shape that drops down on them from above. Where sunlight hits me, I wither and froth. I feel nothing except red rage.

Occupied with their savageries, the swordsmen are too slow to turn. I have them. And oh, Violetta, what a feast they make—of brain and lung and gut, and all the tender visceral sweets you once craved.

The pig farmer is escaping. But Nastya needs me. And though my flesh boils, I hurry into the unforgiving sky.

The men bearing Nastya in their oaken net scurry in terror for the town. They are far out in front of me, but I can have them in seconds. Then the bubbling flesh of my scaled black wings starts to curl in on itself, and the sun in my eyes is like fingers. "Nastya!" I cry as I begin to shudder and fall. "I'm sorry!" And then my eyes are sightless, and I'm crashing through something made of leaves and branches, and it's only the darkness bursting inside my head that stifles my scream.

Chapter Fifty-Eight

Donka watched over me while Petra searched the woods for a safer hiding place. I know this because in my fragmented impressions of the following days, everything occurs to the sound of Donka crying. Hands lifted me, and the cooling touch of the soil was there when I was set down again. Otherwise, the time passed mostly as a slowly repeating phantasm of torn limbs and Violetta's face, of Nameless bleeding his life away while Anya melted with a crackle of grease and entrails and passed like water through my shuddering arms.

I would find on waking it had been a more eventful period for Nastya.

When Nastya finally got to see the town, she was wrapped in rope and spitting like a cornered cat. The oaken threads wound around her had done their work—abraded and torn, she quieted considerably once the men got a chord wound around her head and throat. Before then, she'd managed to bite two of their party, and they were amazed to see wounds considerably more serious than should have been possible coming from such doll-like teeth.

The pig farmer had Nastya inverted and trussed like dead game beneath an oaken staff. Then weeping and licking their wounds, the survivors of the town's ill-starred expedition against the Beast of the Woods carried Nastya into the makeshift church, where the priest waited to receive her.

It's important for us to ask at just this moment: Who is this inconstant prelate and why does he assume so many guises in our story?

First as preening pontificator over the marriage of a rapist to his victim. Next as a seraph of compassion, battling the Angel of Death for the life of an outcast child. Then as the flame-belching sermonizer and hater of the body. And now? Now we will see what cruelties he has in him in the name of defending his God.

In truth, this priest is an unexceptional and perennial type. What links all the steps he's danced for us is one thing: his absolute certainty that he's in the right. Even at his most sympathetic, praying the first time over prostrate Nastya, he had no doubts about the futility of his actions. Like all priests, he's a veteran of a thousand such farewells and knew at a look the girl was past saving. His function as he understood it was to plead for a miracle, ask for God's mercy on Nastya's soul, and be sporting in accepting God's decision in the matter. And so the death of a child—an event that might have shattered the faith of a different man—only strengthened him in his certitude, though it also touched his heart.

Certitude is an extremely powerful energy in the world. It is decisive, because it has already made up its mind. It is persuasive, because its points are bluntly expressed and passionately held. And it's brutal, because it owns the One Truth, and the One Truth must be protected from the universal error of other human beings.

How easy it is for the certain man to win arguments against the faltering stammerers who try to voice the muck and noise of reality as it actually is. What a trifle it is for the certain man to build followings among those like himself who want the explanations for life's buffeting complexities to be simpler and more consoling.

The slippery slope the highly certain man slides down is that he can end up finding beauty in his most heinous acts. He wades through blood and never sees the red stuff come up to his belly, because his eyes are aimed at a higher place.

So it was with this good cleric, as certain a man as ever breathed. Still, if you had seen him perform the daily duties that were his primary station in life—presiding over baptisms, consoling the grief-stricken, cajoling donations of alms for the poor—you would know him in most moments as a man at least as good as you or me. Immovable certainty didn't make this cleric's motivations evil, nor all his actions.

Only some of them.

When he saw it was Nastya they brought before him, the priest rubbed his eyes as if wiping away sleep. "I couldn't save you," he said. "Apparently, the Lord was displeased by that ending and has written us another."

He reached toward Nastya, intending to stroke her hair—

"Watch out, sir. She bites," the pig farmer said. "One of my men's half bled." The cleric removed his hand.

He turned to the pig farmer. "Can she speak?"

"No, sir," the pig farmer said, and he grinned. "Muzzled like a strong-willed cur with that rope around her throat."

"Loosen it then."

"Not me, sir. But I'll aim an arrow at her heart while you do it."

The priest reached for the chord.

Little Nastya didn't recognize the old cleric, but she was learning things—oh, how she was learning things—under the stress and hardship of captivity. Blood, for example. She never knew blood was so savory. She'd bitten the first bearer because he was careless and she could twist and get her teeth into him and then, oh! what was that feeling in her stomach? Like how she imagined it after you stuffed yourself with roast pig the way she was sure town people got to, though the Roma never did. So she bit the second bearer and he was even better because she was ready for it this time, the little "snap" of his skin against her teeth, the rum pum pum of the red stuff, pulsing with life as it ran into her mouth.

She was learning how to hear, too, and it was like she never had ears before. She was anxious and she was scared and she was looking from face to face, wishing she knew what they wanted to do. And then she *did* know; not as words or pictures but like she was thinking it herself, or could remember thinking it. Most of the men's minds were dull and unfocused. It made her sleepy to listen to their thoughts. But the priest surprised her. His brain was as orderly as the *synthronos* (what are *synthronos*) in a church (but I've never been in a church, oh yes you have, oh yes you have . . .).

Oh yes, she had been in a church! With the priest the night she died! She remembered it all now, or at least she remembered his memory of it. She could see herself in the nave, her breathing slow and getting slower. The way she looked as she started to die.

Then she had a memory of words the priest said before, when she was too sleepy to hear them: "Perhaps God wanted his little angel back." And she knew how she could defeat him.

His hand came so close, she could have had the whole thing in her mouth before anyone could stop her. But she knew what was in the pig farmer's thoughts, too; he was sorry they brought her back, and was hoping for any excuse to let fly. She let the cleric loosen the rope and pretended to be grateful, even when he pulled on it to make her look at him.

"Well?" he said. "Have you any account to make of yourself?"

Then Nastya's eyes welled and she was a little girl again, saying, "Bless me, Father, for I have sinned" and other things she overheard in his thoughts. And she begged them not to hurt her, and she cried "Our Father, who art in Heaven," and she cried. "Be ye therefore followers of Christ as dear children," and she cried. "Mary, Mary, Holy Mother, pray for us sinners, pray for us sinners, pray for us all."

Though the Bible words weren't hers, she meant every one of them. She was scared, and all of a sudden she didn't like what was happening to her. She didn't like that she could hear people thinking or that she enjoyed the taste of blood.

Hers was an honest cry for mercy.

When Nastya had finished, she could see they were moved, the old priest most of all. He looked at the others.

"Do you see," he said, brushing back a tear, "what stratagems the devil will use against us?"

And then he pulled on the rope so hard that Nastya's tongue was sticking out through her teeth and she could feel her own blood flowing down her neck. It hurt so badly that she hoped she was dying but instead she just went to sleep.

Chapter Fifty-Nine

Petra brought Nastya's body home to us, torn and broken and frayed and still. She had wrapped her daughter's corpse in a blanket and cleaned the blood off the child's face. Nastya looked peaceful, and so like a baby that Petra sang lullabies to her and rocked her as if she was sleeping.

I'd been unconscious for three days. Enough time for a season to change. For two lovers to meet, exhaust their passion, and grow cold to each other. Enough time for an ocean to wipe away a city.

Enough time for the end of a world.

"What happened?" I said.

Petra indicated she wanted me to touch Nastya's face, and I did so, shivering at its coolness to the touch. She reached around her daughter, taking me by the hand. Then Petra released the memories Nastya had captured from the town before she died, and given to her mother for safekeeping.

Nastya was put on display. The townfolk were brought to the secret sacristy where at first they kept their distance from the tightly bound and frightened little girl, making signs of the cross so the demons inside her wouldn't climb in through their eyes as they looked at her. This soon proved tedious, and so they went out into the street and gathered stones to hurl at her, increasing Nastya's terror but having no physical effect—a sure sign, all agreed, that Nastya was Evil given a deceptively innocent form.

They all knew oaken things were charms against these creatures. A secondary tradition already had it that this was because the Savior's Cross was made of oak, though where the Romans came by that wintry wood in Palestine, the tradition didn't say. The town did what any frightened people would have done with this information. They stockpiled oak objects of every scale, shape, and type, causing a five-times run up in the value of bowls, doorframes, bedposts, commodes—anything at all carved from the holy lumber.

When the rocks taken from the road failed to injure Nastya, some of the goodly folk saw an opportunity for a return on their investment in timber. Soon the streets were full of children, running home on their parent's orders to get a few small objects that might be of use.

All the while the old priest performed unfamiliar rituals full of references to blood and feasting. There were archaic tortures, using thorns and nails, and grisly talk of animal sacrifice, and a lamb whose blood covered the whole world. In perfumed language, their Deity was slaughtered, taken away and returned to them, and then broken into bits for them to feed on. And their God reveled in it, saying, "Eat, for this is my body" and "Drink, for this is my blood."

They formed little lines to get their teeth and tongues into the things they worshipped, and thereby to become more like those things themselves. Then the children returned from kitchens and stables with pieces of oak that were sharp or heavy or hard, and the townfolk stood over Nastya until one of them made a guttural cry that was a kind of signal, and then they—

"Something else," I said, pulling away. "Please. I can't bear it."

And Petra, who was crying too, took my hand.

The old priest wouldn't let Nastya die.

When the initial burst of savagery subsided, he reprimanded the mob for their indiscriminate violence. "This isn't a carnival," he said angrily. "There's a soul trapped inside that thing. The Lord won't get the pearl of great price if you kill the oyster while it's still in its sins." He confiscated some of the more barbaric implements, banished a few over-enthusiastic congregants from seeing Nastya again, and for the next two days, instituted a policy that limited the mob's access to a few morning hours, where they would approach the girl in pairs and only torment her under his watchful supervision.

Between these sessions of public edification, the priest spent hours alone with Nastya. He prayed over her and cleansed her wounds by hurling buckets of water at her from across the room, so as to avoid coming within reach of her teeth. In this way, he maintained his own image of himself as a merciful man.

The priest never once indicated to Nastya what was expected of her. The closest he came was on the third day, after her beating at the hands of the town. He looked at her and said in a quizzical way, "It might help if you accepted our Lord into your heart."

And Nastya, in every way she could, being bound and with the cutting rope laid tight against her neck, signaled her assent, as she would have assented to anything under similar circumstances.

The old priest smiled sadly. "Too easily won," he said. Then he seemed to give up on her, blew out the candles, and left her there, alone in the dark.

Chapter Sixty

Nastya felt the darkness as a current of rolling water, as her mother's arms, a womb. *When was the last time I felt so safe?* she thought. *It must have been years ago, in a field of flowers.* She lay there and sent her mind to a place where the pain couldn't follow, and then waited for nightfall.

At evening, she found the priest again, readying himself for bed. He had spent much of his day in prayer over Nastya, but such was the precision of his thinking and his devotion to routine that he didn't skip over the additional prayer he had offered up nightly for fifty years, which was for the souls of his flock, and in that way a generosity.

Then, worn out by cares of the day, he fell quickly to sleep.

Nastya gave him the same dream she'd given him for three nights running. It was a simple dream, little more than a repetition of the time they'd spent together that day—the same prayers, the same cruelties. But into the day's events, Nastya wove small indications of the outcome she knew the priest secretly looked for—little moments when the devil he saw when he looked at her was weakened by the cleric's persistence, and the transfigured creature the priest struggled to set free could be glimpsed, thrashing inside Nastya for release. She could have performed these small miracles there in the sacristy when they were alone together, but it was the priest's trust in his perceptions she wanted to make sure of, and she could color these if she brought her marvels to him in slumber.

This third day's dream had a crescendo of such moments, ending in the brave priest risking his own security by gathering the poor tormented and still dangerous girl into his strong arms, then holding her as she vomited up evil things, until they wept together, because, though greatly improved and nearer to God thanks to the priest's ministrations, Nastya was still unclean. In this dream, when the priest left Nastya, he still blew out the candles, but he didn't turn his back on her, defeated. Instead, he said with a breaking voice, "We've done much together. We must put the rest in God's hands."

In the same way Donka dreamed of her Sower, the old priest dreamed of a spectacular affirmation that the cause he spent his life serving wasn't just righteous, but destined to succeed. He had achieved a heroic span of years and grappled with the Enemy as he found him every day, but the world seemed no better. Children still cried for bread, men cheated each other in the marketplace, and when the old man looked his congregants in the eye and gave them the Holy Word, he sensed their desire for the footpath and a return to whatever private depravities awaited them around the dull glow of their own unscrutinized hearths.

It wasn't doubt the old man felt. The Book was the True Way, and he had done right to be its servant. But the Lord was in most ways inscrutable, and though the larger victory was certain, nothing in the Book assured him personally of a satisfactory conclusion. Indeed, the Book said most men were failures in God's stern eyes—had he himself, in any way, succeeded? Had he saved anyone? For surely it wasn't vanity, or not vanity only, to seek some response in a long dialogue where his had been the only audible voice.

Nastya heard these thoughts as if they were her own, and she fashioned a glorious answer. And then, just before daybreak on the fourth day, she took the dreams they'd made together for three days running from the forgotten place inside him where they were waiting for her call, and she replaced actual things with her loving fancies, so the priest would be completely ready to receive the tender gift she'd made for him.

Chapter Sixty-One

The priest awoke to a sound of doves cooing and a scent of hazelwood. The lightness he felt in rising and putting on his black vestments told him how heavy this business of recent days had been. But not this morning. This morning the whole world was bathed in a brightness that seemed to have no source, but to be everywhere, in all things.

As he walked the short distance from his quarters to the sacristy, sharp-leafed cypress trees nodded in greeting at his approach. A tradesman hurried past him, cursing furiously as an ox resisted the bridle. The priest normally would have reprimanded the man for his language, but today he simply admired the purple beast's stoicism, the coarse nobility of the man's thick fingers, the cascading estuaries of cracks and wrinkles on the worn reins. He had business to attend to, but he would have liked to linger, and as he moved on he reflected on how long it had been since he gave himself over to the daily beauty of everyday things.

Reaching for the ironbound door, he heard an unfamiliar sound inside the sacristy, of something struggled against, lifted and then dropped. For some reason he thought of his old church before the Turks razed it, and a pigeon trapped inside the nave who beat himself to death against the ceiling trying to find the sky. Such a sad thought. And yet the priest felt anything but unhappy, for surely the sound in the sacristy was an arrival and meant some kind of a decision was near. Serene against all possibilities, he reached for the door, noticing as he passed over the handle a shaft of key-shaped light illuminating his hand.

The Angel inside the net was so beautiful it took a moment before the priest could speak. Her long limbs seemed to swim against the air under the proud force of her noble wings, and her cascading hair was a softly gleaming corona of Pentecostal light.

She had all but worked herself free of her bonds, and was trying to extract something unmoving from inside the oaken web. It was the sound of this effort the priest heard before entering—the Angel, patiently lifting an object tied to a bench, and then dropping it to the floor when the weight of the furniture proved too much for her.

She stopped when he entered, and he saw the object the Angel sought: the unbreathing body of the gypsy girl.

"How have I come to be here?" the Angel asked.

"It was I who called you," the priest said, partially averting his eyes.

The Angel genuflected, and the elderly cleric found himself fighting back tears.

"What do you remember?" he asked her.

The absolute stillness of her exquisite face seemed to cloud imperceptibly. "A place black and sulfurous. Tittering beasts that struck at me and bound my hands. My wings shorn, and pains across my body. And worst of these, an absolute loneliness—the knowledge that I was in the one place where even God would never find me."

The Angel touched the priest's cheek, so gently it was like her hand wasn't there, saying, "But one kept searching." Then she pushed off with her wings and hovered above the still form of the gypsy girl, laughing. "And was that all that confined me? That handful of sand?"

"That," the priest said, "and the swamp she was well mired in."

"Come help me lift her," the Angel said merrily. "I will have need of that modest shape again when the Last Trumpet sounds." Then the knots seemed to melt between the priest's fingers, and the Angel lifted the girl as if she carried a petal or a leaf.

She turned to the priest in the act of her going. "And thou," she said, "oh good and faithful servant. What of thee? What recompense, beyond the eternal one already owed?"

The priest wept. "I am not worthy of this moment. Your shining presence has been reward enough."

The Angel's smile was like all the good things the priest had ever known—the swish of his mother's dress when she held and powdered him, the honest warmth of baked bread, the weight of the Book in his hand. Faces came to him that he had known and loved but that had hurried on before him, and they didn't seem far away any longer, but as close as a sunrise or twilight.

The Angel spoke, saying, "Well said, good father, and for your humility you are instructed that your good work is completed. For from this day, you will take your place at the right side of the Father, and await with the Angels the completion of His divine plan."

And then the Angel held out her hand.

They were flying high above the village when the Angel asked the priest if he had anything on his conscience that he wanted to make right before he arrived in the presence of the Lord. The Angel waited patiently as he made his confession. It was a short one, though closely observed, as the priest was in the habit of meticulously unburdening himself at the end of each day, and this day had had an auspicious beginning.

When the priest finished praying, the corpse of the gypsy girl in the Angel's other arm opened its eyes, which were filled with compassion. "I'm sorry," Nastya said. "I wanted you to see Heaven just the way you've dreamed it, but I don't think I can carry you any farther. They've hurt me so badly, and I'm so weak, and you are so heavy in my arms."

Then her grip slipped. And such was the old man's faith in the immediacy of his next destination that he didn't even scream as he fell.

Chapter Sixty-Two

I will spare you the story of Petra's frantic search, of a mother, dodging the townsmen's arrows and curses, trying to survive long enough to save her daughter. Let us say that the town was now fortified against us. Let us say that the goodly people, having lost near half a dozen on the worst terms imaginable, were jumping at shadows. So when a shadow actually moved in the village, a hail of dread projectiles frequently answered.

The town lost three more men to this enthusiasm for defense. In this way, it also rebuffed Petra's every attempt at rescue.

She saw Nastya take to the sky carrying the priest and could feel the pain and weakness in her. Trying to fly to her daughter, Petra was again attacked and had to flee. She cheered lustily when she saw the priest slip from Nastya's grip and plunge silently to his death.

Then Nastya started to lose control in her flight, and Petra's intonation changed from exultation to anguish.

Nastya made it almost all the way to the dry well before crashing. Petra gathered her gently, and as the town knew the place, she carried Nastya deeper into the woods and washed her in a stream of clear water. She dressed Nastya's wounds the best she could, though they would not stop bleeding.

Wordlessly, Nastya reached for Petra's mind and gave Petra her story. It was almost too much for Petra, and they held each other and cried as they relived Nastya's suffering. But Nastya wanted her mother to have all of it, so she would not have to wonder what her daughter's broken body had been subjected to.

When she had finished, Nastya communicated her love for her mother, her love for Donka, and her love for me. In her inchoate way, she told her mother she would listen to her more closely the next time they found a snake. Then she died, and Petra brought her to us, and shared what she could of the bitter business.

And so this is how my own beautiful angel was lost, like Violetta and Nameless, into the grasping hands of the Adversary.

I buried Nastya beneath a tree in the forest, which was all I could do for her now by way of resurrection. It was an oak, the form she had favored in life. Because despite that rooted changeling's role in what befell her, none of us blamed the timber for the purposes the carpenter put it to.

There was no real haste after that. No urgency to anything, not to anything at all. "There will never be hurry in our lives again," I thought. Because it is men who need to keep moving, to accomplish. This was the curse of their wilting-cabbage carcasses, those cadavers-in-waiting they carried around. We of the twilight could squander a century on a game of cribbage, if only we kept free of those vicious, transient organisms.

And we would keep free of them, once the consummation they kept begging me to bring to them had been delivered into their hands.

But what of us? The three who remained? Three now so weighted it was all they could do to stand upright. Where was the refuge that would welcome such splintered vessels, carrying so much rotted cargo?

I found myself walking along the Danube in the darkness—that wrong-flowing river aimed like an arrow at a seething Slavic shadow even Cyril, with all his churchly runes and magic, couldn't fully illuminate. Cyril, who fashioned an alphabet that looks like knife marks on a baby's throat, and then used it to pour the twin poisons of piety and saintly forbearance down our throats; God-crazed Cyril, who for all his signs and wonders would have stood humiliated and dumbstruck at the rude and pagan force that crackled like a galvanic charge between the Danube's muddy banks—untamed, untrammeled, unconverted.

I stared down into the murk black depths of that intractable and nonconforming waterway, that current as cold and unforgiving as the chilled heart I now carried inside me. And I knew that the path of our exodus was northerly, that we would leave like weightless winged birds, with no cry for the emptiness of the air; we would fly off, without looking back on the scorched landscape of infertile fields and unfruited orchards we left behind us.

A fetid sweetness assailed me, and a dead dog drifted into view, bloated and stinking, turning in lazy circles of seepage where the fish had eaten him away. I cackled at the omen and said out loud, "Soon to be joined by your master." For if these ignorant townsmen were so enamored of sickness and infirmity and the base corruption of their vile imprisoning flesh that they were willing to commit slaughter to preserve the certainty of their mortal outcomes, then I was at last and finally willing to leave them to the maggots and worms. The sky would grow light and darker without them. I and mine would make a fullness of their absence.

In the next few days, we filched pine and cypress and cedar as we could find it, and I showed Donka and Petra how to make boxes of the boards, and how to fill them to the proper level with loam. We would take the nourishing forest with us when we left this place forever.

Then I turned my attentions to the town, and set about the work.

Chapter Sixty-Three

Some nights are for flying. Some nights I crawl.

From the watchtower, the pig farmer could see everything except the streets and lawns, which were covered by an unseasonable and low-lying fog.

Some nights I lie still and do nothing at all.

The pig farmer sighed, as lately he was prone to do. With the spectacular death of the priest and the escape of the girl, they were almost at naught for their efforts.

Some nights I'm the hand that reaches from your dream.

There would be no more excursions into the forest. He had asked for volunteers and received not a one—in fact, had lost three of the original party.

Tonight I am mist. I am steam.

Two of those were stoned to death for having the gypsy girl's teeth-marks on them; he was lucky he had any swordsmen left after that. They would make their stand in the town now, where his men felt safer and knew where to run to if anything went wrong.

And the moon is so bright. And the air is so still.

He looked down over the moonlit buildings and counted the men he could see on the rooftops. Fourteen, fifteen, was that all?

Tonight I can strike at will.

Ah, no. Sixteen. He had missed the one defecating over the side of his house. That made seventeen in all. Hardly an army, but enough if the creatures continued to attack them as they had been—frontally, and one at a time.

This one's afraid that he'll die in his sins. I sigh as he breathes me in.

Someone choking. There!

Here's one whose arrows went wide of the mark. Drag him down into the dark.

Another one! Over there! The vapor—it's alive!

And that one is brown-skinned, and that one is fair. Fill up their lungs with pestilent air.

Leave their eyes focused in a slackening stare.

The pig farmer shouted, "Away! Away!" as two more dropped. And then he was coughing and covering himself, stumbling down the stairs as haze and steam reached for him.

I'm something that vanished before it was there.

Mother of God, is there no end to these torments?

Violetta, Nastya, it is beginning.

Oh, it would be so easy to kill them all this way. Enter them as dew. Probe them for weaknesses. Nourish cancers like bread molds. Find half-stopped hearts readying to burst, and with a little jab of breath, topple them all.

The unprotected streets show me nothing but shutters and silence. I feel the village whimpering under beds and in cupboards. Cowering beneath tables with a hand over its mouth so as not to fright the children with the animal squeal that fights against its teeth. I feel you, I say to sightless windows. I feel you, and I know where you are. Your town could be empty of life by morning.

"Too quick," says Nastya's slow-dying corpse. "Too simple," says complicated Violetta. And wearing my mistresses' colors, I acknowledge their wisdom.

I, too, want these people to know themselves as they are.

It wants only for what's hidden to emerge.

And in kitchens, under floors, in the sweet dung of stables, I make alliance with secret fang and whisker and claw.

We are rat-faced hundreds now, and the villagers seem so scant.

I dig into pelts, soak up pinprick vermin who pierce and feast.

We are insect thousands now, and the villagers seem so few.
Bug veins burst, and feverish parasites gambol and spawn.
We are contagion, infection, and we are millions now.
And the villagers seem not to exist at all.

Chapter Sixty-Four

When the plague came, the town didn't understand what was happening to it. Conditioned to fend against supernatural blows, the villagers weren't ready to accept disease as the final harbinger of the struggle. In their minds, disease came from God as a punishment. Surely in this battle against hell's own spawn, God was on the village's side.

Then people started coughing, just a little, all over town. Within hours they'd taken to their beds. Within hours more, yellow liquid ran from their eyes and they were coughing up red sputum that looked like pieces of lung.

An hour later they were dead. And the people who attended to them were coughing. Just a little.

Still, the ailment seemed to have a kind of intelligence behind it. If someone had done injury to the gypsy girl, their children died first, and then they did, after watching it happen. The one or two remaining slayers of Violetta took sick early and then lingered in agony on the cusp of death until they begged their families to release them—a thing their loved ones could not do, for fear of their own and the sufferer's immortal souls.

This selectivity was a trait no previous illness had ever shown. It might have gone more remarked upon, if the town wasn't demonstrably in the process of losing its mind.

For the plague's lethality was total. It passed over no one, and no one recovered who felt its touch. A kind of mad joy broke out among the townfolk as they realized there would be no deliverance. Winter stores put by in peasant thrift were broken open and strewn with profligate abandon on dirt floors. Eating parties flourished, where in the style of Roman emperors, poor farmers and respectable burghers consumed stock bred for its milk or cheese or wool until they vomited their excess onto the table. And then being emptied, they consumed more.

No one troubled over the demands of cleanliness in such a savage environment, and so the rats came in their hordes. The townfolk welcomed them now, apostles hailing their deliverer, and one group even fashioned a little crown and placed it on a fat and snarling rodent, hailing him the "Rat King." But he was a despotic ruler, for in little more than a few hours' time, none of his subjects remained alive to pay his due homage.

Fires broke out and went unextinguished, coating all with a sulfurous pall. Children were left to cry on floors in their own filth— for why attend to such fragile crops, knowing they will never see harvest?

Licentiousness was practiced in combinations of sixes and fours. Without the normal checks of social order and the fear of ostracism or punishment, these orgiastic displays unleashed jealousies resulting in more than a few casual murders. And all the little cruelties that were in the normal rhythm of things even in the best of times blossomed like canker on the weedy town, so that in ways too vile to set down, the village became its own clarion, trumpeting its own impending doom. Ecce Homo.

We would not stay to greet it, I decided. And so at dusk we gathered up twelve of the scores of horses who had escaped to the fields from the carnage of the town. Then we loaded a dozen casket-sized boxes of nurturing forest loam onto three of the few unburned wagons, and we made ready to take our leave.

As we came within sight of the smoldering village, Donka, who had hardly spoken since crying herself out after Violetta's death, stopped the wagon she was driving and turned to me. "Take me there," she said. "It's the only place I've known. I want to see what it looked like when it decided to die."

The streets were deserted of all life; even the rats were gone. A few feeble flames glowed low and dull against exposed crossbeams, and the entire town had more the look of charcoal in a hearth than anything that had ever been graced with a lover's passion or the laugh of a child. Incongruous and untouched, a few preserved objects pocked the ashen landscape—a straw-haired doll, a spinner's wheel, an hourglass—as if the owners had been called away on pressing business, never to return.

Donka seemed unmoved. She was stranded since Violetta's dying in a more desolate place.

I looked up at the faltering sky. "So, he's got them at last."

"Who?" Donka said.

"The Foe. For surely everything in this death-worshipping village has hurried gladly into the Adversary's withering embrace."

But Donka knew otherwise. She had seen almost immediately some little fluttering movement in the stone watchtower—one of the last unburnt edifices, and the only one of any considerable size.

The pig farmer had eluded me again on the night I took the men of his watch. Seeing my designs from his higher vantage point, he gulped the last available breath of untainted air and stumbled his way into the fields, where he was safe from me as I plotted inside the town.

Upon returning, the pig farmer barricaded himself in his lofty perch with water, stores, and the last of his oaken arrows. The plague found him there, but late because of his isolation. And he lingered, being one of Violetta's slaughterers.

He lingered still, in agony. And hearing our voices, and the general tenor of our thoughts, he realized who we were and saw at last his chance for vengeance.

All this Donka understood and in fact accepted. As I brooded on the dead town, she felt the murderous heat of the pig farmer's thoughts, and she warmed herself against them, as a stranger trapped in a winter storm might warm her hands against an unexpected hearth. It was a kind of relief to know this purgatory she suffered in could be ended.

Her next thoughts were for my safety. She took my arm and, by an affectionate and artful step whose real purpose I did not ascertain, made sure I was protected from the archer in the tower by a half-burned wall. Then Donka turned to me, suddenly coquettish.

"Husband," she said, "you have deceived me."

Glad of her first smile in weeks, I extended the joke with mock gallantry of my own. "I, m'lady? How so?"

She grew serious. "When you took me, you made me a bargain. If I died, I would never see my lover's face again. If I accepted your gift, she and I would never be parted. And so I lived, and now she's hurried off to a place where she can't find me."

There was a subtle shift in her stance, and then I felt the hot flash of triumph that sparked inside the pig farmer's hatred for us as he raised his bow, and I knew what she was about to do.

"I'll go to meet her—"

And Donka stepped out into the square, the bow sang, and the shaft came for her.

But it was slow-footed compared to me.

Because if all these hours had brought me a single wisdom, it was that we are capable of infinity of loves. And if we persevere, some of them will find us.

Hearts crack, eyes bleed with weeping, jilted lovers starve on forlorn mattresses, wasting toward early graves. But outside their windows, the dance goes on, combining and recombining as now two pair off, and two, and two.

We heal, and the pain of the healing is our monument to the scale of the loss. And then we adjust our relationship to whatever's left, to include one more unthinkable possibility.

It was one of the lessons I wanted to teach gentle Donka—I, who had lost loves as great as any, only to find Donka waiting among the later loves for me.

So I flew to her and took the arrow in my side where it would least harm me, turning as it struck so it would not strike Donka when it passed through. "We'll bury our mutual dead together," I said.

And Donka, still unable to imagine that the earth would not tumble into the sun in Violetta's absence, just looked at me.

CODA:
The Book of Stones

There are still places where time barely moves. Barren slopes, without rain or season, where the sulfuric air drives off creatures of a day, and only lean wolves, sharp rock, and brackish shrubberies abide.

When humans nest in such a place, they do so believing as always in the permanence of their own industry. Generations will follow the intrepid pathfinder and hail his fortitude as a tamer of wildernesses—he knows this like he knows the tools in his hands. In fact, as roof-beams rise and are covered in masonry, tile, and thatch, he merely settles the forward outpost of a failed campaign.

For soon the plucky colonizer tires of thin air and soil-less ground in a place where, if he puts a shoe wrong on a footpath, the landscape itself will rise to kill him as casually as he might drown a kitten in a bucket back on the farm he came from. A brown shade settles in him. He grows anxious and finds himself unexpectedly weeping.

So the stone house and livery, erected in expectation, start to languish. The walls crack, the roofs cave, and a process of silent abandonment commences, until the last of those who weren't driven mad or to murder takes his leave. And all returns to its natural state of unchanging corruption, and what's left of a hearth and a hope is a circle of broken stones, like a mouth on a hillside—the statue of a scream.

We left the world of human jostling for such a place. High in the Carpathians, where even the horses refused to go, there was a ruined tower and battlement. A capricious lord once held sway in it, meting out gore and cruelties. The people rose, the tyrant was pulled down, and the lore that accrued to the spot kept the town away from it. For at night, they said, the dread lord still walked his battlement with a bleeding infant in one hand and the head of a priest in the other, hunting for souls to steal.

The legend suited my purpose, for I had turned away from men forever, so I thought. I assumed this dread lord's gorged mantle, brandishing it like a shield as a further hedge against human companionship. And if some beer-bold peasant sneaked into the hills and found me restive, I would make him my agent with a hellish display of picture book horrors that sent him stumbling back to the town, his hair whitened and his hand forever trembling, to hold forth in taverns and churches about the night he barely escaped with his life from the vaporous and abiding ghost-son of Vlad Tepes Dracul.

Donka and Petra became curious about the wider world. For their sake, I traveled to other towns on night winds, picking locks in whispers. Books in all languages I gave to them, tapestries for the walls, a spinet to set beside the cheering fire.

And one night I brought them a sister, a mute mulatto girl named Anyes, whose neighbors had come by torchlight crying "Witchery!" when their own poor planting devastated a harvest. Taking the form of some forked devil out of a sermon, I snatched Anyes from the flames and watched the pious folk scurry. But fire had done its work, and when I revealed myself to her ebbing mind she wanted to go with me, and so I claimed her. For forty days, we raised her like a moon-eyed calf in a little box of forest peat, so that her appetites were matched to ours, as were the things that nourished her.

A chamber where prisoners once begged and moaned I made a library, and we would read there together of the rise and fall of empires, the clash of armies in pitched slaughters, magistrates and hemlines, and other perennial follies.

The highest point of the tower I domed and then installed a great brass telescope in it, and there we would retire to watch the distance separating us from the One Foe. When a comet streaked across the sky, we would imagine a whole world writhing in finishing flames.

And we were comforted by the thought, because it signified what we already knew: He neither watched nor was listening.

He came to us out of the West, a staggering silhouette against a failing sun. His eyes darted but rarely blinked.

His clothes were rags, and hardship rode him close. He would indicate later that this was by choice, that an urge toward annihilation goaded him, driving him toward our barren and treacherous heights and what he took to be obliteration.

The sight of him, so full of breakages and scorn, rended my obdurate heart. And I was curious. Curious about what sort of man mankind had here produced. For he was different from any earlier impression I had of his race—a riot of strange new suppositions and possibilities, of sorrows and cruelties unavailable to those of his kind I had known before him. Did this make him unique? Or was he a symptom of wider tendencies, some fundamental change the paragon of horrors had undergone while I and mine averted our eyes? Was he a novelty? A refugee, like we were? Or the bleeding edge of some unanticipated manifestation, and therefore the potential carrier of new lethalities his tribe might brandish against us?

When he asked hoarsely for water, it was in a language I'd gleaned in pieces down the centuries while gliding through the skies over seaports, where it was increasingly the mother tongue of the impressed sailor and the auctioneer—of greed and acquisition, rapine, profits and loss.

English. He spoke English. He was an Englishman.

But there was something else in this stranger who stumbled in unexpectedly and now greedily swallowed an entire pitcher of Adam's ale, as if he was afraid it might evaporate if he set it down. Something desperate and unalleviated had come to us, and now it glowered at me, with water drooling down its pinched lips, a disrupting Spartan bristling with hidden weapons and set loose amid the Athenian unity the Women and I had made of our lives.

Setting aside my discomfort at his distempers as the reaction of one unaccustomed to having guests, I asked his name.

He blinked his eyes at last, and a cold sneer broke across his grimed face. Then the last rays of day seemed to leave the sky as he said, "Harker. My name is Jonathan Harker."

Special thanks to Jeff Schwager, Dan Lawrence, Vladi and Violetta Grabowski, Beth Swofford, Richard Green, Jacqueline Woolf, Joe McBride, Sarah Duffy, the real Konstantin Kuzmanov, the people of Rousse and Kostandenets, Bob Rogers, Cherish Denton, Sufjan Stevens, Jennifer Van Goethem, the late Petur Penkov (who loved the house he built at No. 1 Rayna Neginya, Kostandenets very much but loved his son even more), Michael Stearns, Simon "You Left Money on the Table" Lipskar, Joe Cashman, Wade Major, Darroch Greer, and others who shall go "Nameless."

Extra special thanks to Ann Kwinn, who bore the brunt of this, and to my twin brother, Thomas John Greene, who cheered it on. "Ah, child of countless trees . . ."

the moon and sun as brother to the earth . . .
T.G. (March 1977)

CPSIA information can be obtained at www.ICGtesting.com
Printed in the USA
LVOW121206290912

300539LV00005B/23/P